RAVEN MASK

By the Author

Witch Wolf

Visit us at www.boldstrokesbooks.com

RAVEN MASK

by

Winter Pennington

2010

RAVEN MASK

ISBN 10: 1-60282-182-8
ISBN 13: 978-1-60282-182-8

This Trade Paperback Original Is Published By
Bold Strokes Books, Inc.
P.O. Box 249
Valley Falls, NY 12185

First Edition: September 2010

CREDITS
EDITORS: Victoria Oldham and Shelley Thrasher
COVER DESIGN BY Bold Strokes Books Graphics

Acknowledgments

Even though preternatural fiction isn't really her thing, my mother has steadily followed this series. She encouraged the writer in me at a young age and taught me not to fear the bloody scratches of the red pen. If I needed her to read something or to listen to me moan and groan, she was always there. My father, too, has shown so much support and encouragement. Thank you for so many reasons and for so many things. Thank you for being a part of this. Thank you for being nothing but proud and for offering love, never shame.

Dedication

To my mother and father,
for always being there and always believing.

CHAPTER ONE

I stared down at the lifeless body of a boy whose face was all too familiar. Timothy's eyes were open, wide and unseeing.

"Shit, Arthur." The words fell softly. I didn't know what else to say. It didn't seem real.

Timothy Nelson hadn't even begun to live. Hell, he was only sixteen. The last time I saw him, I was working on another case. The Nelsons lived on a few acres close to a crime scene that had reeked of werewolf. Timothy had followed me out to my car asking about the preternatural community, curiosity burning in his eyes. Now, fixed on the blue-black sky above, they were completely void.

"I told you it wasn't pretty," Arthur said.

Indeed, he had. I put a hand over my mouth, taking in a deep breath and forcing myself to stand strong.

"He was only sixteen." I breathed the words. "Still a kid. Who would do this to a kid?"

I knew better than to ask such a question. It was like a knife to my stomach.

The paleness of death had lightened Timothy's summer tan, and his lips were half-parted as if life had slipped out between them. I saw no visible wounds, no sign of blood or struggle. One of the cops had placed a towel over his hips, covering his nudity.

He had been stripped of his clothes, as if even in death, the killer had wanted to leave him vulnerable and shamed.

Arthur offered me a pair of latex gloves. "I'm sorry, Kass. I know you spoke with him."

I took the gloves and put them on. I wouldn't find the killer by mourning Timothy's death. I couldn't stop what had happened, but I could stop what might happen.

Most cops look at a body and try to see only it. But you can't, not always. Sometimes, there isn't anything you can tell yourself to chase away the knowledge that the corpse at your feet was someone's loved one.

I could put a face to the people that would miss him. Worse, I could put a face to Timothy when he was alive. I shut the door on sadness and pity. The body at my feet was an empty shell, a piece of evidence. It may seem cold, but at times that line of thinking is the only thing to hold on to, the only thing that keeps you from sinking into the morass of violence.

You have to be able to detach yourself in police work. If you don't, you'll drown. I owed it to Timothy Nelson not to.

As I shut my eyes and inhaled sharply, the smell of death hit my nostrils and the beast stirred, quirking an ear in my direction. For a moment, she seemed curious. But with no blood-tinged life to call her, she let her wolfish neutrality slide into place. I wrapped it around me like a shield and knelt in the dead grass, pushing aside any memory of Timothy Nelson alive.

Using my thumb and index finger I tried to move the jaw, but had to settle for looking around it. Rigor mortis was setting in, so the body had to have been sitting for at least three hours. Maximum stiffness would occur some time after twelve hours.

I didn't see any bite marks. Arthur had said on the phone that the victim had been drained dry, as if he suspected it had been done by a vampire. The skin was pasty, like wet chalk. It was easy to see why Arthur jumped to the vampire conclusion.

But if so, there had to be an exit wound. I checked for puncture marks in the arteries at the wrists. Still nothing. I sniffed, trailing my fingers across the collapsed veins at the elbow.

"Who found the body?" I asked.

"The father."

Mr. Nelson was tall and tan, like an older version of Timothy. Mrs. Nelson, I remembered more. She'd gone ape-shit, calling me the devil's whore and threatening to Bible-thump me out of her house. Fortunately, Arthur had taken over from there. She'd probably gone ballistic and they'd locked her in a loony bin. Hey, one could hope.

"You're right. The body has been exsanguinated," I said.

Even with a vampire attack, there should have been some blood, some hint of it. I sniffed again, thankful the corpse hadn't been sitting long enough to become pungent.

There was an exit wound somewhere. If I couldn't see it, well, I had other senses to rely on.

It was faint, like a miniscule piece of raw hamburger surrounded by the smell of dirt, death, and grass. I focused on it, knowing if I followed it I could find the source. Pushing the towel aside carefully, I made sure certain parts of the body remained covered and gazed near the groin area.

I ran the tips of my fingers over the wound. "The femoral vein was cut."

"Why not the artery?" Arthur asked. "If it was cut he'd have been dead in what? Fifteen to thirty minutes? If they were trying to kill him that would've been the way to do it."

"If they were trying to kill him quickly. Arteries bleed a hell of a lot more and a hell of a lot faster. We'd see more blood too. The medical examiner will be able to tell for certain if it was the vein, but I'd bet my ass it was."

Arthur knelt beside me, already wearing a pair of gloves, and craned his neck to see.

I put two fingertips to the slit. The cut was clean, indicating a steady hand and either a very sharp razor or a really sharp knife. The cut itself was only about two and a half inches long but went deep, deep enough to penetrate. I could've felt around the wound easier without the gloves, but I was screwed on that one. You don't fuck up evidence by leaving fingerprints all over it before a medical examiner takes a look. I kept probing the wound and found a small interruption in the slit.

"I don't think it was just cut."

I tried to stitch the wound together in my mind, like making two pieces of a puzzle whole. I felt the edge of puncture marks.

"You need to make sure someone measures the cut and examines the edges of the wound carefully. From what I could feel through the gloves," I stood and crossed my arms over my chest, "the cut was created to distract from the original wound."

Arthur took his gloves off. "What do you think?"

"Definitely a vampire. It would explain the exsanguination."

"Damn it."

He had obviously been hoping it wasn't a vampire killing. Since he'd called me out, he already was sure that something preternatural was involved. Sometimes, it's human nature to hope the truth is a lie.

Pulling out a small notepad from his front pocket, he began to scribble notes. "I'll ask the medical examiner to take a closer look and see if she can find any fang marks hidden in our cut." Judging from the look that crossed his face, he intended to say something I didn't like.

"How's your girlfriend doing?"

"She's fine…"

"Would Vampira do—"

"No."

"How do you know for sure?"

"I cannot believe you're asking if the woman I'm dating did this."

"The woman you're dating happens to be one of them."

"So, you're pointing your finger at anything with a pair of fangs?" I was exasperated. I wouldn't sit back and let him make Lenorre a suspect just because she was convenient. Sure, we'd been dating for almost a month, but I cared about her, and accusing her of murder crossed a major line with me.

Besides, Lenorre would have more sense than to leave a body where the cops would find it. As owner of The Two Points, Oklahoma City's only vampire club, she wouldn't risk the bad publicity.

"No. You're right." He nervously straightened his blue tie. The suit was gray and neatly ironed. I seriously doubted he'd done it.

He'd probably just taken it to the cleaners. Arthur's not a spic-and-span type of guy.

"You don't have to ask me something like that. I can tell you she didn't do it. If you even think of questioning her," I lowered my voice, "I'll be pissed."

"You're right," he said again. "I'm probably just pointing fingers because I have no idea where to begin finding the sucker that did this."

The corner of my mouth twitched. "Very poor choice of words. That's why you call me. I'm the one that shovels the preternatural shit, remember?"

Arthur gave me an idiotic grin. A younger-looking cop carrying a small grocery-store sack stepped up to us and held the bag open.

I dropped the gloves in it. "Thanks."

Arthur tossed his in. "Fine. Will you let me know if you find anything? Last time you didn't even tell us you figured out who the killer was."

"I didn't exactly figure it out under ideal circumstances. I didn't tell you I suspected Carver because, if he had been a werewolf, he could've kicked your ass."

Arthur didn't know the whole truth and I sure as hell didn't plan to tell him. Carver *is* a werewolf, but he hadn't kidnapped me. That had been Lukas Morris, brother of the alpha female of the local werewolf pack and one sick puppy. He had murdered an innocent woman on Carver's land and left her for the police to find. His plan had nearly worked. It might've, if he hadn't botched it by kidnapping me.

"The last I checked you were human too," Arthur said. "Unless Vampira has taken you to the dark side. You do look kind of pale."

"Show me one person at a crime scene that doesn't look pale."

Arthur pointed toward the yellow tape around the scene. "That guy."

A cop in a dark blue uniform stood by the tape. His swarthy skin was practically camouflaged by night. The cop looked over at us and I gave him a quick smile before turning back to Arthur. "African-American doesn't count, smart-ass."

He laughed.

"I'm going home now," I said. "Call me when you get the ME's report, and stop making bad jokes at crime scenes."

"Will do, but I can't help telling a bad joke every now and then."

"You make a habit of it." I headed for my car parked near the edge of the woods. "I'm sure they have medication for that."

"If they put me on medication you'd miss me."

"Oh, really? I think you're flattering yourself, Kingfisher."

"No. You'd miss me about as much as I'd miss you if they put you on Prozac and made you nice."

I rolled my eyes, laughing. "Good night, Arthur."

Chapter Two

A human would've called the quietness in the car silence. But werewolves can hear every click and tick, which is a bitch when I'm trying to sleep. The only noise was that of the car as it sliced through the Oklahoma wind. At seventy miles per hour, the engine purred. Not that thunderous growl of a serious sports car, but a purr, which worked just fine for me.

I didn't feel like listening to music. I normally do when I'm driving. Part of me felt unreal, disconnected from reality. Timothy's lifeless brown eyes and that angry cut haunted me.

The killer's hand had been steady, not careless or driven by passion. I was betting the murder had been premeditated. Whoever had killed Timothy had planned it and taken the boy when no one was looking. If the vampire had gotten into his mind, Timothy might've enjoyed every minute as he slowly slipped into the abyss of death.

I heard a rumble before lights flashed in my rearview mirror. The car behind mine swerved into the middle lane, speeding up until it was next to mine. The little metal cobras against the shimmering purple paint gave away its model, though I couldn't see the driver through the tinted windows. They hit the gas and the Mustang lurched forward. I shook my head. If they thought I would race, they were wrong.

When I heard another rumble I glanced at the Mustang. "Good Lady, I could outrun your car on foot, you idiot."

They did it again. I was about to give them the one-finger salute when my cell phone rang from the console. I grabbed the headset, placing it in my ear and answering without bothering to look at the caller ID.

"Yeah?"

"What's up?" It was Rupert.

"Oh, trying to get some idiot to understand I don't feel like racing."

"What kind of car is it?"

I told him.

He laughed. "Yeah, you don't have a chance."

"Gee, you think?"

"Occasionally."

The purple car slowed and pulled into the lane behind me.

"Rupert."

"What?"

"They're on my ass," I growled. My agitation caught the wolf's interest. I took a deep breath, forcing a steady hand over my emotions. Had it been closer to the full moon and had there been any actual triggers, it would've been harder for me to squish her. Thankfully, it wasn't, and when I focused on shielding, she quieted. Shape-shifting while driving…could law enforcement ticket for that?

After a long pause he asked, "Can you shake them?"

"Yeah, hold on." I plucked the earpiece out of my ear and tossed it into the passenger seat.

Well, if up my ass was where they wanted to be…

I slammed on the brakes, gripping the steering wheel at ten and two. My tires squealed to a halt, echoed by the sound of the Mustang's. I waited for the space of a heartbeat for the Mustang to slam into my Tiburon. When the impact finally came it was more of a tap than the big crash boom I expected.

The man who emerged from the car looked furious. His dark brown hair rose in porcupine spikes, and a black leather jacket covered his light gray sweater.

"Kass!" he yelled, "what the fuck?"

I waited until he was close to the driver's side window to lower it.

"You asked me if I could shake them."

"I didn't tell you to slam on your fucking brakes!"

I grinned in defiance. "Maybe you shouldn't fuck with me. Did that ever occur to you?"

He tilted his head. "Wait. You knew it was me?"

"No."

"Then why'd you slam on your brakes?"

"Under the circumstances, it seemed appropriate."

"I don't really see the point in risking your life just to get someone off your ass. One of us could've been hurt."

"One of us, yes. I think you're forgetting something."

"You may be a werewolf," his voice was low, "but everyone has their weakness."

"Fortunately, fiberglass isn't one of mine. If you're thinking about trying me, don't, because I am seriously not in the fucking mood tonight."

Rupert rocked back on his heels and put his hands into his jeans' pockets. "Fine."

"What the hell are you doing out here in the middle of nowhere?"

"I had some things to pick up from Texas and was on my way home when I saw you."

"How did you know it was me?"

His smile was feral. "You act like I've never seen your license-plate number."

"Where'd you get the Mustang? What happened to the Phantom?" The last I knew, the Phantom, a smoke gray Hummer H2, was in the shop.

"Sold it."

"Why? You loved that car."

"Because it was my car and everyone knew."

"Ah." I understood. "So the Mustang is your incognito car?"

"For the time being."

"It doesn't suit you."

"That's the point."

"Did you ever get the Hummer out of the shop?"

"No, I sold it to the guy who'd been working on it."

"What was wrong with it?"

"You don't want to know."

I dropped it. When Rupert said you don't want to know, you really didn't want to. Obviously, the car wasn't that bad if the guy from the shop had bought it. You could deal with a bit of blood by getting new upholstery. But more than that would take some serious reconditioning. It probably wasn't just a bloody nose that made Rupert get rid of it.

"Where are you headed?" Rupert asked.

"Home."

"Which home?" He pulled up the leather sleeve of his jacket and looked at his watch. "You still have about six hours until dawn."

I didn't always stay the night with Lenorre. Recently I'd been spending more time at her place. We'd learned we share a common interest in black-and-white movies and cuddling. I'd slept in her bed and she'd held me while I slept, but we still hadn't had sex. We'd gotten close when I was wolf-ridden, but Lenorre would not take me when the wolf was in control. It'd only happened once or twice, but since then I hadn't reoffered. She didn't push it, not really. Neither one of us had made that final leap to cement the relationship.

She was probably waiting for me to act, but beyond kissing and touching, I hadn't been able to.

I could be brave in the face of danger and a chicken-shit when it came to love. Every woman has her hang-up. Why did it feel like I was collecting them?

I sighed. "I'm going to Lenorre's after I stop by my apartment."

"Did the cops call you out here?" His gaze was very blue.

I didn't see a reason to deny it. "Yeah."

"How bad was it?"

"Bad."

"Do you want help?"

"It wouldn't hurt."

"All right, I'll follow you." The keys jingled in his hands. "Deal?"

"Deal, but if you start riding my ass again—"

"You'll slam on the brakes."

"You bet your ass I will," I said to his back.

CHAPTER THREE

I went inside alone to grab a few things and didn't bother turning any lights on. Being a werewolf has its perks, one of which is excellent night vision. Wolves in the wild rely mostly on their sense of smell, but they also have good night sight. In a wolf's eyes, the abundance of rods, or nerves that are sensitive to low light, is what gives it the ability to see in the dark. Unfortunately, rods are monochromatic, and in the dark the number of rods washes away my ability to perceive colors other than those of a black-and-white film. Fortunately, if there's light, my vision is normal. Not being able to perceive color in the dark may seem like a downside. Truthfully, it isn't such a high price to pay given the fact I can actually see. When you make a living hunting and killing things that aren't human, you learn to appreciate life's small mercies.

In the bedroom I opened the top drawer of my dresser and pulled out two pairs of undies, socks, and a clean bra. It really didn't matter what color they were. I fished my backpack from beneath the bed, tossing the undergarments in, along with a nightshirt that was originally black and white. Lenorre had given me the shirt that promoted the club she owned. The two little white Vs on it, like upside-down mountains, were supposed to be vampire fangs. Underneath the fangs in cryptic bleeding letters was The Two Points. I yanked two pairs of jeans off a hanger, what I was hoping was my green thermal, and what I was pretty sure was a black-and-white striped sweater.

I stashed everything in the bag and tossed it over my shoulder. My leather jacket was in the car. I thought about grabbing another coat, but I was just going over to Lenorre's, not to a fashion show. Hell, she had seen me when I'd woken looking like the Bride of Frankenstein. Of course, not a curl on Lenorre's head was ever out of place. Looking perfect in the morning *so* doesn't count if you're a vampire. They don't move. Trust me, I know, because trying to move them is a bitch. I learned not to fall asleep on the very edge of the bed with Lenorre holding me, because when I woke about to fall off, she wouldn't budge. Being a lycanthrope, I could have moved her, but it was easier to just move myself.

There was an upside. I didn't have to worry about accidentally kicking her in my sleep and we never fought over the covers.

I shut all the doors in the apartment, grabbed my laptop, and left. After I nodded in Rupert's direction, letting him know I was ready, the Mustang's lights flicked on and I squinted, stifling a growl. Sudden bright lights shattering my night vision hurt like hell. He was just messing with me. I unlocked the Tiburon, tossed the backpack into the passenger seat, and carefully put the laptop bag flat on the floorboard. Rupert waited for my lead.

He had, after all, never been to Lenorre's house, so I was curious to see his expression when we got there. It was a house worth staring at.

❖

Rupert followed me to the porch with only the sound of our boots crunching the dead grass. I knocked on the door, lightly, waiting for footsteps on the other side. I could usually hear Rosalin, friend and beta werewolf of the Blackthorne pack, bounding down the stairs. She was the one who customarily opened the door. Rosalin was one of the many residents living under Lenorre's roof. She also worked for Lenorre at The Two Points.

Rupert hadn't so much as blinked at the size of the house. What kind of place did he live in? I'd never seen it. We had a bet several months ago, when he'd told me to try and find out where he lived.

But the last case I'd worked on with the police had interfered and I'd never figured it out.

It was silent before the front door opened to reveal Lenorre's blank and beautiful face. The long black curls of her hair were pulled off her shoulders and piled at the back of her head, held in place by a metallic hairpin decorated with rubies.

A stray curl had broken free, falling over her pale cheek. Against her dark hair and pale skin, her eyes were striking. At first glance one might pass them off as the blue-gray some humans have. But Lenorre was not human, and her eyes were the true gray of misty storm clouds that changed to liquid silver when she embraced her power.

I'd never seen anyone with eyes like hers.

Her crimson gown had a spill of white lace around the collar and wrists. It appeared to be a Victorian dressing gown, but when she stepped back, I caught a glimpse of long white leg peeking through a slit in the velvet. As I raised my gaze to the gown's scoop neck, a jolt of longing shot through me. The dress was tight, offering a demure amount of décolletage. It was definitely too risqué to be truly Victorian.

"I see you have brought a guest." Her expression was unreadable as Rupert followed.

"You don't mind?" I asked, hopeful she wasn't irked with me for bringing a friend without her consent. It was her home. I hadn't intended to be discourteous, but you never know how someone will react until they do so, especially vampires.

She gave me a not-so-happy look before turning to walk into the parlor. "You could have asked." She didn't have a thread of anger in her voice.

The calmness of her words surprised me. "I know." I placed my things on a white armchair just inside the room. "I didn't think about it. I apologize."

"I am disappointed you did not ask my permission. You did not take my feelings into consideration," she explained, stepping closer.

I looked up into those intensely smoky eyes and felt like an ass.

"I'm—"

She placed a finger against my lips. "You have already apologized. There is no need for you to say you are sorry again." She touched my cheek gently. "All I ask is that you do not make the same mistake twice."

I suddenly felt like I was being scolded. I began to defend myself against the comment when she moved, catching me off guard. Her arm snaked behind my back and she pulled me against her.

With her body so close to mine, her curves against me with only our clothes as a barrier, I gasped.

She cupped my cheek, and though she held me gently, I knew the strength she carried in her mere fingertips. She bowed her head.

"You are always so torn between love and war." Her words caressed my lips, tickling. I shut my eyes, unnerved by the sudden closeness, by the heat building between my legs. I felt her other hand at my back, tracing the raven tattooed on my skin. The beak started between my shoulder blades. Lenorre's hand swooped downward, following the line of tail feathers to my lower back.

"You're always distracting me from a good fight."

"If you want to fight, we can fight, but neither of us holds our tempers on a short leash." Her lips moved against mine, terribly and utterly distracting. "I can think of far better things to do with you than fight."

She kissed me, drawing me roughly into the circle of her arms. She held me against her like a prisoner. Her lips parted against mine and I opened my mouth, catching her bottom lip between my teeth.

Lenorre moaned.

My stomach lurched. I liked a little bit of pain in the bedroom, but I had not known Lenorre had similar interests. I released her lip, slowly, and started to pull away from her. She buried her fingers in my hair, cupping the back of my skull. She kissed me again, this time exploring my mouth with a recklessness that had nothing to do with control and everything to do with passion, with need. She kissed me until I was breathless, until that need burned between my legs and threatened to buckle my knees. I put my hands on her shoulders, holding on to her like a life preserver as I drowned in her kiss. The tips of her fangs glided over my tongue. My hands trembled on her shoulders.

The room no longer existed. The only thing that mattered to me was Lenorre's mouth, the feel of her, the taste of her. I was aware only of the line of her body against mine, the soft swell of womanly curves hidden beneath the folds of her clothing. I searched for the opening to her gown, trying to free the first button, but my hands trembled too badly to unfasten it. Lenorre caught my wrists, pushing my arms behind my back. Her slender hands were suddenly shackles that trapped me and kept me from touching her. A growl of frustration escaped me.

"Please." Instead of sounding like a plea, it sounded more like a demand.

Lenorre turned her head, brushing her mouth across my cheek. Her voice was breathy as she said, "We are not alone."

"Sorry." Rupert's deep voice startled me and made me come back to myself. "I didn't mean to interrupt," he said, crossing his arms over his chest. "Most guys would feel," he paused, searching for the word, "honored. But this is like watching my little sister make out with her lesbian girlfriend." I felt the blush creeping to my cheeks.

As if on cue Lenorre and I both stepped away from each another, wiping our mouths. It wasn't a sloppy kiss, but a deep kiss like that leaves some evidence. I used the back of my sleeve. Lenorre used her thumb and index finger to daintily dab at the corners of her mouth. The gesture made me think of more nefarious things. She watched me while she did it and I knew what that dark look meant. She was hungry, and it wasn't for blood.

I wanted to kick Rupert out and tell him to shut the door behind him.

"Thank you," he said, stepping out of the doorway. He picked up my bags, moving them over to the couch so he could sit in the chair.

I debated excusing myself to make a trip to the bathroom before I sat down, but decided it was best not to because then everyone would know why. Lenorre took a seat in the opposite armchair. I moved to the couch, slightly narrowing my eyes. *Sitting in a puddle of your own wetness isn't exactly comfortable.*

The corner of her mouth twitched into a smirk.

"What?" Rupert looked at us both.

Lenorre didn't say anything.

I shook my head. "Nothing."

"You may be a werewolf, and she may be a vampire," he glanced at Lenorre, "but you're both still fucking women."

"Yeah," I said, "pretty much."

Lenorre said, "Do not try to understand, Rupert. It will only give you a headache."

Indeed, it would.

Thankfully, Rupert changed the subject. "What did you see tonight?"

Lenorre looked curious enough for me to realize that she too wanted to know what I had seen. I walked over to the fireplace, running my fingertips across the edge of the mantel. I couldn't give either of them a run-down on what I had seen tonight while sitting. I needed to partially distract my mind from the words I had to say.

"Do you remember the last case I worked on with the police?"

I turned, then rested my shoulder against the fireplace, facing them. Rupert gave Lenorre an accusing look, which she met unflinchingly.

"How could I forget?" he said grumpily.

"Why, I am glad you find me so unforgettable, Rupert." Lenorre sounded rather sarcastic, clipping his name at the end. When they'd first met, Rupert and I had followed Rosalin back to The Two Points. Lenorre had helped calm my beast so I didn't shift all over the place. To my knowledge, she'd never been discourteous to him, but he'd made it clear that he didn't trust the vampires.

"You two," I said. They both looked at me. "Play nicely or don't talk to one another."

Lenorre circled the edge of the armchair with a fingertip. "Do not think you can boss me around, little wolf."

"Lenorre, can the crap and put your ego back in its coffin." I couldn't stifle the growl that built in my chest. "This isn't about Rupert or you. Do you remember my last case? I questioned a family and their son. That sixteen-year-old boy is dead."

My words were like a piano crashing into the middle of the room, invoking silence and everyone's attention.

"All right, Kass," Rupert said, "you win. I can ignore my dislike of your bed partner in order to hear what you need to tell me."

"And you?" I looked at Lenorre. "Can you do the same?"

Her tone and the set of her shoulders told me she was being careful. "I do not dislike Rupert."

It didn't seem to bother her that he didn't like her. In fact, his dislike seemed to amuse her.

"Thank you," I said.

"You're welcome," Rupert said. "Go on."

I nodded. "The boy's body was found between six thirty and seven thirty this evening. When I reached the scene rigor mortis had already set in. The body had been exsanguinated."

"Which means he was dead for at least three hours," Rupert said.

I nodded. "Exactly."

"Who found it?" he asked.

"The father."

"He was drained dry?"

I nodded, again. "Not a drop of blood left in his body or on the scene. I checked the jugular and the carotid. Neither of them had been pierced. I checked the ulna and radial, nothing."

Lenorre moved slightly.

"If there were no visible bite marks that leaves—"

"The femoral area. I'm pretty sure it was the femoral vein but anatomy is not my area of expertise. I won't know for sure until Arthur calls me with the examiner's report."

"If it was the vein, that indicates an intentional feeding and a slower death," Lenorre said, impressing me, although she was a vampire, after all. "Choosing a vein over an artery cannot be done in a moment of blood frenzy. The vein would require patience on the vampire's part."

"Right, since veins bleed more slowly," I said. "The artery would be more ideal for a quick fix. How would a vampire know where to bite to get the vein?"

"Pulse," Lenorre said. "Arteries have a beat. Veins do not."

Duh.

"Would the anticoagulant in your saliva make the vein bleed quicker?"

"A little," she said, "yes."

"Someone made a deep cut with a steady hand. So I agree. It was definitely intentional." I took a breath to calm myself.

"They cut the vein to hide the puncture wounds," Rupert said.

"Yeah."

He looked at Lenorre. "Would one of your vampires have done it?"

Lenorre shook her head. "No."

"How do you know for sure?" he asked. "You can't keep your eyes on them all the time."

"They are bound to me," she said, as if that explained everything.

Rupert said what I was thinking. "That doesn't tell me much."

"Rupert has a point," I said. "I don't know shit about vampire clans, or whatever you guys call them."

"Kassandra, it is similar to a wolf pack. To provide control, instead of absolute chaos, clans exist in every state in this country, in every city in this country. Each clan has a ruler, much like an alpha werewolf. A ruler provides for their clan, protects and punishes."

"Rosalin once told me you were one of the most powerful vampires in Oklahoma," I said.

"Mayhap. Every clan has a Countess or a Count at the head."

"All vampires are tied to a leader?" Rupert asked.

"For the most part. There are very few solitary vampires, but as Kassandra is a stray among the wolves, so there are those among our kind who, if powerful enough, break the ties from their original makers. Even then, most wayward vampires do not have the power to conceal and protect themselves. Thus they seek the protection of a more powerful vampire."

"A stray?" I asked. "I didn't exactly follow you to your doorstep. That's a nice way to put it."

"Do not take offense. You are a lone wolf. I apologize. I should not have called you a stray, but that is the term most wolves would have used."

"No," Rupert said, "I like *stray*. It suits her. She did show up on my doorstep when the accident happened."

I flipped him off. He laughed.

"On your doorstep?" Lenorre inquired.

"Yeah, bled all over the damn place. You have no fucking idea how long that took to clean up."

"You never told me that," I said.

He shrugged. "Why bother? You're my friend. I would rather you be alive than dead because I went all OCD at the wrong moment."

I shook my head. "OCD just doesn't seem your style, Rupert. It sounds more like my mother."

"Your mother?" Lenorre looked thoughtful. "You never mentioned your mother."

"I had to come from somewhere."

"Have you met her?" she asked Rupert.

"Once. If you ever meet her you'll see where Kass gets her stubborn streak."

I suddenly had an image of taking Lenorre home to my family and laughed.

Rupert caught it. "You just pictured it too, didn't you?"

"Yes, yes, I did."

"Pictured what?" Lenorre asked.

"The look on my mother's face if I were to introduce you two."

Rupert said, "Your mom wouldn't care."

"She probably wouldn't." I pictured my mother's reaction. *Oh, honey, she's cute. A little tall, don't you think?*

"All right," Rupert changed the subject, "we were talking about the crime scene. Was there any other evidence besides the bite marks?"

"The boy was naked."

"It was intimate," Lenorre said.

"Definitely intimate."

"It must've been someone he knew well to get that close to him," Rupert added.

"Not necessarily." Lenorre looked contemplative. "Did anything at the scene hint at any type of sexual activity?"

"I didn't see or smell anything."

"What did you smell?" she asked.

I made a disgusted face. "Death."

"You should call Arthur," Rupert said. "Let him know that the ME needs to run a test for any type of bodily fluids on or around the body. They may have already done one, but make sure."

Why hadn't I thought of that? See, friends are very important. Especially those with more experience.

"Right, but what about the vampire?"

"I will see what I can do," Lenorre said.

I walked around the couch and sat down, rubbing my temples. "This puts my other investigation on the back burner," I said, and looked at Lenorre.

"What other investigation?" Rupert asked.

"Sheila Morris," I said, "the alpha female of the local werewolf pack." It took a few weeks but I'd finally told Rupert that I'd been kidnapped. I couldn't lie to him. He seemed worried and pissed that he hadn't been there. I assured him that Lukas Morris was one dead puppy. He'd told me he was happy and sad. Happy, because I'd personally filled Lukas's body with silver ammo. Sad, because he didn't get the pleasure of doing it himself. I'd met Sheila once. I don't like her. I especially don't like the things I've heard about her from Rosalin and Lenorre. So, I was watching her and trying to see what dirt I could dig up. I had a gut feeling she would pull some new stunt, probably one that would get people killed. I just didn't know when or how.

"Do you want me to take over?"

"I can't ask you to do that. If she's into the same kicks as her brother, your life would be seriously at risk."

"My life is always seriously at risk."

"She's a werewolf, Rupert. I don't think you could handle that." I wasn't trying to be rude, just truthful. I wanted to keep my friends safe. If I had to tell them something was too difficult for them, that's what I'd do, but I should've known it wouldn't work. Rupert's blue eyes went cold and hard, like water freezing. If looks could've killed, I might've dropped dead. I'd seen the expression on his face only a few times. It'd scare the shit out of any bad guy. To have it directed at me, to feel the full force of it, made my blood run cold. The wolf perked her ears, ready for a challenge. I tightened my shields.

"You have no idea what I can and cannot handle." His tone was grave, dropping a few octaves with each syllable.

"You want the case?" I asked. "Fine, but I want you to call me if you need help."

"I need all the information you have on her, whereabouts, history, etc."

That didn't take long, because I didn't know much. I told him about Sheila's history of being a sadist and where she lived. Some of it, Rupert knew from our talk about my being kidnapped. Lukas had revealed things about his and Sheila's childhood. I told him what I could about the pack.

In the end, Rupert stood. "I'll see if I can find out more about Sheila. I may be your friend and I don't mind taking this load off of your shoulders, but you still owe me." I caught the flicker of a faint smile.

I laughed. "Go figure."

"Twice now," he said.

"For what?"

"For the last time I went hunting with you. I was almost werewolf kibble."

"You were not! We were fine."

His blue gaze flicked to Lenorre. "Then, there was a certain situation where one of her chicks with fangs tried to use me as a punching bag."

"She has been punished," Lenorre said, "as she was not meant to cause you any physical harm."

"Nice to know, but I still don't trust you."

"It is your prerogative to think of me what you will," she said idly. "Only remember your thoughts do not affect me."

Chapter Four

R upert left. Lenorre and I remained seated. I glanced around the cream-colored room, trying to find a clock. Some days it's easy for me to keep track of time. But other times I'm so preoccupied with other things that I forget about it. Being with a vampire, I tried to be aware of time more at night than ever before. I certainly didn't want Lenorre to burst into flames because of some unexpected vitamin D.

As if Lenorre had heard my thoughts, she said, "Do not fret. We have a few hours until the sun rises."

"Was I that obvious?"

"Yes, and I assure you, I will not burst into flames if I am not in bed when it does rise."

"What happens if you're not? Do you just die wherever you're standing?" I sounded harsh, but couldn't think of any other way to put it. I wanted to know, so I asked.

She watched me for several moments. "No. I wouldn't just stand there."

"You'd flee?"

"More or less."

I stood. "I need to shower and to put my things away." I didn't want to talk about death anymore tonight. Even if my girlfriend technically personified it.

Lenorre moved gracefully across the room, picking up my laptop bag and swinging it over her shoulder. I grabbed the backpack, tossing one of the straps over my left shoulder.

She waited in the doorway, watching me with a blank yet thoughtful expression that I couldn't decipher.

"What?" I asked as I walked by.

"Is it so wrong to enjoy watching you?"

"No. I just don't understand it."

We made it to the basement on the other side of the house and through the large steel door into the underground lounge. As always, I had to wait a few seconds for my vision to readjust to the light.

Lenorre led me through the labyrinth of hallways, then opened the double doors at the end of one hallway. Her bedroom was about the size of most living rooms. The king-size canopy bed, placed a foot or two from the wall, was draped with black and burgundy silks. I never knew what colors would decorate it. Unlike mine, Lenorre's bedding changed a couple of times a week. My bed doesn't see enough action to warrant such frequent upkeep.

On the other side of the room was a sitting area, with a black sofa pressed against the farthest wall near a matching armchair. The sofa's back curved in almost a heart shape. Its arms were wide and curling, and on the inside of the curl was a spiral of light gray. The sofa stood on four black-clawed feet.

Once a beautiful painting of the night sky hung on the wall behind the armchair, but now it was gone. The painting had been from the perspective of someone standing on a cliff, gazing at the deep waters of the ocean, with the horned crescent moon high overhead, reflecting off the water. The picture was shattered the first night I had stayed with Lenorre. I learned not to play touchy-feely with the vampire before she died at dawn. I had noticed the pain buried deep in her eyes and tried to distract her from it. The distraction cost both of us, because when she woke, the hunger she had felt before dying channeled into blood lust. Let's just say, it wasn't pretty. The picture didn't survive. I'd have offered to replace it if it hadn't been one of a kind.

Lenorre placed the laptop in the armchair while I let the backpack slide down my arm and onto the couch.

"I will start the water," she said.

She disappeared into the bathroom, and a moment later I heard it running. Bath? I walked quietly into the huge room.

Lenorre sat on the edge of the tub.

"I thought you were starting the shower?" I narrowed my eyes.

"The shower is too large."

"So? What's your point?"

Lenorre tilted her head to one side. "I shall be tempted to join you."

I closed my eyes and focused on breathing. "You just had to put that image in my head, didn't you?"

I heard the water shut off before I felt the weight of her presence in front of me. "That look on your face," she said, voice low, "hearing the way the breath catches in your throat, listening to your heart as it skips a beat. Such intimacy pleases me greatly."

The word *intimacy* made my body tighten and the breath actually catch in my throat.

"Why are you doing this?"

"Because I want to know you want me."

"Can't you see I do?"

I heard her move around me, her energy like a gentle breeze, cool and untouchable.

Her whisper echoed. "Kassandra, I want you to succumb to your desire." She didn't try to hide her British pronunciation, lilting the words in places I couldn't imitate. Then again, I'd never been very good at accents. Lenorre didn't accentuate her words harshly. Her smooth intonation was soft and purring, delectable and soothing at the same time, like silk and chocolate.

I inhaled a shallow breath. "You want me to lose control for you?"

"No, I want you to consent to succumb to your desires."

I turned and looked at her then. "I won't."

"You will not allow yourself to succumb because you are afraid," she said with an unblinking stare.

I nodded and stared at the floor, not entirely thrilled that she was right. I hate admitting that I'm afraid more than I hate actually being afraid.

Lenorre touched my jaw gently with two fingers, lifting my gaze back to hers. It reminded me of when we first met, only this time she wasn't trying to help me control my beast.

"You have been hurt," she said, "as have we all. I want you to lose your fear, to lose your control, to lose the distance you place between us. I want you to stop running from me."

"I'm not running. I'm still standing here, aren't I? If I was running, I wouldn't be in this relationship."

"No, you are not running in a physical sense, but you have placed chains and shackles around your heart, trying to keep it safely in a cage, trying to force it to behave." Lenorre placed a finger over my lips, and I frowned. "You gave yourself to Rosalin, you allowed your wolf to rule your head in a moment of passion, because she was not a threat to your heart. You were able to distance yourself, to give your body to her, to have that release with her, because somewhere in the depths of your mind you knew Rosalin would not scratch below the surface."

I had been thinking practically the same thing after Rosalin and I were together. In truth, I hadn't done anything to her. I had tried to walk away, but she persisted. I had submitted to the energy of our beasts. Lenorre knew afterward that our encounter had been casual. Rosalin and I were friends. She still flirted with me every now and then, but when she saw Lenorre's anger after that one incident she didn't cross any lines. Fine with me. Rosalin was pretty, but we were better as friends than lovers. Besides, I had my hands full with the vampire in front of me. I didn't need a werewolf too. I'm not greedy, nor do I need that much difficulty and drama.

"What are you thinking?" Lenorre asked.

"I agree with what you just said." I didn't continue. It'd be too uncomfortable to admit the truth aloud. Lenorre already knew what had happened. I didn't need to say it.

"I have brought you to the brink," Lenorre said, "but every time you reach that point you back away a little more and pretend nothing has happened."

Was I backing away? I felt like she was luring me into her intricate web. Then again, what we force ourselves to see and what's really there can often be two different things. The authority I'd worked so hard to exert over the beast was the same mastery I was trying to exert over my heart.

"I lost control for you once," I told her. "You could've taken me then."

"I desired you, not the beast that was riding you," she said coldly.

"In that moment, Lenorre," my voice was breathy, "I wanted you, more than I'd ever wanted anyone, more than Rosalin. I can't even begin to describe the things I craved for you to do to me. How can you say I'm the one running away from what happened earlier? I forgot about everything, everything but you—your mouth, your hands, your body." Just admitting it out loud made my stomach flutter uncontrollably.

A dark look slid through her eyes before she closed them. "Kassandra, I desire more than just your body."

I unbuttoned the leather jacket, letting it fall to the floor. The Mark III and shoulder holster were in plain view. Lenorre's eyes flew open, then flicked from my face to the gun.

"If that's what you want," I stepped closer, "then take it, but stop analyzing the situation. When you analyze, when you talk instead of act, you give me time to think, and when you give me time to think, you give me time to distance myself."

I heard her sharp intake of breath and suddenly understood why she enjoyed listening to the breath catch in my throat. I watched as her chest rose and fell. The undead don't have to breathe to survive. I knew she had taken that breath for my benefit. Her gaze filled with an otherworldly light. Her eyes that had been smoky were suddenly liquid silver.

"I should have known," she said softly, but before I could ask what she should've known she grabbed me. Her arms snaked around my back. She kissed me as deeply, and as passionately, as she had earlier. With her body against mine, with her tongue filling my mouth, all thoughts washed away like words written in sand. Her hands slid down the arch of my spine, over the slight swell of my ass. A moment later I felt her nails through my jeans and the pain made me moan. In one fluid motion Lenorre picked me up. I wrapped my legs around her thin frame, burying my hands in her long silken hair, crushing the curls with my fists. Lenorre didn't break the kiss when she carried me into the bedroom.

CHAPTER FIVE

She broke the kiss when she placed me gently on the bed, then climbed on top of me and turned off the bedside lamp.

I looked at Lenorre and felt like I was stuck in some erotic, thrilling black-and-white movie. Her curls fell around her incredibly pale face, making it appear even more striking. With her on top of me, the cut of her gown pulled away from her body. It was loose enough that my gaze was drawn to the swell of her white breasts.

A new wave of desire filled me. The anticipation speeded up my pulse, made my heart beat faster. Could she see me as well as I could see her in the dark? But before I could ask, she grabbed the front of my shoulder holster, pulling my face to hers.

She kissed me, gently at first like the brush of a moth's wing. I pressed into the kiss, begging her for the depth my mouth craved, my body craved. She pushed me down on the pillows, her pale face looming like some dark beauty. With both hands she grabbed the strap of the holster, and before I could tell her not to, the leather snapped.

"There are things I want from you, Kassandra," she said, words like a susurrus wind tickling autumn leaves. Lenorre's power rode the air and pulsed against my skin like a clinging mist.

Her voice sent chills up my spine, encouraging my body to rise to meet hers.

"Things that might frighten you," she whispered against the fall of my hair. Her hand traveled the front of my body. She placed her hand between my legs, and even through the jeans, I could feel the weight of her power. The promise of what we were about to do.

The wolf stirred, rising in me like some great wave. She pushed near the surface, but instead of threatening to break through, she waited. I placed my hands on Lenorre's hips, sliding them up the curve of her body until I cupped both of her breasts.

Her dark eyelashes fluttered.

"You won't frighten me, Lenorre."

"Are you so sure?" Her body went inhumanly still. I sat up and caught her shoulders. Lenorre let me push her onto her back.

I climbed on top of her, grabbed a handful of her gown, and tugged. The buttons popped in a small orchestra of ripping thread and little pings as some of them hit the wall. I pressed my mouth against her collarbone, nibbling lightly. Lenorre moaned.

Her hands were cool as she raised my shirt and stroked my stomach, but instead of taking off my shirt she tucked her fingers under the waistband of my jeans. At the touch of her fingers so dangerously close, I reached down to unbutton them. I was going through far too many clothes these days. And I hate shopping. I don't mind the new clothes, but I don't enjoy trying to pile-drive through a maze of shop-crazy women. This little werewolf is not that courageous.

Her mouth was suddenly against the side of my neck, tongue lingering over my suddenly thudding pulse. "No." She pushed my shoulders and I fell back.

Lenorre didn't bother to unbutton my jeans. She caught the two folds of material and jerked, dragging them down in an achingly slow manner. The line of my black satin panties showed against my pale skin. She lowered her head, planting kisses across the jagged slant of my hipbone.

"Are you afraid?" she asked.

"If saying I'm afraid will get your mouth between my legs, then yes, I'm afraid, very afraid."

Lenorre's laugh vibrated against me, caused my spine to bow. She licked a slow path across the top of my underwear, sealing a kiss against my skin. The muscles in my stomach contracted, rigid against the pleasure. She placed those small kisses on the lower half of my body until her hands slid up over my hips, across my ribs.

"Lenorre," I moaned. "Please…"

"Please what?" Her words were muffled against my thigh.

"Make love to me."

"We will get to that, my love." The lilt in her voice told me she was amused. Her velvet tongue slid across my thigh.

"Are you laughing at me?" I groaned, frustrated and desperate.

She slid her fingers across the hollow between my thigh and groin, then slipped two of them effortlessly beneath the damp satin that covered my crotch. The edge of one finger brushed my clit, and I gasped again, but it didn't stop there. She teased my opening, stroking back and forth, making the muscles low in my body contract, making me wetter than I already was. But I didn't need to be any wetter. I was ready.

"Lenorre!" I said, somewhere between a pant and a growl. I dug my hands into the comforter on the bed as I yelled, "Please!"

She did what I wanted her to. She gradually, oh so gradually, eased two fingers inside of me.

"More," I begged. "Lenorre." I moaned as her fingers glided over a very pleasurable spot. "I need more." My hips rose as her long, slender fingers hit the back of my cervix. Caught between pleasure and pain, I didn't want her to stop.

Need. I was a throbbing, pulsing, aching thing filled only with need. I needed her, my entire body trembled with need, but this, this was too slow, and too small a taste of what she was capable of doing to me. I craved chaos and oblivion, while she gave me order and acute awareness. Desire burned between my legs. Lenorre fanned that flame, made it burn brighter, more painful as she drove her fingers in and out of me. Each stroke was excruciatingly slow, making the fire stretch and grow until I felt as if it would consume me. My body ached for release.

"So wet."

My muscles contracted. She hit that spot inside me and slowly began to withdraw.

"Lenorre," I pleaded, holding myself on my elbows. My vision blurred around the edges. In a move too quick for me to register she tore the satin underwear away with an angry hiss. She put our faces dangerously close, keeping her hand between my legs.

"Kassandra." Without warning she shoved her fingers inside of me. This time, there was no order, no teasing, no careful restraint. She simply fucked me with supernatural strength. Her lips were hot where they met mine, and wet, like she had just licked them. Her mouth was unyielding, with nothing chaste or gentle about it. I opened to her, spreading my legs wider, slipping my hand under her gown. I cupped her breasts and her nipples stiffened like tiny darts. Distantly, in some part of my mind I managed to hear the wooden posts of the canopy hitting the wall.

I drove my nails into her and Lenorre broke the kiss, rearing back with a hiss that revealed her fangs. I tugged at her clothes trying to pull them from between our bodies. It took me a moment to realize that Lenorre was bracing herself with her knees, and the gown was stuck under her.

The only way to get the dress up was to tear it, so I lowered my shields and focused on the wolf, calling her. Her warm energy pressed against the inside of my skin like soft fur. I wasn't aiming for a full shift. What I offered her was a peek through a door with a chain and lock. Control is strength. If you can't control your beast, it will control you. Some days, it's an internal battle for dominance. How much the wolf fights depends on how badly she wants out. If she wants to investigate or munch on something in the immediate surroundings, it's a little more difficult to sway her. Fortunately, Lenorre wouldn't show up on the wolf's radar as food. The wolf craved life, a fresh kill, not the undead.

Energy spilled down my arm, into my hands. I gazed at her through the eyes of the wolf.

Lenorre spared a glance between our bodies. When she raised her face, the look she gave was challenging.

I got a better hold of the gown, digging claws into it. Her laugh thrummed through me when she saw my transformed hands and she pushed against me, forcing my hips to meet her thrusts.

She buried her face in the bend of my neck. "I had no idea just how untamed you are."

My claws tore through the velvet and it gave way. The side of her dress slipped off to expose a long line of flesh from ankle to torso. Though she might not have been wearing a bra, her dark lace underwear stood out over her body like a cloud trying to obscure the moon. I grabbed a fistful of the material at her shoulders, tearing it away. I snaked my arm between our bodies, grasping her underwear. The underwear tore more easily than the dress.

All the while, her fingers never ceased their rhythm.

"I may be a vampire," she said calmly, "but I cannot expend this much energy without feeding soon."

She shoved her fingers deep inside me, curling them, pressing into my deepest corners.

When I had enough breath to speak, I said, "Problem."

Lenorre began flicking her fingers over that spot as I writhed beneath her. "Yes?"

"I..." I had to grab on to something. My claws pierced the mattress as my spine bowed. "Can't do...Ah, fuck!"

Lenorre's voice was a hell of a lot more even than mine. "You can't do what?" she asked, obviously amused again.

I wrapped my legs around her as she sat back on her knees, keeping the new rhythm she'd found. She slid a hand beneath my ass, raising my lower body off the bed. At this angle, her fingers went deeper. I'd never gotten off on penetration. I'd enjoyed a woman's fingers inside of me, but no woman had ever made it feel quite so mind-numbingly pleasurable.

Lenorre read my body and my hips bucked against her hand.

"Kassandra," she said, and I fought against my fluttering eyelashes to look at her. Her fingers flicked again, and this time I had to close my eyes to keep them from rolling. Lenorre laughed as I jerked helplessly. "Save your breath," I felt the heat of her breath against my clit, "you will need it."

She covered me with her mouth, sucking lightly at first, and when that awarded her with a moan, she sucked harder. Her fangs pierced that sensitive skin, and I was too taken with the pleasure to care. The tip of her tongue glided over my clit, as fast as her fingers had inside of me. The orgasm wasn't gradual. It didn't build and slowly spill over. It pierced me and tore a ragged half-moan half-scream from my mouth.

Lenorre didn't let me catch my breath. She pushed me further, into the abyss of pleasure so wondrous, it hurt to feel it. My claws convulsed in the mattress. I hadn't let the shift take me over completely, but I hadn't exactly pushed the beast out of my hands and eyes. My canines lengthened, sharpened, and I could no longer hold her at bay. She intended to take her chance to get out.

There were sounds, sounds of destruction as my claws tore sheet and mattress, springs popping, and the sounds of a woman's screams caught somewhere between ecstasy and agony.

A part of me understood whose screams they were, understood I was the one screaming, but I no longer cared. The orgasm stripped away all my precious control. I tried to cling to the fragments of it, but it was too late. I tried to hold the wolf at bay, tried to shove her back into her invisible crate somewhere inside of me. She'd found the weak spot, discovered the door in my shields that the orgasm had opened further. She shoved her furred body against that door, fighting with everything she had, wiggling and squirming in her frenzy to get out and run amok.

The wolf burst from my skin and the darkness swallowed me.

CHAPTER SIX

Voices woke me and I started pushing away the last fogs of sleep.

"How long has she been out?" It was Rosalin's voice.

"She has been asleep for nearly nine hours." I'd recognize Lenorre's honeyed voice anywhere.

A woman's voice I didn't recognize asked, "Did you bite her?"

Lenorre's voice was empty. "Yes."

"Has this ever happened to you?" Rosalin asked, and I didn't know what the hell she was talking about.

"No," Lenorre said, "but I heard rumors of it when I was with my old mistress."

Mistress? I was growing more curious. I kept my breath slow and even, pretending to be asleep. Call it a hunch, but I had a feeling I'd get more from their conversation that way.

"Rumors?" The woman's voice sounded familiar, but I still couldn't place it or picture the face that went with it.

The back of my thigh itched with a tickling sensation that you can ignore at first, but then it grows until you can't do anything but scratch it. I held my breath, which was a bad idea.

The room was suddenly quiet. I thought about trying to pretend I was sleeping again but figured I'd already blown my cover. Rosalin and Lenorre had most likely already heard the glitch in my breathing. What the hell. I scratched my thigh and rolled over.

Rosalin was sitting on the couch. Lenorre met my gaze from the armchair, and not too far from her, Zaphara sat with long legs crossed at the ankles. At nearly six feet, Lenorre was tall. Zaphara stood even a couple of inches taller than Lenorre. The first time I had met her, she'd been encircled in Lenorre's arms. The two had been necking. I might've been jealous except that necking by vampire standards is very different from human standards. If a vampire wanted to neck with someone, they didn't necessarily want to have a hot and steamy make-out session.

Of course, the biting could be erotic and sensual. But generally, when a vampire wants to neck, blood will often be drawn.

The idea of Lenorre's mouth on Zaphara didn't really sit well with me.

Zaphara's gaze was beautiful and alien. An air about her screamed, "Not human." I just couldn't figure out what the hell she was. Her eyes were the color of amethyst and shone in the dimly lit room. The hair that she normally let loose to fall past her waist was pulled back at the nape of her neck in a low ponytail. I could never tell if her hair color was natural or if she had a really good dye job. When the light reflected off the glossy tresses, I realized they were purple-black. With her hair drawn back, the pale triangle of her face stood out to perfection. It brought out the delicate curve of her jaw and her model-high cheekbones. She looked to be in her mid-twenties, but something I couldn't peg about Zaphara made her seem a heck of a lot older.

"How long have you been awake?" Rosalin asked.

"Long enough to be confused."

"How do you feel?" Lenorre asked.

"Like I need coffee." I shoved my arm under the pillow, unable to remember falling asleep on Lenorre's side of the bed. "When did you wake?"

Rosalin and Zaphara glanced at one another. Lenorre remained silent.

"What?" I asked.

Rosalin stood from the couch. "Where's your cell phone?"

"In my jeans, I think. Why?"

She glanced around the room. "Okay, where are your jeans?"

I sat up and glanced at the floor, finding my jeans in a crumpled heap. "What do I need my cell for?" I asked. I turned to find Rosalin's eyes fixed somewhere below my face.

"Shit." I grabbed a handful of black sheet and used it to cover my chest. "Thanks for telling me." Why did I feel like I was always accidentally giving Rosalin a free show?

"I did." She grinned, baring her perfectly white teeth. "I looked, didn't I?"

"What do I need my cell for?" I asked again. I dug out my phone, keeping the sheet pinned to my chest. How had I not realized I was naked? In fact, where were my clothes?

"What time is it, Kassandra?" Zaphara asked.

I opened the phone. "Three. Wait, I slept until three in the morning? Are you fucking kidding me?"

"Kassandra, look again," Lenorre said. This time I noticed the little PM by the time.

"You're awake?" It was part question, part statement.

Lenorre leaned back in her seat. "So it seems."

"Why are you awake? You're supposed to die at dawn."

"Yes," she said.

"You said something about a *mistress* and rumor."

Lenorre's face was emotionless. "Every vampire has a creator."

"Yeah, but you called her a *mistress*." I managed to make the words sound empty and focused on controlling my facial expressions. I succeeded. Most cops and investigators are good at having a blank expression.

"She is my creator," Lenorre explained. "Mistress is what she wished to be called. It is what she was to me, once."

"Is?" I questioned. "As in, she's still alive or, well, undead?"

She nodded.

I spoke my thoughts out loud. "I guess it's better than her Ladyship."

"Far better," Lenorre said.

"So, why are you awake? What do the words *Mistress* and *rumor* have to do with it?"

"You weren't this coherent when I woke you that one time…" Rosalin said.

I gave her an irritated look. When we had first met, Lenorre sent Rosalin home with me. She'd snuck into my room and woke me up. I was pretty sure she'd woken me on Lenorre's orders, as Lenorre had planned a big, spiffy date. I had to choose between going or not going and pissing off a Countess vampire. Guess which option I chose?

I responded to Rosalin's statement with, "Apparently, I got nine hours of sleep."

"As I was saying before you woke," Lenorre changed the subject before either Rosalin or I could say anything else, "I had heard a rumor when I was still in my creator's care that some days she was able to escape death at dawn."

"How is that possible?" I asked.

Zaphara's expression was detached when she said, "Powerful food."

"Indeed," Lenorre said, "powerful food."

"I am not food," I said. "Stop, both of you. Use a word other than *food*."

"Dessert?" Rosalin asked with a giggle.

"Ha, ha, fuzzy butt, very funny."

"Fuzzy butt?" Rosalin burst into laughter. "Oh, you're cute when you throw childish insults at me."

I glared at her.

Lenorre said, "Rosalin," and Rosalin closed her yap. I knew I was being childish, but I had to smirk at the now-silent werewolf.

"As I was saying," Lenorre continued, "my mistress was able to escape death by drinking the blood of one who was powerful enough to offer such sustenance."

"The question is," Zaphara looked at me, and something in her gaze made me want to squirm uncomfortably, "is Kassandra that powerful?" She seemed to be talking more to herself than anyone else in the room. No one answered, and neither Rosalin nor Lenorre attempted to stop her when she began to walk toward me. She moved in a predatory way, using all her height. The pants Zaphara wore were so tight I could see the play of muscles beneath them. If the room hadn't been carpeted, I might've heard the clacking of her heels, but as it was, her boots were quiet. Why was that suddenly very unnerving?

Zaphara reached out to touch me and I recoiled. Though I didn't know what she was, I didn't want her to touch me. Somewhere inside, the wolf agreed, pacing back and forth. I closed my eyes. Calm. Calm was a good idea.

"Are you afraid of me?" she asked.

"I don't like strangers touching me."

"Am I that strange to you, little one?"

I didn't like being called "little one." It made me feel like a child.

"Yeah, you are."

Her laugh was rich and throaty, and so abrupt I actually jumped. What the hell was she? I felt my eyes widen as she reached out to touch me again. Though I resisted the urge to slap her hand away, I couldn't stifle my low rumble.

When I growled, Zaphara hesitated, and a wary look slipped through her eyes. "I do not want to hurt you."

"Then, what do you want?"

"A taste."

"A taste of what?" My voice was beginning to fall into the huskier, deeper tone of the wolf.

"Your power. I promise I won't bite, though, from what I have heard, you enjoy that."

"You don't know what I enjoy."

"One can take a guess."

"No, you're being presumptuous."

A look of amusement flashed through her amethyst eyes. "Maybe." She reached for me again. This time when I tried to move out of reach I was too slow. Zaphara showed me that she had been polite during her first two attempts. She caught my arm, digging her fingers into my skin hard enough to bruise. If I hadn't been a werewolf, it might've. She pulled me roughly toward her.

"I told you I won't bite," she murmured. A shudder rippled through her body and through the fingers that were digging into my skin. "But now I'm tempted to."

Before I could frame a reply, Zaphara pressed her mouth against mine. I brought my arms up to push her away and the air was suddenly warm, so warm, like the glow of the sun kissing my skin. The magic hit me, and I forgot why I had been trying to break free of her hold. Her lips that had seemed harsh were soft and yielding. Her breath filled my mouth, like autumn wind unadulterated by pollutants. Fresh, like the air might've been a million years ago. The wolf and I turned our faces into the warm pulse of Zaphara's power.

The heat of that metaphysical sun intensified, suddenly too hot, threatening to burn the skin, and then it changed… Stillness.

Her power slammed into me, crushing the breath from my lungs. The smell of fresh dirt and decaying leaves filled my senses. Ice. The harshness of winter pierced me. I screamed against her mouth and the wolf howled with me, alarmed and angry.

Something stirred at the center of my being, rushing past the wolf's alarmed rage. It spilled from that center in a breeze of heat, trying to push away the coldness that threatened to eat me alive. The raven swooped from its perch somewhere inside me. It opened its large black wings and pushed against the weight of Zaphara's magic, fought against the unforgiving cold.

The frost melted. There was only water, and with nothing to hold on to, I was suddenly drowning. I tried to breathe but the air was too heavy.

How do you fight against a magic you do not understand?

A voice flowed through my mind. "You explore that magic, find its weakness."

Weakness? Zaphara's power was overwhelming. I did the only thing I could think of. I willed myself to be still, as I often did in meditation. This was a place inside myself not even the beast within could touch. It was not her room to retreat to. It was mine. All the emptiness and heartbreak I'd ever experienced was in that one place of my psyche. All the pain and loss and resentment came tumbling like a ball of yarn into my hand.

I cast my will into Zaphara's magic like a spear.

Her spell wavered, and I was suddenly able to feel her rough grip on my arm. I let my anger call me back to my body and tried to keep my focus on my shields. I swallowed, stifling the wolf's rage. I didn't need her anger. I had my own, thanks.

"The problem with your magic, Zaphara," I said harshly, "is that it's not real."

She let me go, climbing off me. At some point, we'd both fallen back on the bed.

Lenorre and Rosalin stood close by. Lenorre's face was as blank as it usually was. Rosalin seemed ready for a fight, her shoulders tense. It looked like they had been ready to interfere if Zaphara had decided to take things too far. I would've appreciated them interfering before she kissed me.

Zaphara stopped and looked at Lenorre. I heard her say, "She is more than she seems."

Lenorre gave her a disapproving look. "You need to leave now."

Zaphara laughed and directed a sweeping bow at me. "It's been a pleasure, Kassandra." She made my name sound disturbingly intimate.

"You keep pushing me," I growled, "and you'll make it on to my shit list."

She raised her brows. "Oh?"

Zaphara made it to the door before she stopped. "One day we will see who is the more fey of us. You and your Goddess, or me and my blood." With that, she left, shutting the door behind her.

Fey? What the hell was that supposed to mean?

Rosalin let out a breath she'd been holding. "You know," she said, "I can usually tolerate Zaphara, but sometimes she's so arrogant."

"Zaphara is not a modest creature," Lenorre said.

"Creature," I mumbled. "I could think of other words to call her right now."

"Now that I think of it," Rosalin said, "so could I."

Rosalin and I both turned to look at Lenorre, who spared a glance at Rosalin and then steadily met my gaze. If I had thought she would share her thoughts with me, I was wrong. Lenorre kept whatever opinions she had to herself, which only made me more curious to know what was going on inside her head.

CHAPTER SEVEN

R osalin offered to go make coffee. I knew there was a kitchen somewhere in the basement level, but I didn't know where. I'd only seen the one in the main part of the house.

Lenorre paced in the middle of the room like some dangerous black leopard slinking back and forth in a cage. She stopped, as if feeling my gaze, and turned to look at me. The bell sleeves of her black robe fanned out gracefully about her wrists. The sash was tied loosely at her cinched waist, showing off her hourglass figure. Lenorre's figure wasn't exactly subtle, but it wasn't sickly looking either. Was she old enough to have worn corsets most of her life?

"What are you thinking about, Kassandra?" The curls falling over her shoulders and to her lower back were messy. It was nice to see her hair less than perfect for once.

"You wore corsets, didn't you?" I wanted to know and didn't want to know how old she was. Why? I'd dated women older than me. I never looked at age, but if Lenorre had been alive during the Victorian Era, that would make her over a hundred.

That's the thing with vampires. They don't grow old in appearance. Whatever age a vampire is when they die is the age they appear for the rest of their lives. Had any vampires been turned when they were already old humans? How much would that suck?

"Are you trying to figure out how old I am?"

I shrugged guiltily. "Kind of."

"Kind of?" She gave me a curious look. "Are you fretting over the generation gap?"

I shook my head. "No. It doesn't bother me."

"Yes, I wore corsets." She looked amused. "If you must know, I was changed before that era."

"So, you're over two hundred?" Yeah, I was guessing.

"Yes." She sat on the bed in front of me, and I reclined against the pillows, keeping the sheet tucked up under my arms so that I was covered. I still needed to take a bath, or a shower. "How old were you when you were turned?"

"I was in my early thirties when she turned me." I knew when she said "she," Lenorre was referring to her old mistress.

"When I first met you I thought you were younger. Until you smiled, and I saw the tiniest of lines here." I brushed my fingertip across the corner of her eye.

Lenorre smiled and showed that faint line where crow's-feet would've set in. How many women chose to become undead just to avoid having Botox injections and face lifts?

She slipped her arm around my waist, between my naked back and the pillow. "She did not like them young," Lenorre said, "nor old. She delayed the change until a woman's body had fully developed, till she was at the height of her womanhood and beauty. When we were truly women she turned us."

"Us?" I asked.

"She was a Countess," Lenorre explained. "I was not the only one in her care."

I put my arms around Lenorre's back, pulling her into me. The V of the robe pulled away from her body and I followed the line of her neck, and lower. "Tell me more about this...mistress. You said she was still alive?"

"Mmm-hmm." Lenorre kissed my neck, nibbling a path toward my shoulder. A twinge of heat ran through me.

"Why are you not with her?"

She spoke against the sensitive skin behind my ear. "I was strong enough to break away and create my own clan."

I gasped when she placed her hand over the sheet, sliding it up the front of my body to cup my breast. "Are you trying to distract me?"

"Mayhap," she purred, tucking the tips of her fingers under the sheet and inching it down. She kissed my shoulder, her mouth working its way toward my clavicle.

"Well, it's working." I moaned as her hand stroked my breast, the barest of touches. "But if that's not something you want to talk about, Lenorre, all you have to do is tell me."

Without warning her hands slid under my ass, pulling me lower so I was no longer propped against the pillows. Lenorre grabbed a fistful of sheet, tossing it aside with a whoosh. The cool air caressed my naked skin.

"It is not something I wish to talk about."

Her head bowed and she kissed the pentacle scar on my sternum, just above my breasts. Goose bumps broke out on my arms.

Lenorre began tracing the circle around the pentacle scar with the tip of her tongue. "You never told me just how this happened."

My legs spread wantonly. "I told you it was an accident, didn't I?" I wrapped my arms around her, hands stroking small circles on the back of her shoulders. The robe was smooth and slippery. I arched, raising myself off the bed as my hands sank lower. She was so tall that from this angle I had to settle for playing my nails along her spine.

"Nay, you have not told me." Her tongue licked over the first diagonal line of the star. "Mmm, I know witches are fond of their symbolic jewelry. Silver?" Her breath was cool against the damp lines. The combination of her tongue and words against my skin made my neck prickle.

"Yes." I shuddered as her lips found the side of my breast.

"Yes?"

The warmth of her breath against my nipple made my body tighten. She traced me with her tongue, as slowly and intricately as she had traced the pentacle scar on my sternum. "Yes." I moaned, trying to remember the conversation. She cupped my other breast in her hand, thumb circling the sensitive skin, matching the slow luxurious strokes of her velvety tongue. I moaned again as she caught my nipple between her teeth.

My pulse beat between my legs like a trapped hummingbird.

Lenorre's eyes burned brighter with power, and the breath caught in my throat.

"Lay down."

When Lenorre lowered herself on top of me I touched her shoulder with a hand. "No," I said, "I want you on the other side of me. On your back."

The amused expression didn't leave her face as she gracefully rolled onto her back. "Like so?"

I held myself above her on hands and knees. "Yes." I nuzzled my face in the bend of her neck, burying myself in the ebony curls of her hair. She smelled of cool night air, as if I could smell a frosty breeze on a cold winter night, but mingling with that smell was my scent, the scent of wolf, earthy like musk and pine. I drew the skin of her neck lightly between my teeth and she made a small pleased sound.

I pressed my mouth against the pulse in her neck, feeling it beat like a bird pounding its wings between my jaws. Strangely, at times she had no heartbeat at all, and others, it was there. Did vampires have an on-and-off switch or something? Did it beat when they were well-fed? I traced the vein in her neck with my tongue. I could've bitten her, could've called some of the wolf to my aid and driven canines into her skin, but though blood was a delicious and sweet candy even to the wolf, it was not substantial food.

Besides, werewolf saliva isn't like vampire saliva. Vampire saliva has an anticlotting enzyme in it called Draculin. I shit you not, that's what it's called. It's the same anticoagulant vampire bats inject into their victims. It keeps the blood flowing steadily while the vampire is drinking. Their saliva, much like a vampire bat's, keeps the red blood cells from sticking together and the veins from constricting. How do I know this? Vampire-bat saliva has been used in genetically engineered drugs to help stroke and heart-attack victims. Werewolf saliva just isn't that nifty. Scientists might've been brave enough to take on a vampire bat, but I didn't think they would dare follow an actual vampire around with a spit cup just to see if their saliva could work medical wonders.

"Kassandra."

"Hmm?"

"What are you thinking about?"

I sat back on my heels and started untying the sash of her robe.

"Vampire saliva," I said, watching her lips part seductively.

Her eyes sparkled. "You're thinking about my saliva?"

"Well, yes and no. The anticoagulant in your saliva, to be precise." Yeah, like that made it sound any better. Romantic, that's me. "Why did it feel so good when you bit me?"

Lenorre moved, allowing the robe to fall open. My gaze went from her face to her pale breasts with their soft pink nipples.

"Skill."

"What?" My wits were scrambled by the beauty of her body and the scent of her desire.

I saw her hand moving out of my peripheral vision and caught it, keeping her from slipping it between my legs. "Would you stop trying to distract me?" I gave her a push on the shoulder. "Lay back down."

She did what I asked. "Kassandra, there are few areas in which your mind is easily distracted."

"You're implying the bedroom is one of those?"

"Yes."

My fingers found the sash and I started pulling it free. Lenorre raised her dark brows as I caught her wrists in my hands, pushing them toward the head of the bed.

"What are you doing?" Her voice lilted with amusement. But I wasn't going for that.

"Making sure you can't distract me."

I looped the tie around the black wooden beam. She let me do it, remaining passive while I tied the silken shackles.

Her passivity broke and before I could move she rose, licking a wet line between my breasts.

"Even bound," she murmured against my skin, "I assure you, I can distract you."

I lowered myself until our naked bodies touched completely. "I think it's time I do the distracting, not you."

A pleased sound escaped her as my breasts slid over hers. I shuddered, feeling her nipples harden against my skin, and slid low enough to kiss her breasts.

Lenorre sighed my name and I looked up, rolling her nipple lightly between my teeth. Her head fell back with a soft moan and she tugged gently at her bonds. If she wanted to, she could snap them. Hell, she could snap the bed in half. Being in complete control was solely an illusion.

I grazed the edge of my teeth across her breast, kissing her, taking her into my mouth and sucking. I licked and nipped my way down her body, settling between her legs.

Lenorre draped her legs over my shoulders and I wrapped my arms around them, using my grip to pull her closer to my mouth. I placed a chaste kiss on the inside of her thigh, leaving kisses until I found the hollow between her thigh and groin. I flicked my tongue against that sensitive area and was rewarded with a longer moan. I brushed my lips across her sex, turning my face to the sensitive skin of her inner thigh. This time, it was not a chaste kiss. I drew the skin into my mouth, tucking it between my teeth, careful not to cross the line from pleasure and pain to absolute pain. I ran my left hand over her hip, over the slope of her groin, tracing the hot, wet slit between her legs. Her thighs blossomed like a night-blooming flower opening to the seductive glow of the moon.

I wrapped my arms around her thighs, using them as an anchor. I could smell her, cool and immaculate, like the first sprinkling of hoarfrost on a cold winter night.

Gazing up the length of her porcelain body I realized her fingers were working at the knot at her wrists. While I'd been trying to distract her, she'd been busy. She gave me a challenging look as the silken material fell from one wrist.

Obviously, I hadn't been distracting her well enough.

I dug my nails into her thighs and her back arched. "No," I said.

Lenorre laughed, her voice shaky with pleasure. "I will get out of them eventu—" I pressed my mouth between her legs.

"Kassandra."

I sealed my lips over her, sucking her clit into my mouth. Her hips rose and my pace quickened. I gave myself to her, losing thought of anything but the way she felt in my mouth and her desire coating my lips. The world narrowed to my tongue dancing over her hot flesh and to her moans filling the room like music.

Her muscles tensed beneath my hand and I sucked harder.

"Kassandra." She moaned my name again.

The sight of Lenorre throwing her head back in pleasure almost undid me. Passion drove me as I pushed her to the edge. The sound of her pleasure filled my ears, sweet and encouraging. Lenorre moaned, going rigid under my touch.

Then I moaned, the sound muffled against her. My hands tensed, nails digging into the skin of her thighs. An invisible pleasure built unexpectedly at the base of my spine and spilled through me. I tore my mouth from Lenorre and cried out.

CHAPTER EIGHT

Everything was hazy as I tried to breathe past the pulse thundering against the side of my neck. Lenorre seemed to be doing the same. I rested against her thigh, and she met my gaze with a light and breathless laugh.

"What?" I panted.

"You."

I frowned. "Why?"

"You look so…spent."

I drew a deep breath. "What the hell was that?"

"Wondrous," she said, falling back on the pillows. "Exciting. What is the term they use nowadays? Mind-blowing?"

"Yeah, but that's not what I'm talking about."

"Your orgasm?" she asked.

I nodded.

"Projection," she said.

"You pushed your orgasm onto me?"

"Yes." Her expression was damn near mischievous.

"I've heard of people projecting," I said, "but never of someone projecting an orgasm."

"You've been amongst the humans too long, Kassandra."

To that, I didn't know what to say, except, "I need a bath."

A shower was out of the question. One, I didn't feel like standing up. Two, I wasn't sure I could.

"So do I." Something about the way she said it sounded suggestive.

"Oh, no." I sat up. "No more. After last night, and this afternoon…" Thinking about last night, I looked and, sure enough, I'd torn her mattress all to hell again. The first time I'd torn the mattress apart was when the beast was trying to rip through my skin. It was also the first time I'd shifted into a bird.

I gave Lenorre an apologetic look. "I'm sorry. Did you have to replace the last one?"

"The last mattress? Yes."

"Lenorre, I'm—"

"Kassandra, do not worry about it." The corner of her mouth twitched. "Besides," she smiled like a lazy cat, "that is not the only thing you tore."

My hands were still on her thighs. Confusion made me furrow my brows. A moment later, something warm trickled over my hands. I flicked my gaze to Lenorre's thigh. I'd lost myself to a moment of passion, and when the orgasm had shaken my body into pure oblivion I had cut her. The blood was very bright against the stark white of her skin, but the wounds were already beginning to heal. I stared for several moments, wanting to run my tongue across those scratches. It wasn't entirely the wolf's desire that motivated me, although the scent of fresh blood was making the wolf pace, disturbed by the fact that it was Lenorre bleeding but wanting a taste nonetheless.

I shook the thought away.

"Kassandra," she mused, "if I was so afraid of your nails, I would've asked you to cut them before we went to bed."

I hadn't cut her with my claws, but with my human nails. Not a lot of women in law enforcement have long nails. In fact, for obvious reasons, not many lesbians that I know have long nails either. Maybe it had to do with being a werewolf. I was used to having that defense and felt naked without it. But if I did this kind of damage with them, I could hurt someone I cared about in human form or in wolf form. Thoughts of what I could accidentally do to

Lenorre during a moment of passion overwhelmed me. I started to draw away.

Lenorre untied the knot at her wrist with quick, light movements. She stood, holding the robe closed around her glorious body. "We should bathe."

"We?" I called after her.

She turned on her heel, arching a smooth dark brow in my direction. The look in her eyes told me she'd already made up her mind.

I raised my hands. "Fine."

The corner of her mouth quirked in subtle amusement. Suddenly, I didn't feel so bad.

CHAPTER NINE

The bath hadn't exactly cleared my mind, but the coffee Rosalin had made did the trick. At least as much as it would. I could still smell the scent of Lenorre's skin like some heady perfume.

Rosalin was watching me from her perch on the small bar.

"You look," she tilted her head to the side, "unusually relaxed…"

"Unusually relaxed?"

"Yeah. You're not holding your shoulders as stiffly."

Rosalin was a werewolf, and our kind pay attention to body language. It didn't shock me that she'd noticed the subtle change. I'd have spotted it in her.

"I told you when we first met you needed a good shagging. Looks like I was right."

I almost spit out the sip of coffee I'd taken. "Rosalin…"

She shrugged, rinsing her mug out in the sink and putting it in the dishwasher. "I have to admit, I'm a little disappointed it wasn't my doing."

"Rosalin…"

She waved a hand in the air, absentmindedly. "I know, I know. I'm not hurt." She laughed. "My ego is just a little bruised."

"Well, it shouldn't be," I said, remembering what had transpired between us. "You were," I searched for the word, "persuasive."

"Please." She practically snorted the word, pushing the auburn locks out of her face. "You just hadn't ever had sex with another lykos."

I nodded. "There is that."

Lenorre walked into the kitchen wearing a pair of tight black pants tucked into knee-high leather boots. The blouse she wore was a metallic silver far lighter than the color of her eyes. The collar and cuffs were folded neatly. She had tucked the shirt into the pants, so that it showed the slim perfection of her waist. The entire outfit accentuated her height and made me think of the word "slinky." The few top buttons on the blouse were left undone, but modestly so, just enough to tantalize and tease. My heart raced at the sight of her.

Rosalin shook her head, catching my attention.

"What?" I asked her.

"Ah, *amore*," she said breathily, touching her hand to her heart.

"I don't like to be teased."

"I'm not teasing," she grinned, "just pointing out the obvious."

"Kassandra." Lenorre caught my attention before I could respond to Rosalin. "What do you have planned for this evening?"

"Working on the case."

"Were you off work today?" Rosalin asked.

I nodded. I'd asked Rit, my partner at the office, to take over unless otherwise notified. She was a good sport. I'd had too much on my plate the last few weeks to contract any new clients. I was glad Rupert was helping me out, digging up what information he could on Sheila Morris. Hell, maybe he'd have better luck than I did.

"Where's your gun?" Rosalin asked.

The green thermal was too tight to successfully cover the Pro .40 in the small-of-the-back holster without a jacket. I hadn't thought to bring my extra gun, and since I wouldn't wear the Mark III without a holster, I wasn't wearing one.

I looked at Lenorre.

"You took her gun?" A perplexed look crossed Rosalin's face. Her confusion turned to disbelief.

"No."

Rosalin looked confused again, trying to figure out what had happened.

"So, then…where's your gun?"

"The shoulder holster is out of service."

"Out of service?" She gave a quiet laugh. "What is that supposed to mean? Do we need to stick another quarter in it?"

"Lenorre broke it."

Lenorre lifted her shoulders. "I am willing to replace it."

In fact, after our bath, she had offered to get me a new one.

"I told you not to worry about it, and I mean it. I just feel… naked without any weapons."

I heard soft footfalls to my left and glanced toward the dining room door as Zaphara entered. Her long dark hair was still pulled away from her face, falling in a tight braid down her back. She wore a long trench coat. When she moved the light hit the coat, igniting the iridescent colors in the black vinyl.

"Ready?" Zaphara looked at me.

"For?"

"I was talking to Lenorre."

"Then perhaps you shouldn't look at me," I said, stifling a growl.

"Yes," Lenorre said, "give us a moment."

Lenorre explained that she needed to drop by The Two Points and that she wanted me with her.

I glared at Zaphara. "Please tell me she's not going with us?"

"She is."

"I would rather Rosalin go with us than Zaphara." The way I said her name wasn't exactly friendly, but then again, I was beginning to dislike Zaphara. Why bother hiding it?

"Rosalin does not inspire fear in others," Lenorre said.

"Thanks," Rosalin said. "That makes me feel really good about myself."

I touched her arm, briefly. "If it's any consolation, I really do prefer your company over hers."

I glared at Zaphara again. She laughed.

Yeah, this was going to be fun. Not.

Lenorre said my name to get my attention.

"Fine," I said, "but I'm driving."

Lenorre sat in the passenger seat next to me. No way in hell would I let Zaphara sit there. It was bad enough she'd chosen the seat behind mine. Every time I checked the rearview mirror, her mouth quirked in a devilish smile. Why we couldn't just strap her to the hood of the car like a prized deer was beyond me.

"Zaphara, your head is in my way." I tried to keep the irritation out of my tone, but a little of it slipped through. She chuckled. A second later I heard the sounds of her moving across the seat, into the one behind Lenorre. I hadn't argued with Zaphara when she'd decided not to wear a seat belt. Lenorre put hers on without questioning, probably because she knew I wouldn't start the car until she did. Zaphara could handle her own if we got into a wreck and she flew out the front window. Mean, maybe, but the thought amused me.

Lenorre was unnervingly quiet, though I heard Zaphara messing with something in the backseat. I tossed a glance over my shoulder to find she was going through my CDs in their black binder.

"What the hell do you think you're doing?" I turned my gaze back to the road. We were almost to the highway.

"What does it look like I'm doing?"

"Fine. Why are you going through my CDs? Is that better?"

"Much better." I glanced back to see she was still flipping through the pages with CDs in them, as if it was all so very interesting. "I was curious," she said.

"Just because you're curious doesn't mean you've got the right to snoop around," I grumbled loud enough to be heard. I drew in a deep calming breath. It wouldn't do any good to let Zaphara get to me and let my anger call to the wolf. She wasn't worth it.

Zaphara lifted her index finger, pointing toward the floorboard, and made a small circle in the air, suggesting I turn my gaze back to the road. I was really, really beginning to dislike her.

I heard a CD sliding out of its little plastic holder, then Zaphara was suddenly hovering between Lenorre and me. She tried to push the CD into the player, but since there was already one in it, it wouldn't go in.

"That's it!" I slammed my foot on the brake. The last stop sign before I would make a left turn and take the on-ramp to the highway was a good twenty feet away. Lenorre flung a hand out, bracing herself against the dash as the car skidded to a halt. Zaphara, having nothing to hold on to, flung a hand out to grab the corner of my seat, but most of her upper body was flung forward between the seats against the dashboard. I hoped her ass landed on the gearshift.

"You need to fucking sit back and shut the fuck up," I said, a bass growl vibrating against my chest. "I am not fucking playing with you. I am not playing your fucking little game. I don't give a damn how much fun you think it is. Stop it. If you don't, you can get out of the car and walk your happy ass home."

I glared at Zaphara, knowing the wolf stared through my gaze. In human form, my eyes were green, but when the beast rose they changed. The few flecks of gold around my pupils spread out like a bursting star. It was unnerving to watch. I'd seen it only a few times in the mirror. Zaphara's expression went from surprised to curious.

Lenorre said, "Zaphara."

One word and Zaphara moved to the backseat. She sat down and, surprisingly, did what I had asked. She kept her damn mouth shut. The CD had fallen to the floorboard when the car jolted to a stop. Lenorre handed it back to Zaphara, who picked the case up off the floorboard and returned the CD to its slot.

Her expression was free of satisfaction or devilishness. She didn't even look smug. I was surprised. Slowly, she inclined her head and I relaxed a little.

I took my foot off the brake and drove in silence the rest of the way to the club.

CHAPTER TEN

When we got to the club the parking lot was empty with the exception of a few cars here and there. I guessed they were employee cars. The club was open to the public from Thursday to Sunday. Since it was Wednesday, they were closed. You had to be eighteen to enter and twenty-one to drink in The Two Points. The patrons were eclectic, ranging from high-school and college students to hard-working adults. As with most clubs, business hopped on the weekend.

Rosalin had informed me several weeks ago that the club had a gay-and-lesbian night. It was held in a different part of the club, with a bouncer on each door. I was heading toward the main entrance when I heard Zaphara mumble, "Quite the mouth, she has."

I turned back to see she was walking beside Lenorre. She'd spoken as if I couldn't hear, but I was guessing she actually didn't care if I did.

Lenorre's stormy gaze met mine, glinting softly in the streetlight. "You have no idea," she said, her voice low. I ignored the twinge between my legs.

I waited by the two double doors as they approached. Zaphara reached for the door and looked back when she noticed Lenorre had stopped to stand next to me.

"Go inside and tell the others I wish to speak with them privately," Lenorre said.

Zaphara did as she was told without question. I nearly had to put her through the windshield to get her to stop looking at my CDs, but Lenorre asks and off she goes.

Lenorre touched my shoulder, and I jumped, turning back to her.

"I know she makes you uncomfortable," she said softly, "but you must believe me when I tell you that she is not as bad as she pretends to be."

"Not to you. You've got her wrapped around your finger."

Lenorre shook her head, curls dancing against her back "No, she is not wrapped around my finger. You merely have to give her a reason to respect you. Until she does, she will continue to challenge, tease, and even sink to the level of irritating you intentionally. It is similar with wolves in a pack. She taunts you."

I pictured various ways of gaining respect from Zaphara…none of them exactly pleasant for her. But if I wasn't careful Zaphara would literally flip my bitch switch. I wanted to jump on her and make her…well, make her do *something*. The words "shut up" came to mind.

"I don't really care if she respects me or not."

"You should. Zaphara is not one you would enjoy having as an enemy."

"What is she?"

"That is for her to say."

I gave a frustrated growl.

"I'm not putting myself out there and trying to be her friend, Lenorre. You'll just have to deal with that. So far, I don't like her, and my dislike grows every time she opens her damn mouth."

The corner of Lenorre's mouth twitched and humor illuminated her gaze.

"Don't," I said.

Her smile was genuine, but awkward, as if she was trying not to but couldn't help herself. "I do not expect you to befriend her. I think you have gained some of her respect with your little stunt in the car. You caught her off guard and showed her she has underestimated you."

"She keeps pushing my buttons. It's really annoying. If you're asking me to try to control my anger, to not start a fight with her, I'll try, but I want to know why."

Lenorre put a hand on the brick wall behind me. "Because she is my friend."

"Wait. That's not fair. You can't pull the friend card on me." I tried to glare at her and knew I failed. The smell of her skin so close was intoxicating.

"Just as Rupert is your friend, Zaphara is mine." She leaned in until I could feel her body scant inches from my own.

"I hate it when you do that," I mumbled.

"Do what?"

"Distract me while you drive home your point. It's not fair."

Her lips were against my brow. "Isn't it?"

She took a step back and I reached out to stop her, burying my hand in her thick curls. I pulled her mouth to mine. "If you're trying to distract me, distract me properly."

Her tongue traced my lips before she pressed into the kiss.

"Better?"

I cupped her face, pulling her back toward me. "Not yet," I mumbled, but I didn't kiss her. I inhaled her scent. Our scents mingled like a wintery forest. Gently, I used my cupped hands to tilt her head. I pressed my mouth against her brow and stepped out from between the wall and her body.

"Now we're even."

The onyx crests of Lenorre's eyelashes rose. That otherworldly silver light made my pulse race, made my body tighten. She went entirely still, predatorily still…and then…her laughter filled the night like something sweet and touchable.

"What have I gotten myself into with you?"

"I should be asking myself the same thing."

She reached into her blouse pocket, holding out a square of black material. I took it from her, realizing it was a handkerchief.

"What?"

"Your face." She sounded amused.

It took me a moment to realize I was wearing most of her lipstick. I set about using the handkerchief to wipe it off.

"Come here," I said. She did what I asked and I wiped the faint imprint of my lips off her brow.

"You win."

"I win?" she asked.

"For now, I'll try to play nice with Zaphara. Though I'm not happy with you for not telling me what she is. Clearly, she isn't human. She doesn't seem to be a vampire and she sure as hell isn't a wolf. But I'll wait, if you trust her so much."

To that, she was silent.

"Does my face still look like a crime scene?"

"No." She opened the door.

CHAPTER ELEVEN

W e met in the same room Lenorre had escorted me to when I first met her. The room was upstairs, past the dining area, in a shadowed corner of the club. I followed Lenorre as the throng of vampires parted before us. The candles in the room had been lit and cast flickering shadows along the walls. Lenorre took a seat on the couch and I followed. Zaphara stood next to it, arms crossed, watching each vampire enter the room with a cautious gaze. Although she was likely an occasional blood donor, she played another role in Lenorre's life. Zaphara was a bodyguard. But what the hell was she hiding under the trench coat?

"My lady." The vampire who had spoken moved to the middle of the room. His long brown hair fell around his shoulders like a sandy waterfall. He went to one knee before Lenorre, bowing his head. "You requested our presence."

Like most of the other vampires in the room, he was incredibly pale. My skin was almost as light as the vampires', but human and lycanthrope skin doesn't take on that luminous paleness.

"Futhark," Lenorre said, "you may stand."

The vampire rose. Futhark? Was that his name? I wasn't oblivious to the Norse path. In fact, I'd studied the Futhark runes, once upon a time, but a vampire named Futhark? He was tall, about six-five. Guiding the long silky tresses behind his shoulders, he looked at me with incredibly blue eyes, but they were not true blue. Specks of chestnut brown ringed his pupils. He was slim, with a slim face, his cheekbones high enough to make his eyes seem deeper and give him a wise, thoughtful expression. Suddenly, the name suited him. He was named after the old Germanic alphabet. He dipped his head in greeting, and I returned the gesture.

"Thank you, my lady," he said. By the way he carried himself, I was betting he was an older vamp. He moved with casual grace, as if it was second nature. He seemed mild-mannered and candid, qualities I hadn't seen much of among the vampires. His aura of intelligence and power continued to scream, "Older."

"Kassandra." Lenorre's voice wasn't exactly empty, but it had taken on a polite, almost political edge. "I would like to introduce you to Futhark. He is one of the Primes in this city."

Futhark actually bowed to me.

"Prime?" I asked.

"Yes." He looked a little confused.

"My apologies, Futhark," I said as politely as I could. "I'm a little ignorant of vampire society."

"There is no need to apologize. You are wondering what the title means?"

I nodded.

He looked at Lenorre again. "I can see why you like her, my lady. She has a sense of honesty and forwardness you do not often see."

Oh, yeah, he was an old vampire. I'd bet my ass on that one.

He swept his arms out in front of him. "A Prime vampire," he explained, "is a stronger vampire within the vampire community. We are older and offer our loyalty to the Count or Countess of a territory."

"You seem old enough to have your own clan," I said.

Futhark nodded. "I am powerful enough to become a Count if I did so choose. It is not a burden I wish to carry."

"Thank you, Futhark."

He gave a slight bow. "You are most welcome. My lady Countess has always had impeccable judgment. Any friend or ally of hers is a friend and ally of mine."

I didn't really know what to say. I felt like I was suddenly stuck in some type of old court. Which, in a sense, I guess I was. Vampire court. Whoohoo.

"Countess." A woman's voice rose from the group of vampires, and the speaker stepped forward, her sable hair gleaming where it fell past her shoulders. "Might I ask why you have called us into council?"

"You may." Lenorre looked at the vampire, her voice now empty. "One of our kind has murdered a boy. I want those of you assembled to be on the lookout. Gather what information you can. Either a traitor is among us or a stray is in town."

"Very well," the woman said, smiling. Her gaze shifted to mine, and the breath caught in my throat at its intensity. Her sea green eyes were unflinching as she stepped toward me. "Is this your new pet? I have heard a little about you." She watched me intently, as if memorizing my every expression. I resisted the urge to squirm. I wasn't a child, and I wasn't human. I refused to let the big bad vampire scare me or make me uncomfortable.

"Kassandra is no pet," Lenorre said, and although she looked calm, I could feel the tension in her body where it touched mine.

"Kassandra," the vampire said, as if tasting my name on her tongue. "A lovely name for such a lovely young woman."

"Eris," Lenorre said.

She looked at me, and something in the way she did so made me think Lenorre wasn't the only vampire with a taste for women.

Eris turned her full attention back to Lenorre. "Countess." She lowered her head, though unlike Futhark, she didn't fall into a bow or curtsy. "You have done well for yourself." Her sea green gaze met mine again and the tension between us was like a cord being pulled tight. I didn't like it.

There were less than thirty vampires in the room, and not all of them introduced themselves as Futhark had. As I watched from my seat beside Lenorre, I remembered Stanley, a vampire I'd met during my first visit to the club. It was hard to miss his eyes, which were as blue as any Siamese cat's. It was equally difficult to miss the labret piercing beneath his lower lip. I'd thought he was a younger vampire, but apparently I was mistaken. He stood in one corner of the room, wearing a knee-length velvet jacket the color of a green apple with a pair of tight black pants. I watched his slight nod in profile, the chin-length black hair swaying as he listened to a gothic-looking doll-like woman I didn't recognize. As if he sensed my gaze, he turned, offering a wink.

Lenorre advised them to find out what they could and report back to her. The vampires were taking their leave when I caught Eris staring at me. I was standing with Lenorre, waiting to leave, when she visually dissected me as if I stood naked in front of her. I fought my own discomfort and forced myself to look away, sensing the wolf's agitation at my refusal to rise to the challenge. But I knew better than to take on a vampire in Lenorre's club just because she was staring at me.

I sensed more than saw Eris turn her attention back to Isabella. Isabella was the girlfriend of a guy named Trevor, and I had met them both at Lenorre's when I was working my last case. Isabella lived in Lenorre's house, but I hadn't known she was one of the older vampires, though I remembered seeing her wearing a frilly, old-fashioned nightgown. That should've hinted at her age, but the first time I'd met her she'd worn a miniskirt.

Once the room was near empty, we left. Zaphara sat in the backseat as I drove back to Lenorre's. On the way home, she even managed to keep her mouth shut. I was tempted to swing by a gas station and buy her a damn cookie.

CHAPTER TWELVE

I had just stepped into the house when the cell phone rang from my back pocket. Zaphara hadn't said a word to me as she left the room, and for that, I was thankful. I answered on the third ring. It was Arthur.

"Talk to me," I said.

"Dirty or—"

"Arthur, just tell me why you're calling me at almost one in the morning. Did a medical examiner take a look at the body?" How the hell did he get any sleep? He seemed to be up most hours of the night, though he usually didn't phone unless it was something important. That thought worried me.

"She didn't get the chance." Arthur was talking in a low voice, as if he didn't want to be overheard.

"What do you mean she didn't get the chance?"

"The body went missing."

Distantly, I heard Rosalin coming down the stairs. I turned my back on both Lenorre and Rosalin and walked into the parlor.

"When?" I asked.

"No one can calculate the exact time of the body's disappearance. We're not sure if it went missing before or after it got to the morgue. We do know that it happened somewhere between eleven and one yesterday morning."

That made sense. They were still trying to wrap things up when I'd left the crime scene.

"Where was the ME?" I asked.

"On break. She didn't get the chance to look at the body. We're thinking they snatched it then, when it had just arrived."

"Which means it was never even signed in? Have you questioned the carriers?" My mind was racing.

"Yes. The two of them don't remember anything. When we asked them what time they got to the morgue, they couldn't even recall arriving there or that they had a body to transport."

"Shit."

"You're telling me. Kass, I need to ask you a question and I want you to answer honestly."

"If you plan to accuse me or anyone I know, I will fucking hang up on you."

"I won't accuse you or your girlfriend. I know you didn't do it. You're probably too busy doing one another." He chuckled.

I shook my head again. "Get to the point, Kingfisher. What?"

"You said you were pretty sure it was a vampire bite."

"Yeah..." Where was he going with this? A thought came to mind. "You're going to ask me if I think he was turned?"

"Damn, you're good. How'd you guess?"

"Is that sarcasm I hear?"

"Maybe," he said lightly. "Do you think he was turned?"

"I honestly don't know how to tell."

"The only way is to have an experienced witch or vampire look at the body," Lenorre said from behind me and I jumped, only a little startled. "A turning does not leave any physical evidence."

"What does it leave?" I asked her while Arthur coughed in my ear.

"A change in the aura. You would have been able to sense it, but you keep your shields drawn too tightly." I believed her. I shield like a son of a bitch to keep a lot of things from getting through them.

"How long does it take for a vampire to rise?"

"It depends on the strength of the vampire that turned him. It drains both participants." She didn't bother to conceal the thoughtful expression that furrowed her brows. "Only an older vampire has enough power, or energy, if you wish, to sire a subaltern. If the vampire that sired the lesser is strong enough, the youngling would have risen by nightfall this evening. The longest period of time it would take is four days."

"Are you hearing this?" I asked Arthur.

"Some of it. It's all vampire-speak to me. What does she mean?"

"It means, if the vampire that sired Timothy is strong enough, he'd have risen tonight."

"Fuck. We're in deep shit. Not only will Holbrook rip me a new one, but the boy's parents will tear into me if they find out their son is an evil, undead minion."

"Being an evil, undead minion isn't illegal in America, Arthur. His parents can't do shit unless they've hired someone to stake the body and signed a consensual release. Did they? Did anyone tell them it might've been a vampire attack?"

"No, and no," he said a little more lightly. "We withheld that information. The parents believe it was a cult."

"Why doesn't that surprise me?"

"Kass, I don't like them either. The dad's okay, but the boy's mother is a fucking right-wing lunatic. What am I supposed to tell them? In the end, we have to say something. You remember how it goes."

"Arthur, I know, but we're still not certain. The only way we can be certain is to find Timothy's stolen body, dead or undead. If he consented to being turned, you can't do anything."

"Except tell his parents. Kass, he's only sixteen! I've had to tell parents their child was murdered, but never that their child was turned into one of the walking dead."

"Arthur, he's not a zombie. He's not the walking dead. If he's a vampire, then he's undead." Why didn't more cops have preternatural training? No offense to Arthur, but they were simply clueless most of the time. Oh, wait, I'd be out a job if all of them had the training I did. Scratch that thought.

"Can the parents press charges?"

"On you or the vamps?"

"Both."

I sighed. "Here's the deal. If Timothy consented to being turned, then no, no one can press charges. In Oklahoma the age of consent is sixteen. That's applicable to vampire turnings. If Timothy was taken against his will and protests, then he can press charges against the offender. The parents cannot take action against the department. So take a deep breath, pop a Valium, and relax. We'll figure this out."

"I wish I had a Valium."

"Welcome to the joys of being a detective, Kingfisher."

"I heard Holbrook offered you the position once. You turned it down. Why?"

I sat on the couch with a sigh. After I was infected with lycanthropy, when I told Captain Holbrook I was leaving, he offered me the position of detective if I agreed to stay. I couldn't. The pay was a little higher, but the hours were erratic and unstable. It was also a heavy burden I wasn't willing to carry, werewolf or no. I didn't know how Arthur had heard. Maybe he'd spoken to Holbrook. That was the only thing I could think of, because no one at the department knew.

"I didn't want that much responsibility."

I heard his heavy sigh. Being a detective was really beginning to take its toll on him. If he didn't take it easy, he'd crash and burn. As much as he sometimes irritated me, he was a good guy, and a good cop.

"Arthur, you need to get some sleep. You're not any good to the department exhausted and sleep-deprived. Go home and get a good night's rest. I'll do what I can. Lenorre's got her vampires looking into it. If I hear anything, I'll call your cell phone. You'll fold under this much stress if you don't take care of yourself."

"You should've taken the promotion." His words were empty, his usual jesting tone gone. Arthur always made jokes. He always saw the bright side of any situation. If he didn't see a bright side, he'd light a match and make one. He was always eager about working a new case, solving a crime. He enjoyed his job, even with the horrors he saw. This level of seriousness worried me.

"Arthur, you're a good person and a good detective. You were the one meant to be a detective, not me. That's not my path in life. It never was. I knew that. That's why I turned down the promotion. Even now, you're sacrificing your well-being to make the world a better place."

"What for? We take out one bad guy and another one shows up."

The vulnerability in his voice made my throat tight. I'd never heard Arthur sound like he was on the verge of breaking.

"That's how life is," I said bluntly. "Arthur, just trust me. You'll feel better if you go home and rest. Okay?"

"You'll let me know me if you hear anything?" The moment seemed to have passed. He wasn't joking, but his tone was firmer, more like he was getting a grip.

"Yeah, I'll call."

With that, he hung up. I closed the phone and slid it back into my pocket, then rubbed my temples, taking a deep breath and holding it. "What now?" I said to no one in particular.

Lenorre answered. "We wait."

"I hate waiting."

Rosalin sat on the other end of the couch. "Me too." She looked at me. "You haven't eaten all day, have you?"

I shook my head and she tsked softly. "Come on, I'll make you some dinner. I know coffee is God for you, but it's not substantial."

Rosalin stood, pulling her bright orange shirt over her hips.

"You like taking care of people, don't you?" I asked.

A look of compassion crossed her face. "I like taking care of those I care about."

"Couldn't tell." I grinned and looked at Lenorre, and as if she saw my thoughts written across my features she asked, "Kassandra, what are you thinking?"

I didn't even know if Lenorre could cook. It was the thought that amused me. I kept grinning, and Rosalin laughed.

"Uh-oh, she has that look."

"What look?" I asked, feigning innocence.

"The one that says you're up to something."

"I'm not up to anything."

"Kassandra," Lenorre said, "do not try to play innocent. What are you about?"

"Well, Rosalin does an awful lot of work around the house—cooking, cleaning, and taking care of things. I'm sure she'd appreciate a respite."

Rosalin laughed. "How do you think I earn my keep?"

"Even if you're working, you should get a day off."

"Are you offering to cook dinner?" Lenorre expertly tried to turn the table.

I laughed. "Oh, no, you don't want me to."

"Yeah, that scares me," Rosalin said. "Let's not, but we can say she did."

"I can cook, if I have to."

Rosalin rolled her eyes. "What? With the microwave?"

"I was thinking that Lenorre should make dinner." I was.

"If you can get Lenorre to make dinner, I'll do a freaking backflip."

Lenorre crossed her arms over her chest and flashed dainty fangs. "Done."

"What?" Rosalin's jaw hung open.

Lenorre spoke over her shoulder on the way out of the room. "Do not be surprised if you find I have talents even you are not aware of, Kassandra." To Rosalin, she said, "When I am done fulfilling my part of the bargain you owe us a backflip."

Rosalin stared when Lenorre, appearing completely dumbfounded, left the room.

I tried not to laugh.

"Yeah, laugh it up," she said. "Has anyone ever told you you're manipulative?"

I pushed myself off the couch and headed for the kitchen. If Lenorre was cooking, I had to see this.

"All the time." I grinned like an imp. "I just can't believe I managed to get two birds with one stone, that time. That's fucking talent."

CHAPTER THIRTEEN

L enorre had made fettuccini Alfredo, and I had to admit it was excellent. The sauce was creamy with just the right amount of freshly ground black pepper and chicken. I bit into a warm breadstick smothered in butter and sprinkled with Italian herbs.

"Lenorre, you have a phone call." I nearly dropped my fork at the sound of Zaphara's voice. I hadn't heard her enter the room nor had I heard a telephone ring.

"Downstairs," Zaphara told Lenorre, as she stood. I watched Lenorre leave the room until she was out of sight. Zaphara stayed in the doorway, staring at me. I resisted the urge to throw my fork at her because a fork probably wouldn't hurt her.

She'd taken off the spiffy trench coat and was wearing a form-fitting black shirt with slits up the sides of her torso. A line of white skin peeked through the buckles that held the slits together. Zaphara propped herself against the archway, turning at the hip to reveal the silhouette of her small breasts where the fabric clung to them. It took me a second glance to realize her nipples weren't hard; they were pierced and she was showing them off.

I met her amethyst stare, giving her the blankest expression I could muster. The expression must've worked because the grin on her face faltered.

"Those must've hurt," I said.

"It felt good to me." She raised her hand as if to touch them.

I busied myself by twirling a small amount of fettuccini around my fork.

"You don't strike me as the masochistic type."

"I have varied tastes."

"Goody for you." I raised the fork to my mouth and drew the noodles off with my teeth. If she wanted to have a stare-down, fine. I could do that.

"You would be such fun to play with." She said it almost wistfully, and I relaxed. I could win this round.

Rosalin remained silent, as if she didn't want to draw attention. I ignored Zaphara's comment. She was just trying to get under my skin, and if I threw a witty reply at her, she'd find one to throw right back. Rosalin leaned over her bowl and I suddenly realized just how submissive Rosalin could be, even though she was beta wolf of the Blackthorne Pack. She might as well be on her back, offering up her soft belly. That said something about either Zaphara and whatever she was or Rosalin. I wasn't sure which.

"How long were you in gymnastics?" I asked, changing the subject and referring to the backflip she had done when Lenorre set a beautiful dinner on the table. Rosalin's gaze flicked nervously from my face to Zaphara, who laughed before she turned to leave the room.

"Five years," Rosalin said. "She wants you to top her."

"What?"

"Zaphara. She wants you to top her."

"As in?"

"BDSM."

"Yeah, I got that. She wants me to top her?"

"Um, yeah. At least, I think that's what she's doing."

I actually laughed. "No, I think Zaphara would rather top me than play the role of the bottom."

"You heard what she said about having varied tastes. I know for a fact she went to see Eris once."

"Wait, Eris? As in the vampire Eris?"

Rosalin nodded.

"What does she have to do with it?"

"She's a pro-domme."

I knew a little about BDSM because I'd entertained the idea once or twice. I'd done a little nail digging and biting with the women in my past, but after being infected with lycanthropy, rough play seemed like a bad idea, especially with a human. I hadn't been intimate with a human woman since then. Remembering what I'd done to Lenorre's thighs and what might've happened if I'd lost control or if it had been closer to the full moon confirmed that not being with a human was a wise decision. Lenorre could handle me and my beast.

"What does that mean?" I asked.

"Eris is a professional dominatrix."

I stared at her. "You're kidding me. She gets paid to spank and fuck people? Isn't that close to prostitution?"

She gave me a look. "Prostitution is illegal."

"It doesn't mean people don't do it."

"A pro-domme isn't a prostitute. A lot of people have that misconception. A true pro-domme doesn't have sex with her clients."

"She just spanks them?"

Rosalin grinned. "And a little more, I'm sure. She's not allowed to sleep with them. I don't think she'd want to and Lenorre would tear her head off if she solicited uncivilized behavior at the club."

"She's a pro-domme at the club?"

"Yes."

I shuddered, remembering Eris's piercing sea-green eyes. Her presence made me weak in the knees.

Is that why she had been staring at me? Is that why she had called me a pet? I straightened my spine. I never had been, and never would be, someone's pet werewolf.

Rosalin was watching me intently. "It's very professional. Both parties have to consent." She gathered our bowls and the breadstick plate from the table. "You sign a contract and everything. A lot of the time, there's an undercurrent of sexuality to it," she said, "but sex is never involved. It's more about the power exchange. The submissive gives most of their control to the dominant. For some bottoms, it's a therapeutic release."

"How is giving all your control to someone else therapeutic? Doesn't the submissive give all their power to the dominant?"

Rosalin looked thoughtful, standing near the curtain. "It may look that way, but in reality the submissive has the power to use the safe word."

"Safe word?"

"Or sign, depending on the agreement. The safe word is what protects the submissive. It keeps the dominant from going too far."

I leaned back in my seat, "You sound like you have experience."

"My ex-girlfriend was a little freaky," she said, balancing our plates in her hands. "That's all I'm saying."

When Rosalin left the room to put dishes in the dishwasher, my mind reeled. Eris was a dominatrix. Rosalin had made a valid point. Was she right? Was Zaphara pushing my buttons because she wanted me to get pissed and try to hurt her? If I hurt her, would I be doing exactly what she wanted?

Lenorre emerged from downstairs, calling me out of my thoughts. "Rosalin, a visitor will arrive shortly. Will you escort her to the parlor?"

Rosalin walked back into the room. "I will."

"What's going on?" I asked Lenorre, searching her blank expression for an answer.

"Eris thinks she has found the vampire that turned Timothy."

"Are we sure Timothy's been turned?"

"If he hasn't been, why would the vampires have stolen the body?"

I pulled my hair up. "Right. Maybe a pedophile with a thing for necrophilia is on the loose." I dropped my hair. "Oh, Gods."

"What?" Lenorre looked worried.

I shook my head. "Nope. I'm not saying that thought out loud. It'll sound so much worse if I do."

"Kassandra, tell me."

"Just because you're undead it doesn't make me a—"

"A necrophiliac?"

I gave a slight nod.

"I am quite sure the term is only applicable to predators that enjoy their prey cold and unmoving." She touched my cheek gently as if trying to wipe the horror from my face. "As you said to your detective friend earlier this evening, I am undead, not dead." She caught my wrist, placing my hand on her chest. I felt the air swirl into her lungs. "Do the dead do this?"

"That's the thing," I said, "you don't have to breathe. Hell, sometimes you don't even have a heartbeat. It's like you guys get this on-and-off switch."

"Not quite. It is only a natural part of our survival ability to shut off our bodies. It aids a vampire in hunting." She pulled me into the circle of her arms, and I didn't struggle or try to pull away. She didn't feel cold and empty, which was enough to chase the thought away. The reality was she died at dawn. Well, most of the time. As far as I was concerned she was alive, not the way I was alive, but alive enough to will her own heart to beat.

I stood on my tiptoes, offering my lips. She kissed me.

"Better?" she murmured.

I nodded, not needing to explain. She knew it was taking me time to get used to everything. Even before I'd been infected I hadn't exactly been great at relationships. I loved being in them but hated having them blow up in my face. In the past, I always got with women I had absolutely nothing in common with.

Lenorre understood me. She saw me, not what she thought I could be or what I could do for her or how I looked in the crook of her arm. I didn't have to explain myself to her because she paid attention.

Your lover should always see you.

The doorbell chimed loudly through the house. I heard Rosalin open the front door and greet Eris in a soft voice. She offered to take her cloak, sounding not quite subservient but utterly polite.

Looking at Lenorre I thought, *It just might get worse.*

My fear was confirmed when Eris thanked her in a silky tone that made my stomach fall.

CHAPTER FOURTEEN

"It is a pleasure seeing you again, Kassandra," Eris said, taking a seat in one of the armchairs in Lenorre's parlor.

I looked at her then, briefly. What was I supposed to say? I wasn't exactly up on vampire etiquette. For some reason "ditto" didn't seem like the polite response.

I widened my eyes at Lenorre just a touch, letting her know she needed to jump in before I stuck my foot in it.

Lenorre asked her, "You said you had information on a stray in this territory?"

Eris leaned back in her seat, crossing her legs and clasping her hands in her lap. "Yes. Well, strays, to be precise."

"Tell me," Lenorre said, and I was glad she'd diverted Eris's attention. I pulled my feet under me, listening.

"One of my patrons at the club divulged information regarding a rumor of a new and ambitious vampire in town. You should be on your guard."

Eris idly rolled her thumb across the arm of the chair. The dress she wore was midnight velvet, similar to the cloak she had been wearing, but where the cloak added an air of mystery, the dress clung to her skin, showing off her curves. She noticed me and smiled beautifully, flashing only a little bit of fang. I looked away again, trying to keep my curiosity to myself. Rosalin shouldn't have told me Eris was a pro-domme. I was having a hard time keeping my mind from wandering.

Lenorre nodded solemnly, a lot calmer than I would have been. "As I had suspected. How did your patron hear of this rumor?"

"I am not certain. You know as well as I that most of my patrons are vamp-sluts. They'll straddle the first pair of fangs they see." She actually laughed.

"Vamp-slut," I mumbled. "That's a new one."

"Not really," Rosalin said. "There's death-banger, fang-whore, blood-bitch, coffin-thumper, coffin-bunker, fang-fucker—"

"I get it. Are there any nice, politically correct terms?"

"A willing donor," Eris said coyly.

"A fang-cushion?" Rosalin added.

"Apparently not. Forget I asked."

"Only the pitiful ones get the bad nicknames," Rosalin said.

"Pitiful?"

"Vamp-addicts," she explained, "bite-junkies. You wouldn't miss one if you saw one."

"No," Eris said softly, "they're not easy to miss."

I glanced from Eris to Rosalin.

Rosalin said, in all seriousness, "They resemble a pin cushion without the pins."

"That's lovely," I said sarcastically, then asked Eris, "So one of your patrons told you about a new vamp in town?"

"Correct."

I looked at Lenorre. Eris had started staring again. "What do we do?"

"We seek out the truth. If there is a new vampire in my territory, without my permission..."

"They're in a shit-load of trouble." Rosalin's words were more blunt than Lenorre's would've been, but they worked.

"Precisely."

"It goes without saying you have my aid," Eris said, her eyes on me.

"Good," Lenorre said. "For we shall need it."

"Why do you think I offered? I will see what further information I might obtain using my skills."

Though I was curious, I didn't ask what those skills were. Point for me.

Eris stood in a swish of velvet and declared, "The sun will rise soon."

Lenorre rose gracefully to her feet. "I will have a room prepared for your stay." She looked at Rosalin, who, as if knowing what to do, nodded and left the room. I resisted the urge to grab the arm of her shirt and say, "Don't leave me."

It took me a moment to realize Eris and Lenorre were staring at me. With the attention of two devastatingly beautiful vampires on me, I forced myself to sigh.

Chapter Fifteen

"Are you throwing one of your infamous Halloween parties this year?" Eris asked Lenorre. The four of us were sitting in the living room in the final hour before the sun rose. Although Eris's room was ready, she hadn't left for it yet, much to my disappointment. And relief, which pissed me off.

"I have considered it."

"You haven't made any plans?"

"When is Samhain?" I was trying to remember what day it was.

"Friday," Lenorre told me.

"This Friday?" She nodded and I shook my head. "This schedule is really throwing off my sense of time."

"You'll get used to it," Rosalin said.

"I haven't been to work in how many days now?"

"I thought Rit was taking care of things?"

"She is, but it's not fair for me to just dump everything in her lap. I'm going into the office for a few hours tomorrow. Or today. Whatever."

"What do you do?" Eris asked, seeming genuinely interested.

"Work."

She looked amused at my defiance.

"Kassandra is a preternatural investigator," Lenorre said smoothly.

"That little business near the café?"

My office wasn't little. It wasn't anything fancy either. It was work, and as long as we brought in enough income to support ourselves, most everyone at the agency seemed to agree that the establishment was fine. Besides, I liked my little two-story business.

"I did not mean to insult you," Eris stated.

"None taken. I don't have size issues."

"I would hope not. You are rather petite."

I searched her face, trying to figure out if the comment was supposed to be a joke but couldn't tell. "Your point?"

"It doesn't bother you?"

"Why would it?"

"Some feel compelled to make up in attitude what they lack in physical size."

"She does," Rosalin noted.

"My attitude has less to do with my size and more to do with who I am."

"You'd get an attitude with someone that talks down to you because of your stature, though, right?" Rosalin asked.

"I'd get an attitude with anyone who talks down to me for anything." Before either she or Eris could say anything else I switched my attention to Lenorre. "Tell me about your infamous Samhain parties."

Lenorre pulled her legs up into the seat. "I throw one every year."

"Are you having one this year?"

"I have been thinking about it. Eris?"

"Yes?"

"What do you think of a masquerade?"

Eris looked thoughtful. "It's a good idea."

"I hate to ask," I said, "but don't you think you should give people more advance notice for the party?"

They looked at one another and Lenorre shook her head. "They will show up in costume either way."

"The club is open on Halloween," Eris said. "Most will wear costumes."

"What about the vampires dressing in masquerade?" Rosalin asked. "They could float into the crowd, and the guests could get a shot at dancing with masked and mysterious vamps?"

Everyone looked at her. A soft blush rose to her cheeks. "Sorry, it was just an idea."

"No," Lenorre said. "It's a very good idea."

"Lenorre is right," Eris said. "I like it. A patron doesn't often get the opportunity to spend an evening dancing with a vampire."

I was beginning to feel a bit like a fly on the wall. The club scene just didn't do it for me. Lenorre decided to use Rosalin's idea. Decked out in mysterious garb, the vampires would each pick a single date for the evening and work their magic. Not literally. Lenorre kept her charges under control. They were not to do anything illegal with their dates. They could present themselves with an air of mystery or use subtle seduction, but they were working. It was a job.

How many people would go home that night swooning or with a pierced vein? And how could Lenorre think about a party some days away when she had stray vampires hunting and turning teenagers in her territory? Tired, I closed my eyes and let my head rest against the back of the couch. I wanted to let go of death for a while—no more dead kids, no more hunting vampires, no more calls from the police saying they had found another body. But my world revolved around all of that. Lucky me.

"Kassandra."

Their conversation had come to a halt.

I forced my eyes open, having started to doze off while they talked clothes and music.

Lenorre stood in front of me, offering her hand.

I took it, allowing her to help pull me to my feet. Eris stood and inclined her head, and Lenorre mirrored the gesture. In a sort of tired daze I made it to the bedroom. Once the double doors closed behind me, I started stripping, pulled on a pair of shorts and an oversized T-shirt, and went to brush my teeth.

Lenorre entered the bathroom while I was brushing. I met her reflection in the mirror.

"They could use their disguises to their advantage." I spoke around my toothbrush. "Your place is the only vampire club in the city and, to any other vamp, probably good hunting grounds. We might be able to trap the strays without having to go find them."

"True," Lenorre said, propping her shoulder against the cabinet as she began to brush her teeth. "If they are so bold, then yes, my vampires will find them." She was clearly deep in thought, so I stayed quiet as I finished my nightly routine. I didn't want to talk about it either. It would be even better if I could get the thoughts to go away too.

We finished getting ready for bed in silence. Lenorre had her moments of unreal quietness, but right now I sensed she had a lot on her mind. I let her have her thoughts without prying. She was a Countess. Lady only knew what kind of good publicity the vampire killing would ruin for her. Not to mention that the public would have a massive freak-out if the news broke that crazy vampires were turning teenagers. It could cause chaos and might blow up into open season on vampires, protective laws or no. I crawled into bed, snuggling into the cool sheets.

Lenorre slid against me and I breathed a sigh of comfort and relief.

"We will find the vampires that hurt Timothy, Kassandra, and when we do, they will pay dearly."

Her voice sounded lethal, but the arm she draped across my stomach was light and tentative. I took her hand, holding it close to my chest, and sank into the exquisite feel of her against me. "I know."

I fell asleep before the sun rose and Lenorre died.

CHAPTER SIXTEEN

The bell chimed softly and June, my secretary, looked up from her desk, peeking over the plastic rims of her reading glasses. Her silk blouse was the color of sun coral. She was never happy when I left someone else in charge of the agency, whether it was she or Rit. June, an older woman, had one of those attitudes that people often mistook for rudeness. She wasn't rude. Well, okay... sometimes she was, but I didn't take it personally. June was just very blunt. She could rip the bullshit out of anyone before they got a chance to start with her. Which is why she did an excellent job.

"Well, well, well." She didn't look happy. "Where have you been?"

I stopped just inside the doorway, trying to balance the tray of coffee cups in my hands. "Good morning to you too. I brought coffee."

I rested the carrier tray on my left hip, retrieving a cup. June opened her mouth, but before any words came out, I stopped her. "It's decaf. I promise. Where's Rit?"

"Where do you think she is? She's where she always is. In her office. By the way, it's noon, not morning."

I was wondering why I hadn't spiked her coffee with Prozac when Rit walked into the room. She was wearing a pair of navy blue slacks with a white button-up blouse that accented her thick waves of black hair. Though it usually fell around her shoulders, today it was pulled back into a tight ponytail that made her coffee-and-cream complexion with its cinnamon highlights glow.

I held out the cup of coffee to her as a sort of peace offering, a way of apologizing for dumping everything into her lap.

"Coffee?" I asked.

Her dark gaze flicked to the cup as she took it. "Extra shot?"

"Yeah."

She gave me a concerned look. "Have you been all right?"

"I'm fine." I climbed the stairs and walked toward my office with her.

"I've been a little worried. The last time we spoke you sounded like there's a lot going on…" It was her way of asking what was happening in my life. Rit was polite and respected my privacy. She wouldn't demand I tell her everything. If I brushed the comment off, she'd drop it.

I decided not to. "I've been working with the police on another case, and it's eating a lot of my time. I'm sorry I really haven't given either June or you an explanation."

"Don't worry about it. I know there's a reason you asked me to take care of things here for a few days."

I plopped into the seat behind my desk. "How's business?"

Rit was quiet for several moments. I glanced up and noticed her watching me. "You're not wearing a gun?"

I hadn't bothered to stop by my apartment before coming to work. I still felt naked without the gun, but I refused to tuck it in my pants, and well, guns don't go in pockets, and purses are a good way to lose one, ask any woman. Somehow, we're capable of losing elephants in our purses. It's like magic.

"No."

"Are you sure you're okay?" she asked, again.

"I'm fine. My holster isn't."

"What happened?"

"The snap broke."

I checked my desk calendar to see if June had written anything on it, but it was blank. Yay. The little full-moon symbol marked at the beginning of the month caught my attention. The last full moon, I'd gone out of town to shift like I did every full moon. Rosalin had told me I was welcome to go with the pack, along with Claire, a brand-new wolf she'd taken with her. The wolves gather on the night of the full moon to shift and run through the forest. In truth, we're pack creatures. The only lone wolves are the ones that choose to be, or the ones that don't have the connections to join a pack.

I spared a glance at next month's calendar. The full moon would be on my birthday in November. Werewolves can sense the full moon like a woman can sense when she's about to start her menstrual cycle. A few days before the full moon, I get restless. A lot of the time, I try to go running to burn off the restless energy, but the energy won't dissipate until after a complete shift on the full moon. When the moon mother calls, you obey.

Rit sat on the other side of the desk and crossed one leg over the other. "What's going on with the police?"

The image flashed through my mind. Timothy's lifeless brown eyes, the slit on his thigh trying to mask the puncture wounds, his youthful body left vulnerable and exposed, a killer's trophy in the night. Rubbing my temples, I sighed.

"The police found a boy's body." I focused on keeping my tone even and undisturbed by the visions in my head.

"What's the boy's name?"

"Nelson. Timothy Nelson. Why? Have you heard something? It hasn't been on the news, has it?"

She nodded again. "It's been on the news, but that's not how I heard of it." She paused. "Kassandra, his older brother was here."

"Here?" I pointed at my desk.

"Yes. He came in to speak with you about his kid brother's case, but since you weren't here I talked to him. His brother's murder is one of the ones I'm dealing with."

"Avani." I rarely called her by her first name, and I hoped it would help drive the seriousness of my point across. "You need to drop it."

"Why?"

"I'm already covering it. Why the hell would his brother come here? Is that the one that was away at college? Texas University?"

"Same one. Why do I need to drop it?" Her expression turned suspicious. "What do you know that I don't?"

I got up and closed the office door. If I told her, I didn't want anyone to overhear, even if it was just June downstairs. You never know when something supernatural might come in. Granted, most of the business we did was with humans, and I've had to turn away a lot of potential clients just because they wanted me to tell them whether their house was haunted. There were still a lot of "not humans" out there, and any one of them could show up at any time.

"Do you remember the last time I took a few days off work?" When she nodded, I continued. "I was investigating a killing out near the Nelsons' family home. They didn't have any connection to the killing, and it wasn't anyone they knew well. They were in the wrong place at the wrong time. Mrs. Nelson practically threw me out of her house." I shook my head. "I met Timothy. Rit." I nearly choked on the words. "It was there." I forced the words out of my mouth. "I saw it. I knew it. I sensed it. I tried to warn him…"

I hugged myself, closing my eyes.

Her hand was on my shoulder, a gentle touch. "Kassandra, what was in his eyes?"

"Curiosity. When I mentioned that a werewolf had to have made the attack, he pressed me for more information. I told him to be careful. I should've told his parents." I looked at my desk. "No matter how neurotic Mrs. Nelson seemed, I should've warned one of them that Timothy was curious and to watch him, but I didn't." My throat was tight. "I told a sixteen-year-old with an insatiable curiosity about monsters not to do anything stupid." I blinked, which only made my vision blur.

Distantly, I was aware that Rit had put her arms around me, pulling me against her. "It's not your fault," she murmured. "It is *not* your fault."

I don't do well with compassion, and hers broke through the careful walls I'd built around myself. No matter how untouchable people try to convince themselves they are, they are not. Whether it is a werewolf, vampire, or human, pain is pain. Heartache is heartache. The question I'd feared thinking swam to the surface of my mind like some great oceanic beast. Could I have saved Timothy's life if I had acted differently? If I hadn't shrugged him off with a quick *be careful*, would he still be alive? If I had told someone to watch him, would it have kept him safe?

I closed my eyes as tears threatened to break free. I would not cry, damn it. I would not. I took a deep breath, trying to steady myself, feeling Rit's arms around me like a friendly anchor. My body jerked with a silent sob. I could never truly open up to Rit, because she had no idea I was a werewolf, and I was pretty sure I would break up our little office. And I liked Rit. We weren't close, but I'm not really close to anyone.

I heard the door open before June's voice carried into the room. "Someone's here to see you, Kass. She says she's a friend."

Rit turned at the hip. "She'll be out in a minute."

June grumbled unhappily as she left, but I didn't think Rit heard her.

"You know this isn't your fault." She brought my attention back to her. "I'll drop the case if that's what you want."

"I'm not asking you just because I'm already working on it, Rit. I don't want you to get hurt."

She squeezed my shoulder and stepped back. "I know."

"Good." I wiped my eyes, glad I'd decided not to wear makeup. Mascara is a bitch when you cry, no matter how much a brand promises it's waterproof. There is virtually no such thing. If you cry, you still end up looking like a raccoon.

"You should talk to the brother," she added. "There were things he refused to tell me. I told him I couldn't help find his brother's killer unless he shared everything. He's pretty determined to talk to you."

"That's fine." My voice was hollow.

"You want me to schedule an appointment?"

"Yeah, see if he can make it this afternoon."

Noises outside the door made both of us turn to look.

June raised her voice. "You can't just go up there!"

"I'm a friend!" Rosalin said. "Would you stop pulling on my shirt?"

"Get your ass back in that lobby." June still wasn't yelling, but she was getting close.

"If you don't let go of my shirt," Rosalin growled, "I'll take the damn thing off! I told you, I'm her friend. She won't get pissed." There were sounds of a struggle, then she said, "Lady, you need to take a freaking chill pill!"

"I'm about to show you a freaking chill pill." June sounded like she was ready to knock Rosalin through the wall.

Rit looked at me. "Friend?"

"Yep." I tried not to smile, but damn, it was hard.

Rit laughed. "Are you going to save her?"

I thought about it. "Nope. She can take care of herself. They both can."

Rosalin burst through the door holding June in a fireman's carry. She was pounding on Rosalin's back. "Put me down!"

I bit my bottom lip, trying not to laugh. Rit attempted to cover hers by pretending to cough.

"Would you tell her I'm a friend?" Rosalin pleaded.

"June?" I took a step forward. "I'd like to introduce you to my friend Rosalin."

June's hand resembled a snake about to strike.

"June!" I was too late. She hit Rosalin's ass with a loud smack, and Rosalin's eyes flew wide with shock as she dropped June, catching her just soon enough to break her fall.

"What the fuck did you do that for?" she asked.

I went around the desk to help June, but she swatted my hands away. I retreated, holding them up in surrender and backing off.

She got to her feet on her own, turning on Rosalin. "You deserved it! I told you to wait in the lobby. You should've listened to me. I don't care if you're the President of the United States. If I tell you to wait in the damn lobby, I mean it."

"You smacked my ass," Rosalin said.

"You're damn right I did!" She shoved a finger into Rosalin's sternum. "You," poke, "wouldn't," poke, "put me down," poke.

Rosalin tried to get out of June's reach. "Look." She put her hands up as I had earlier. June had a way of making people surrender, even big bad werewolves. "I just wanted to talk to Kassandra. I told you I'm one of her friends. I told you she wouldn't mind if I just came up here."

"Next time, you listen to me, you got that? If I tell you to sit and wait—you sit down and do just that. I work here. You don't. I'm doing you a service. Therefore, you listen to me."

"Fine, whatever. Just get out of my face, please."

June turned an angry look on me. "Your friends!" She tossed an angrier look at Rosalin, practically stomping out of the room.

"Is she always like that?"

"Yes," Rit said.

"June has a hot temper," I said.

"Gee, really?" Rosalin asked. "That woman needs to get laid."

"Why do you always think everyone's problem is that they need to get laid?"

"Because it is."

Rit laughed. "You've got balls."

Rosalin looked as if she had eaten something sour. "I don't like balls," she said, then grinned. "I've got pussy."

"No," Rit corrected her, "anyone that stands up to June like that has to have *balls*."

Rosalin looked a little green around the edges. "That's just... gross."

Rit laughed again. "A lesbian friend, I take it?" she asked me.

I shrugged. "I don't know what her sexual preference is." It was true. I mean, I knew she liked women, but she could've been bisexual.

"I am a lesbian," Rosalin said, giving me a look that said I was supposed to know better, or something. "I thought I had made that obvious."

"Rosalin..." I warned.

"That kind of friend?" Rit asked.

Rosalin said, "No, Kassandra already has a girlfriend."

"When did you get a girlfriend? The last I knew you were happily single."

"Long story. One day, I might tell it to you. For now," I looked at Rosalin, "what do you want?"

"To see you." She was smiling sweetly. Yeah, right, like I believed the innocent werewolf act for an instant. I stared at her for several moments.

"Rosalin. Why are you here?"

"I told you, I wanted to see you."

"That may be true." I fixed her with a hard look. "But that's not all."

Rosalin continued to smile.

Rit clasped her hands together. "Well, I'll leave you two to your awkward silence. It was nice meeting you, Rosalin." Rit moved around her to walk out the door, then looked back at me, shaking her head before disappearing into the hall.

"I want to take you to lunch," Rosalin said finally. "Honest, that's it. Lenorre didn't ask me to spy on you or anything. If she wanted someone to do that she would've sent Zaphara."

"You want to take me to lunch? What do you plan to do? Give me a piggyback ride?" The last I checked, she didn't have a car.

"I'll pass on that. I'm not scared of your driving."

I was quiet.

Rosalin sighed. "You know, this isn't as difficult as you're making it. Do you want to go to lunch with me or not?" She put her hands impatiently on her hips. "I promise, I won't pounce on you or start table dancing or whatever scenario you're—Kassandra? Why are you looking at me like that?"

I couldn't help it. I lost my cool and started laughing.

"What? What did I do?"

"Rosalin, I'll go to lunch with you."

"Then why didn't you just tell me that to begin with?"

"And miss this?" I put my hands on my hips and pushed my bottom lip out at her.

"I wasn't doing that."

"Uh-huh." I grabbed my coat, then put it on.

"I wasn't…"

I snatched my keys and started heading for the door. "Since I'm driving that means you're buying, right?"

I drove the few blocks it took to get to the Skyline Café. At one of the tables outside, a couple laughed together. An older man took a sip of his drink, reading the newspaper. We walked through the glass door and up the stairs that led to the roof.

I hadn't felt dressed up next to Rit, but next to Rosalin I did. She wore a long-sleeved black shirt layered under a light pink short-sleeved tee. The pink T-shirt had three black rings around the sleeves. The back of the shirt had the word BITER written in black letters, like the last name on a sports jersey. A pair of light blue flare-legged jeans clung to her figure. Her black, pink, and white skate shoes matched perfectly. I felt better that I wasn't the only one over twenty that owned a pair of skate shoes.

"How'd you get a ride?" I asked, waiting for the hostess.

"Trevor. He had to go to The Two Points to help put up decorations."

"Ah."

A blond-haired girl with lips painted a shade of pink that was brighter than Rosalin's T-shirt smiled at us and asked cheerily, "Two?" We weaved through the crowd of round tables and chairs to a spot in the middle. "Is this all right?"

"It's fine," I told her. "Diet Coke for me and…"

"Water," Rosalin took her seat, "extra lemon."

The waitress smiled again and placed the menus on the table. "I'll bring them right out. My name is Leslie. I'll be your waitress this afternoon."

"Thanks, Leslie," Rosalin said. With one last smile Leslie left to get our drinks. I opened the menu, trying to decide what I wanted to eat.

"When did you start drinking diet? It's not like you need it."

I glanced away from the menu to look at Rosalin. "I always have."

"Why?"

"The corn syrup in regular cola makes me nauseous."

"Oh."

When Leslie returned with our drinks we placed our orders. Skyline Café had a variety of foods, from pasta to burgers. It amused me to find that Rosalin and I had both been checking out the list of steaks. We both ordered the eight-ounce sirloin, medium rare, with baked potatoes.

"Why didn't you join a pack?" She plucked a lemon from the small saucer and squeezed it into her water.

I looked around to make sure I didn't see anyone I knew. I didn't but still kept my voice low. "I've come out of a lot of closets and put my job on the line more than once." I shrugged. "It used to seem important to be able to be who I was without fearing rejection or oppression. It still is, but I've learned to keep work and my personal life separate."

"You're afraid joining a…group," she said carefully, "would make everyone look at you funny and suspect you're a…witch?"

I smiled at her discretion. "Something like that. I just don't want it interfering with what I do for a living. I mean, a lot of people have accepted that I'm Pagan and lesbian." I took a sip of my Diet Coke. "My life is complicated enough. I don't want to complicate it further. I'm solitary and have been for years."

"True, but by being solitary you've alienated yourself from your community." She glanced around. "Kassandra, look at them. We're not like them."

"I know. We are and we aren't."

I gazed out across the array of tables and listened to a woman with her child order a tofu burger. They were on the other side of the rooftop, and the woman was soft-spoken. A human wouldn't have heard them from where Rosalin and I were sitting.

"You belong with us," she said strongly.

"Are you against them now?"

She shook her head, auburn tresses glistening deep red in the sunlight. "No. We were like them once. I'm not against them, but you're one of us. We're your family. I knew it the moment I saw you in the parking lot outside your business. I knew it the moment your energy brushed mine." Her voice fell. "You threw your power at me. Do you remember?"

I'd met Lenorre in The Two Points when Rupert and I had been following Rosalin, and I'd eventually confronted Rosalin and questioned her about her dealings with the pack. Our beasts had displayed their power, and my wolf had proved dominant to hers.

"Do you remember what Lenorre said to you?"

"Which part?"

"Your power hit me. It hit me hard. The only other *witch*," she emphasized the word like a dirty word, "who's hit me that hard with her power was Sheila."

Rosalin, as Beta werewolf, was the second most dominant werewolf of the Blackthorne Pack. In order to remain Alpha, Sheila had to pack more punch with her power.

"You're stronger than she is." She spoke like something sour was in her mouth.

"I want you to tell me something." I looked at her then and her light brown gaze held mine.

"What do you want to know?"

"Do you remember when Lenorre sent you home with me?"

She grinned. "Yes, why?"

"How did you get the scars on your back?"

Rosalin leaned back in her seat. "I can't tell you."

"What happened, Rosalin?"

She shook her head. "Kassandra, please, don't do this."

"Does it have to do with the pack?" I didn't intend to let it go. It irked me that she didn't trust me enough to tell me the truth.

"Yes," she said, and that one word fell heavy between us. Shadows of pain were in her eyes, as if the memories were unfolding in the back of her mind. She closed them, clearly because she didn't want me to see what was there.

"It was her, wasn't it?" I asked, lowering my voice. "Sheila. She did that to you?"

Her eyes flew open. "How do you...how would you?"

"I'm an investigator and she's a sadist. It wasn't hard to piece together. Besides," I watched the waitress approach with our food, "I'm your friend."

Sheila Morris, I thought, tasting the rage on my tongue, *now it's fucking personal. If you ever lay a hand on her again, I'll tear your world apart.* The wolf's energy rumbled through me. Rosalin was as close to a pack as I would ever get, and damn it, I wouldn't let anyone hurt her.

Rosalin picked up her fork, watching me. Then she put it down. "Kassandra..."

"I won't do anything." I forced myself to smile, knowing it was a dark smile that said I'd enjoy hurting someone. Funny, I didn't see it as hurting, but protecting. Did that make me a monster?

"Kassandra, please, you can't."

I bent over the table. "Rosalin, if she ever so much as lays a fingertip on you again, I'll break every one of them. I will not sit idle and let her harm you." I touched her hand on the table, and a sudden jolt of energy made mine twitch like the shock of static electricity, only more.

Rosalin's eyes widened with surprise and her lips parted. "Oh, no." She covered her mouth with a hand, shaking her head.

"What?"

"Why did you do that?"

"Why did I do what?"

"You don't know what you just did?"

"Um, no."

"You just claimed me as one of your wolves, like an alpha claims their pack." Her voice was incredibly low, low enough it'd take another werewolf or vampire to translate.

"I did what?"

"When you offered your protection. You felt it. I saw your body react to it."

"I felt...something. I figured it was just static."

"I wish it was. 'Cause if *she* finds out, I'm in deep shit."

"It was an accident." I shoved a piece of steak in my mouth, chewing. I would say I didn't believe her, but Rosalin didn't freak out over nothing. "Besides, wouldn't I have realized I'd just claimed you? That didn't feel like much of anything."

"It was a spark, promising and binding. What were you expecting? Fireworks?"

"Yeah, considering I didn't even notice what I'd done, fireworks would've been nice."

CHAPTER SEVENTEEN

I paid for lunch. I wouldn't have felt right having Rosalin do it after what I did to her. I didn't really intend for her to in the first place. In the privacy of the car we'd spoken about what had transpired.

Even when Rosalin explained that Sheila and any of the other wolves in the territory would sense my claim on her, I wasn't worried. What a strange thing. The clock on my desk said almost five o'clock. Rosalin sat in the corner of my office flipping through a magazine that must've come from the lobby or Rit's office.

June opened the door and glared at Rosalin, who ignored her.

"Your five o'clock is here."

"Send him in."

Ethan Nelson looked like he was in his early to mid-twenties. I was surprised that he resembled his mother since Timothy had looked so much like his father. Ethan's blond hair was pulled back at the nape of his neck in a ponytail. I studied his pale face, relieved that his eyes were hazel, not brown like Timothy's. Not many people consider how difficult it is for someone to look into the lively eyes of a person that looks so familiar to someone they've lost. The only thing that didn't remind me of his mother or father was the fullness of his lips.

I stood, then rounded the desk to offer my hand. "Kassandra Lyall. You have my sincerest condolences, Mr. Nelson." I stopped myself before telling him that what happened to his brother was truly terrible because we both knew it. Useless to point out the obvious to someone grieving. Ethan took my hand in a strong grip, and I returned the handshake firmly.

"You're the investigator the cops have working on my brother's case?"

I took my hand away and sat back behind my desk. "I am. Why?"

"You're just not what I expected."

"Why do you say that?" I tried to keep my expression polite.

Ethan took a seat, pushing up the sleeves of his blue-and-white flannel. "I'm sorry. I'm not trying to be rude or discourteous. You're just younger and a lot smaller than I expected."

I forced myself to smile. "Appearances are deceiving."

Ethan nodded, looking uncomfortably around my office and finally at Rosalin.

She peeked over the magazine and said, "Howdy."

"Hey."

"Rosalin is my very unprofessional assistant." I lanced her a disapproving look.

She got the hint, putting the magazine down and offering Ethan her hand. "I'm sorry to hear about your brother."

"Thanks. I appreciate it."

Rosalin walked back to her seat and Ethan stared at her as if he couldn't help himself. She opened her magazine. Either she was ignoring it or she was completely oblivious to him.

"Ethan." I had to say his name twice to get him to pay attention to me and was tempted to snap my fingers in front of his face.

"Yeah?"

"What did you need to talk to me about? I'm already looking into your brother's murder." I folded my arms on top of the desk.

"I came here initially to talk to you. The other lady told me she didn't know when you'd be back."

I nodded. "Why are you trying to pull another PI in on the case?"

"I wanted to talk to you. I figured if I hired her she'd say something to you."

I crossed my legs, finding a pen to scribble notes if I needed to. I usually didn't take them because I had a pretty good memory. "What do you need to talk to me about?"

"Timothy mentioned that about you." A look of sorrow flickered in and out of his hazel gaze.

"He mentioned me?" I couldn't keep all of the surprise from my voice.

"He said you were tough and to the point. He also told me about the cops coming out to the house when that man was attacked. I was at school so we spoke over the phone. Is it true my mom threw a fit and that you threatened to take her to jail?"

"I didn't threaten to throw her in jail. The cops did."

"Oh."

"What else did your brother say to you? Were the two of you close?"

"Yeah, he talked to me. I was the only one in the house that didn't listen to everything Mom says. Timothy and I had each other's backs. He couldn't talk to our mother. I'm sure you noticed."

"I did notice, and I'm sorry," I said, because I was. I couldn't imagine growing up in their situation.

"Dad's always got Mom's back. We couldn't talk to him either. So Timothy and I, we talked a lot. He was able to tell me things he couldn't tell our parents, and he knew I wouldn't rat him out."

I thought of several things to say and finally decided to ask, "Did you know about your brother's interest in the preternatural community?"

"He mentioned it a few times. He said he tried to talk to you and you told him to drop it. Is that true?"

"True enough," I said. Those weren't my exact words, but the gist of it was pretty damn close.

Ethan laughed. "You're not the only one that tried to tell him that. I tried too. I think," he sounded uncertain, "I know something you need to know."

"What is it?"

"Timothy met a girl a few weeks ago. He told me the last time I spoke with him over the phone. She's a girl from school, Alyssa

Cunningham. I think that's her name." Ethan sighed heavily. "Man, he thought he was in love. Said she was interested in all the things he was—role playing, monsters, video games." He shook his head. "I should've said something sooner. I should've told him it was a stupid idea. How was I to know?"

Know what? Outwardly, I shrugged. "People make their own decisions, even sixteen-year-old boys."

"Especially sixteen-year-old boys," Rosalin added.

Ethan jumped as if he'd forgotten she was in the room. When he looked back at me it was with fierce determination. "Timothy was meeting this chick at night when our parents went to bed."

"It sounds like Timothy was drawn to her because they had similar interests," she said. "Alyssa might have connections to a rogue group of vampires."

Rosalin seemed to be unknowingly following my thoughts. I nodded in agreement.

"What if Alyssa's the vampire?" Ethan asked.

"You said Timothy met her at school?"

"Yeah."

I shook my head. "She's not a vampire unless she's attending night school."

"Timothy went to a public school," Ethan said, clearly disappointed that whatever scenario he had come up with regarding a vampire Lolita wouldn't work out.

"Alyssa's connected somehow," Rosalin said.

I said what I was thinking. "Alyssa's connected to Timothy's sire."

Ethan had a lost look on his face. "Sire?"

I stood and closed the office door. "Ethan, can you keep a really big secret from your parents? Your brother's...life may well depend on it."

"I won't tell them anything. Why? What is it?"

I told Ethan Nelson my suspicions about his brother. Someone in his family needed to know, and since he was the only one prepared to speak to me without a Bible and some holy water in hand, it had to be him.

CHAPTER EIGHTEEN

"Detective Kingfisher," Arthur answered on the fourth ring.

"Arthur, it's Kassandra. I need you to pull up information on a student named Alyssa Cunningham that attended Timothy's school."

"All right, let me get to a computer."

I waited until I heard him typing. "Alyssa Cunningham?"

"Yes, she's around Timothy's age, attends the same school and everything."

"She doesn't have a record."

"That's a relief," I said.

"What do you want me to find, Kass?"

"I want her address. We need to interrogate her."

"Where are you?"

"Still at work. I'm about to go home."

"You want to do this tonight?"

"Could you make that happen?"

"If you intend to interrogate her, I'm going with you. I've got her address. Huh," he said, "she doesn't live very far from your girlfriend's club. Kassandra, do you think she's connected to the murder?"

"She gave Timothy to the vampires."

"Can you prove it?"

"I can prove that I know someone that knows Timothy was talking to her before his disappearance, and when I find Timothy, I can prove it."

"Meet me outside your girlfriend's club at eight thirty," he said, hanging up before I could answer.

"Does that mean you have time to give me a ride home?" Rosalin asked.

"Yeah," I said, "barely."

❖

I dropped Rosalin off at Lenorre's. Afterward, I went by my apartment to get the Pro .40 and small-of-the-back holster. I was surprised to see I still had twenty minutes when I got back behind the wheel.

I liked the Pro .40. I'd taken the Mark III out to the shooting range and found it was pretty good, but I didn't like it as much as the .40. I kept telling myself I would get a Kimber Eclipse, but they were so freaking expensive it'd be a while until I could afford the one I saw in a weapons-and-ammo magazine a few weeks ago. I didn't even know if Rupert could get me a good discount on it, but I planned to find out. Some femmes collect diamonds, I prefer guns. Seriously, what will the diamond do for me? Sparkle? Unless you're certain you can temporarily blind an opponent, I wouldn't recommend wearing anything that sparkles in a fight. Otherwise, you might as well hold a flashing sign over your head that reads: Right here.

I parked next to Arthur's black sapphire Crown Victoria. He stepped out of it and met me halfway. "She lives with her parents," he said.

"I figured as much."

"We have to talk to them first, you realize that? It'll take away the element of surprise if they tell her we want to talk to her."

"I know how it goes." The sign of The Two Points burned more brightly into the night than the few old-fashioned street lamps in the parking lot. The asphalt was so dark it looked like black water. I was glad it was Thursday and that the line at the door was surprisingly short. It'd lengthen later in the evening.

I preferred to drive, and I didn't want to ride with Arthur. Sometimes it's best to be able to drive away quickly, without worrying about where you have to drop someone off or whether they want to go hunting monsters with you if you don't have time to dump them somewhere. Arthur gave me the address and was telling me how to get to the house when I heard a woman's voice call out over the small crowd. "Kassandra."

I whipped around to find the face that went with that voice, and her sea-green eyes met mine. With the distance between us, it wasn't the inviting smile that made it hard to look away. It was the outfit. A pair of form-fitting vinyl pants hung low on her hips. A matching corset was cinched at her waist, over a frilly white renaissance shirt that seemed to bloom out of the corset like the petals of some demented flower. Somehow, the outfit worked for her. She managed not to look like a gothic barmaid. I would've looked absolutely silly in it, but Eris didn't. No, she looked the complete opposite of silly.

"That doesn't look like your..." Arthur stammered, staring in the same direction I was.

I noticed most of the people in line outside the club were staring at her too.

"That's because she's not," I said.

Eris stalked toward us in spiked heels. It took more effort than I'd like to admit not to watch the way her hips swayed. I forced myself to turn and look at Arthur, whose eyes were wide. I couldn't tell if he was scared, or...well, I really didn't want to know what the alternative was.

I met the full weight of her gaze and said, "Eris."

"Kassandra." She said my name again, this time lower, like silk flowing through my hands. She tilted her head to the side. "To what does one owe the pleasure of seeing you again, so soon?"

"I'm working." Ignoring the fluttering sensation in the pit of my stomach, I buried my hands in my coat pockets and tried to look casual, but probably managed to look exactly what I was feeling... uncomfortable.

"Business," she murmured, sparing a glance at Arthur's car. She trailed one startling white finger across the trunk and looked at Arthur. "Police business, I presume? Have you any lead on the boy?"

I said, "No," and Arthur said, "Yes, ma'am."

I wanted to get in his face and call him an idiot. I didn't know Eris enough to trust her. Why was he being so compliant? And "ma'am"? Come on!

Her face fell into a blank mask, and even though her features were expressionless, her eyes burned intensely.

"You do not trust me." Something in her tone made me feel bad, like I had sincerely hurt her feelings.

I took a step forward, one step, placing my body daringly close to hers. "What game are you playing?"

Arthur wouldn't have noticed it, but I noticed her very slow, deliberate blink.

"Kassandra, if I was playing a game with you, you would know it."

My cell phone rang and I jumped, which kind of ruined the tough-werewolf attitude I was trying to project.

"That is most likely Lenorre," Eris said.

"I doubt it." But sure enough, the number on the caller ID was Lenorre's.

"Yeah?" I answered, knowing I sounded utterly bitchy.

"Kassandra." Lenorre's voice made my stomach swan-dive. I walked away from Arthur and Eris.

"What is it?" I said angrily, without really meaning to sound that way.

"I take it Eris has found you?"

"Yeah. Why?"

"Take her with you." It wasn't a command, but sounded pretty damn close to one.

"Why?"

"Rosalin has informed me of what you and the detective plan to go do. I want Eris with you."

"I can take care of myself."

"Kassandra, do not be stubborn. Just listen to me. I want Eris there."

"Lenorre, I'm working," I said more strongly. "This is police business."

"It is also vampire business. If something happens I want you to have more than just one human detective on your side."

Eris leaned against Arthur's car, crossing her arms over her chest. She wasn't smiling and didn't look amused. It looked like she was waiting to hear what her orders were.

"We're just going to ask questions. Why do I need your backup? Give me a good reason to take her with us, and I'll take her. If you tell me because you said so, I'll leave her ass where she's standing, because we don't need her. If anything, a vampire will make people uncomfortable, and when people are uncomfortable answers are hard to come by. Why should I take her?"

"Can you smell another vampire? Are you capable of perceiving if the girl is marked or has been bitten? You may have the supernatural ability, Kassandra, but if you do not know what to look for, you will not see it."

"Lyall," Arthur said, and I turned to him with narrowed eyes. He'd never called me Lyall, not ever.

"What?"

"Tell your girlfriend it's not a big deal. We'll take her super vamp with us."

"You're not serious."

Arthur said nearly the same thing Lenorre had. "Hey, if we're out of our league it'd be nice to have a vampire along. She can hear and smell things we humans can't." He spread his arms out, trying to appear reasonable. "Come on, it won't hurt us any to have the extra muscle."

"Are you happy now?" I grumbled into the phone.

"I am not happy you are displeased with me, but I am happy to know you will be far safer with Eris than without her. As you did not ask me to join you, then I believe you should take her." Her words were careful, so careful. Which meant she wasn't *trying* to piss me off. "At the least," she said, "keep in mind I did not send Zaphara."

The thought almost made me cringe. I would've really freaked if she'd sent Zaphara, but at least with Zaphara my insides didn't feel like they were twisting and falling from a great height. At least with Zaphara I was absolutely sure I could tell her to shut up and leave me the fuck alone.

I hung up the phone, and Arthur gave me a pat on the back.

"Chill out," he said. "The more the merrier."

I shook my head and went to the car. I was fastening my seat belt when Eris slid into the passenger seat and buckled up without being asked. I tried to ignore her presence. At night, the car seemed darker, more private and intimate than it would have during the day. What was Lenorre thinking? Hell, what was I thinking? My eyes flicked to the vampire beside me before I made a right turn onto the main road. I sucked in a quick intake of breath when her gaze met mine.

Shit… I was attracted to her.

How not? She was gorgeous. The thought that probably a million other people were attracted to her made me feel better. Maybe Eris was just one of those women that everyone thought was beautiful? Yeah, that had to be it.

CHAPTER NINETEEN

Gwen and Dennis Cunningham's house was small with white siding and yellow trim along the edges of the roof. Probably a three-bedroom, one-bath home. Arthur pulled into the driveway behind the Cunninghams' old red-and-white pickup. I didn't fret too much about parking the Tiburon at the edge of the yard because a few other parked cars already hugged the curbs in front of other yards. If someone hit my car, they'd have to take another one out with it. It wasn't the greatest part of town, but it wasn't the worst.

I stepped behind Arthur onto the small porch. It was almost nine o'clock, a little late to go question a school-aged girl, but I was with Detective Arthur Kingfisher. As if they would get the luxury of complaining about time restraints? Yeah, right. I don't think so, folks.

Arthur knocked on the door, twice. The curtains in the big window next to the door moved aside as someone looked out, then let them fall back. A woman asked who was at the door.

A male's deep voice grumbled. "I don't know, some guy and a gal that looks like one of Lyssie's little friends."

"One of her friends," the woman asked, "this late?"

"I don't know." I was guessing it was Dennis Cunningham, the father.

Eris propped herself against the white wooden post on the porch, standing in the shadows. I sighed. Why do people assume a short woman is underage? As if I'd asked the question out loud, Eris slowly lifted her shoulders.

The door cracked open and a man with steel gray hair and clear gray eyes looked at us. Before anyone could say anything he asked in a gruff voice, "Who are you?"

"Mr. Cunningham?" Arthur asked politely.

The man looked him up and down. "Yeah? What do you want? Lyssie's not here." He glanced at me.

I folded my arms over my chest.

"Mr. Cunningham." Arthur drew the father's attention back to himself. "I'm Detective Kingfisher and this is—"

I stepped forward. "Preternatural Investigator and Paranormal Huntress Kassandra Lyall. You said your daughter isn't home?"

The man kept the door cracked a few inches and gave me a disbelieving look. "That's a mouthful, girly. If you're looking for ghosts you won't find them here."

"It's Ms. Lyall and I'm not looking for ghosts. I'm looking for Alyssa Cunningham."

His eyelids flickered so quickly that I didn't know if Arthur had caught it.

"We need to talk to you about your daughter," I said. "Do you know where she is?"

"No. She left around five thirty and hasn't gotten home yet."

"Denny?" a woman called from the other side of the door. "Denny, who is it?"

Dennis looked over his shoulder and raised his voice. "No one important."

"Have they heard from Lyssie?" There was worry in her tone.

"No," he said sternly, then ignored her. "What d'you want?"

"Mr. Cunningham." Arthur kept his voice nice and even. "Do you know where your daughter is?"

He opened the door a little wider, speaking in a defensive tone. "No, I don't. What do you want with her anyway?"

"We need to talk to her," I said again. "You have absolutely no idea where your seventeen-year-old daughter is at this time of night?"

I found it hard to believe loving and caring parents would let someone so young run around after the sun went down. I let him see my disbelief and took another step forward, letting my wolf rise just enough that the power washed from me and flooded the area. He flinched slightly and Arthur tensed. Arthur wasn't a sensitive, but apparently even non-sensitive humans pick up on energy frequency.

The smell of whiskey hit my nostrils like something old and sour.

"How much whiskey have you had tonight, Mr. Cunningham?"

"Little lady, what I do in my own damn house is my own damn business."

Arthur said, "May we come inside and speak with you and your wife?"

"No."

"Arthur," I motioned toward the front yard with my head, "a word."

Arthur followed me out onto the lawn.

"What is it?"

"He won't talk to us unless we force him to."

Arthur ran a hand through his hair, which was long enough to cover his ears, making it look tousled. "Suggestions?"

I told him what I had been thinking.

"Stuff 'em and cuff 'em?" Arthur asked. "How can we get him to step out of the house?"

"Leave that to me."

"Kass, don't get hurt. If he's drunk, there's no telling what he might do."

"He's not drunk, but I'm pretty sure his BAC level is over the limit." A few years ago all of the states had passed the .08 per se law, which meant anyone caught driving with a blood alcohol content at or over .08 was considered to be driving under the influence. However, since he wasn't driving we had another option. If we got Mr. Cunningham to step out of his home, especially in a fit of anger directed at me, Arthur was within his rights to cuff the son of a bitch and stuff him in the back of the police car for public intoxication.

"From what I smell, it is," Eris said coolly.

I jumped. "Don't do that." Why the hell did these vampires always sneak up on me? You'd think being a lycanthrope I would hear them, but no. I was getting sick of them springing up like vampiric jack-in-the-boxes and trying to scare the werewolf piddle out of me.

Arthur just looked at her. "You're sure?"

"If I was not sure I would not have said anything."

Arthur stepped back onto the porch. Mr. Cunningham was still in the doorway, watching us.

"Mr. Cunningham." I returned his stare unwavering. I detected something almost criminal in it, something that said he didn't mind hurting people. "We really need to speak with you and your wife. If you care for your daughter at all, you'll talk to us."

"Bullshit," he said. I heard his wife's slightly panicked voice from somewhere beyond the door. "Denny," she said, "just talk to them, please? Just talk to them!"

"Shut up!" he yelled, turning his upper body away from the door. I had a moment to assess the situation, a second to sense the tension in the air and to realize what he was about to do. Dennis Cunningham turned on his wife. I heard her footsteps hesitate, felt her uncertainty fluttering in the air. His beefy arm came back into view a second before he hit her.

"Arthur," I said impatiently.

"Mr. Cunningham!" Arthur's voice rose, trying to get the man's attention.

The door slammed shut, but even with the door closed Arthur had to have been able to hear Mrs. Cunningham sobbing and saying, "Denny, please don't!"

I didn't need supernatural hearing to know what was about to happen. Dennis yelled, "I told you to stay out of this, you ungrateful bitch!"

There were sounds of struggle on the other side. I heard a soft thud like a body hitting the tiled floor.

Arthur tried to open the door, hit it once, and yelled, "Dennis Cunningham!"

"Eris," I said.

"Yes?"

"Would you do the honor?"

"I'd love to." Her response was almost a growl.

I touched Arthur's shoulder and he jumped. "Move it or lose it, Kingfisher."

"What?" he asked as I pulled him to a corner of the porch.

Eris wrapped one hand around the doorknob, bracing her other hand against the door. She pushed her body forward and the door creaked; a little more pressure and the hinges cracked as they snapped. I moved away from Arthur and the corner, slipping up behind Eris and pressing along the wall beside the door. I reached under my coat, pulling the Pro .40 free of its holster in a practiced draw and flicked the safety off with my thumb, holding the gun in a teacup grip.

Mrs. Cunningham was crying and her husband screamed as glass shattered on the tile. Eris looked at me and I nodded. She gave one last nearly effortless push, turning her body into it from the hips up, enough to angle the door so when it fell, it didn't hit anyone. I swept into the room. Mr. Cunningham was on top of his wife, his fist pulled back, ready to strike.

"Dennis Cunningham," I said.

His wild eyes flicked to me, gray and furious. If he thought anger would scare me, he was wrong. There are only a few things worse than a wife beater. If he wanted to fight fire with fire, he was looking at it. I didn't try to hide my rage. I let the son of a bitch see it while I pointed the gun directly at his fist, struggling to keep my shields in place and to resist the desire to drop my weapon and rip his fucking throat out. "Mr. Cunningham. I suggest you get the fuck away from your wife or you'll be missing something."

"You know how to use that thing, girly?"

"What do you think?" I sighted down the barrel, standing in a Chapman stance. Straightening my right arm, I locked it in place behind the gun. My left arm was bent slightly at the elbow, pulling back to provide tension. It's a woman-friendly stance and doesn't rely as heavily on upper body strength as the Weaver. A lot of people naturally fall into a comfortable stance when they first start learning how to use a gun.

He scoffed at me. "You won't shoot me. You don't have the balls."

I glared at him. "Are you willing to test that theory against a .40 caliber semi-automatic weapon?"

"Mr. Cunningham," Arthur said, weapon drawn and aimed. "Move away from your wife and slowly put your hands on the top of your head."

Denny boy didn't look very happy. His fist trembled where it was still curled in the air, poised for a strike. Arthur had his gun trained on the back of the man's head.

"Which path do you choose, Mr. Cunningham? The easy way or the hard way?" I asked.

Slowly, his fingers uncurled. Out of my peripheral vision I could see Mrs. Cunningham covering her face with her arms, trying to protect herself. The points of her elbows stuck up in the air and she was sobbing now. We had to get the bastard off her without all hell breaking loose. Oh, I could've dropped the gun and gone for him. I could've picked him up and thrown him across the room, but how was I supposed to explain to the cops that I effortlessly sent a man three times my size flying into a wall? Somehow, I don't think I could write that off as normal.

"Lace your fingers on the back of your head," Arthur commanded.

Mr. Cunningham did what Arthur told him to do and glared at me.

I felt Eris move behind me like some ghostly shadow but didn't turn to look. "Get up," I said, "slowly. Keep your fingers laced."

Once he got to his feet Arthur holstered his gun and moved in. He jerked the handcuffs off his belt and slapped them on Mr. Cunningham's wrists, then read him his rights. I turned the safety back on, holstering my gun.

Eris and I moved in, helping Gwen Cunningham get to her feet. Her pale cheeks were wet with tears and mottled with bruises. Bruises crawled the length of her slender arms. If a person could inflict harm on the person he claimed to love, that was truly criminal. I'd been called out on domestic-violence cases when I was a cop and had witnessed far worse than this, but either way you sliced it, it still pissed me the fuck off. And now that I was a werewolf, it was that much worse. I silently thanked Goddess it wasn't close to that time of the month. The full moon, that is.

Arthur was guiding Mr. Cunningham toward the door when he froze, finally noticing his doorway. A few splinters of wood from the frame littered the white tile.

He looked back at me. "You do that?"

"No."

"Couldn't," he said snidely. "You're just a little slip of a girl."

"I'm not the one in handcuffs, Mr. Cunningham."

Arthur gave him a shove that sent him stumbling. Dennis grumbled incoherently as Arthur pushed him through the door and to the car. Eris was stroking the woman's wheat-colored hair, trying to calm her.

I went to them and touched the bloody bruise under Gwen's blue eye. She didn't even flinch. I guess if you've been hit often enough you forget how. "Gwen, will you do me a favor?"

"What?" Her voice was soft, but her tone was defensive.

"Press charges. You have a teenage daughter to think about and need to get the hell away from this guy. He's dangerous and unpredictable. Will you press charges and get a restraining order?"

"Where would I go? What would I do? I can't leave Denny."

"If you don't leave, you're putting not only your life at risk, but your daughter's, and don't say he hits you every now and then or when he's drunk. You're covered in bruises, probably some under your clothes I can't see," I said with heat, trying to get my point across. "He'll do it again. I can promise you that it will only get worse. I've seen it often enough." I put a hand on her shoulder. "You'll figure out what to do after you take the first step. Just take it and stop letting this jerk push you around."

Her cheeks were damp with tears. "Gwen," I said. "Mrs. Cunningham, look at me." She did. "You deserve better than this."

Gwen Cunningham had to be at least ten years younger than her husband. She was a small woman, either in her late thirties or early forties. Her gaze met mine and she nodded. "Thank you," she said, and I had a feeling it wasn't just a thank you for getting her husband off her. I'd told her what she probably hadn't heard in years—that she deserved to be treated better.

I sensed the pain buried deep in the fabric of her soul. It would take every ounce of strength left in her to walk away from him. By mentioning her daughter I hoped I gave her something to hold on to. She would have to overcome her fears and insecurities, and ultimately summon an unwavering amount of willpower. I'd seen women do it, but I'd also seen women return. I prayed to Goddess she found the courage to leave and never look back.

Arthur returned and offered to take Gwen to the hospital, but she refused to go. He took her statement and assured her the cops would do all they could to make sure she was safe tonight. Which meant Dennis Cunningham would be spending the night in jail.

"You wanted to know about Alyssa," Gwen said, clutching a Kleenex from the coffee table. "He wouldn't let me tell you this," her voice shook, "but she ran away."

I didn't doubt the truth in her words. "When?"

"Three days ago. I haven't heard from her. She didn't leave a note. Some of her clothes are missing. Denny wouldn't let me call the cops." She sobbed. "He thought I'd call them on him."

"You wouldn't have," I said, "would you?"

She shook her head. "No. No, I wouldn't have."

Gwen Cunningham was intelligent enough to realize the awful truth. I nodded. If it hadn't been for Dennis' display in front of us, he'd never even be going to jail. Gwen would've just sat back and taken it, thinking she deserved it, believing the lies he fed her. He'd torn her down in more ways than just physical.

"We will do what we can to find your daughter," I told her. "If there's anything else you need to tell us, here's my cell." I handed her my business card. *Lyall Investigations* was written in plain black font. The simple white card contained my last name, title, office number, and my cell-phone number.

Gwen took it, nodding. "I will. If she comes home I'll call you. Why are you looking for her?"

"I'm working on a missing persons case." I told the partial truth. "I don't think Alyssa is alone. A boy of her age has gone missing, as well. Do you know if Alyssa was friends with a boy named Timothy?"

"Off the top of my head, no. Lyssie doesn't share much with me."

"What about any friends or relatives she may have gone to?"

Slowly, she shook her head. Sadness clearly haunted her. "No, Denny doesn't let her have anyone over so I never get to meet her friends from school. We don't have any immediate family here, other than Denny's folks, and Alyssa's not close to them." As if she felt the need to explain, she said, "Denny's problem runs in his family."

I nodded, sharply. "Thank you, Mrs. Cunningham."

Heading for the car I stepped over the splinters in the doorway. Gwen would have to call someone to come fix the door. Arthur had spoken briefly about it with her, and she'd assured him she would be fine for the night. Eris did the best she could, picking it up and leaning it against the opening. The hinges were shot, jutting out from the door frame. I was pretty sure Gwen could call someone to replace a door at ten in the evening. At least I hoped so. After all, I had asked a vampire to rip it off its hinges.

CHAPTER TWENTY

A rthur agreed to call me after he took Dennis Cunningham into custody and let me know if they got anything out of questioning him. I doubted they would, but it wouldn't hurt to try. I was a little shocked that Arthur and I had talked Gwen Cunningham into pressing charges. People that accept abuse generally have very low self-esteem and an even lower sense of self-worth.

I really hoped she didn't let him treat her like shit again. If she went back to Dennis, that's exactly what she'd be doing. I hated to see it happen, amongst heterosexuals and homosexuals, but it wasn't my decision to make. It sounded cold, but that was the truth.

When I asked Eris if she wanted me to take her back to the club she declined. I pulled up to the speaker box in front of the black iron gate blocking the driveway that led to the house. Iron fencing circled the entire property. I punched in the key code on the little metal keypad and the gate creaked, sliding open on its tracks.

I parked outside the front door since I didn't have a garage opener. Rosalin opened the door when we stepped onto the porch and held it for us. I unbuttoned my coat and draped it on the black wooden coat rack just inside the doorway.

Rosalin and Eris followed me into the hallway, which was lined with statues.

I glanced at Eris as we approached the basement. At the Cunninghams' I had been able to ignore the tug of attraction that she caused, but now that we were in a hallway and I could smell the subtle scent that was hers alone, it flared up again, suffusing my body with warmth.

I asked her, "Did you choose the name?"

"Yes. Why?"

"Eris. Goddess of Discord?"

"Out of chaos comes order. Occasionally," she practically cooed, "chaos can be quite fun."

I shook my head. "And to think I considered women weird. Vampire women just get weirder and weirder."

At that, Rosalin laughed. "Touché."

Eris put her hand on the wall in front of me, blocking my way. "And is weird such a bad thing, Kassandra Lyall?"

"That depends." I forced myself to keep eye contact with her. "On how weird."

"Weird is just another word for something strange. Strange is the unknown. Would a thing be so weird if you were to become familiar with it?"

"No."

Eris took a step back, no longer blocking my way. A spill of light flooded the hallway, making my vision shift from black and white to bright white around the edges.

I pivoted to find Lenorre standing in the doorway. "I take it things went well?"

"No," I said. "They went the opposite of well."

"Ah." She looked behind me. "Eris." She dipped her head slightly.

They stared at one another for a few seconds before Eris greeted her. "Countess." She inclined her head as Lenorre had. I didn't understand the stiffness to the set of her shoulders so I gave Rosalin a questioning look.

She shrugged, as if to say, "Don't ask me. I have no idea."

"What happened?" Lenorre asked, sitting next to me on the couch.

I touched her. I couldn't sit close to her and not want to do that. The silky night pants she wore were incredibly soft. "It's a long story." I dropped my gaze to the pale triangle of flesh peeking out from between the folds of the midnight blue silk shirt. The shirt was long-sleeved, with the collar neatly folded, flowing into a wide V at the base of her neck. It looked good on her, distractingly good, like a plate of brownies in front of you when you're PMSing. "The girl is missing. The husband is abusive. Arthur has him in police custody. The mother is a wreck. I have no idea how we'll find the girl."

Lenorre pulled me against her, distracting me even more. "I am sure we will figure something out."

I sighed. "I certainly hope so." I rested my cheek against her shoulder, wrapping my arm around her sleek frame. The soap she'd used was seductive and warm. Beyond that intriguing smell was the airy scent of vampire no perfume maker or soap manufacturer could do justice.

Eris cleared her throat. "I hate to interrupt, but I need to feed."

Lenorre looked at her. "By all means, go ahead. I am sure you are more than capable of finding willing food."

"If you want," Rosalin said, "I don't mind opening a vein."

"My apologies, wolf, but you are not the one I wish to taste." She looked at Lenorre. "You said you'd grant me a boon if I went with Kassandra tonight. I am within my rights to ask what I am about to, as well you know."

Lenorre's gaze hardened. "Tread lightly. What you seek is not mine to give."

"Is it not?" Eris mused.

"You had to bribe her?" I asked.

"In a sense," Lenorre said. "'Twas not necessarily a bribe so much as it was an offer of payment in return for her services."

"What did you offer her?" I asked warily.

"She offered a choice amongst her people, so long as the donor was willing," Eris explained.

"Eris is a Prime. She is within her rights to ask for something."

"What exactly is she asking for?"

"You."

It took a moment to sink in. What was I supposed to say? Thanks, but no thanks?

Eris laughed, almost purring. "Kassandra, I ask only for a taste of your blood." She grinned. "You can close your mouth now."

"Do I look like the poster woman for a blood drive?"

Her grin faltered slightly. "No…"

"I told you it was not a wise idea to ask her," Lenorre said.

Eris looked thoughtful as she stared at me. "You would refuse when I at least have the courtesy to ask?"

"I haven't said yes or no."

I tried to relax against Lenorre's body, but I was tense. After Eris and I had stepped out of the car the sexual tension had been minimal. Now, it skyrocketed again between us. The thought of her mouth against my neck tightened my stomach and sent a wave of something close to anticipation through me. Lenorre had only bitten me twice, once when I was wolf-ridden and the second time during sex. The reminder of that mingling sensation of pleasure and pain was exciting.

"If it alleviates your discomfort, a wrist will suffice."

I shook my head, summoning my will. "No."

"Might I ask why?"

"I don't think it's a good idea."

She looked at Lenorre. "Is she always this willful?"

Lenorre touched my hair. "Yes."

"Do you dislike me?" Eris asked.

"It's not that I dislike you, Eris. I don't know you, and from my experience being nibbled on by a vampire is—"

"Erotic." The word made my stomach dive.

Sweet Goddess, make her go away.

I looked at Lenorre. If I accepted, how would she take it? Eris was right, for me there was something erotic about sharing blood with a vampire. I couldn't share my blood with Eris and disconnect the two sensations. The fact she was attractive also made things worse. Not that I would have preferred to be food for an ugly vampire. I didn't want to be food, period.

"I should take her up on her offer," I whispered against Lenorre's hair. "You didn't stop Zaphara from pouncing on me."

My remark was a little spiteful, but I was still upset about the whole Zaphara thing.

"Sharing blood with Eris will not make me jealous. Nor will it upset me. Do I seem jealous thus far?"

"No. Why? You'd seriously let her sink fangs in me?"

"It is Eris. If it were any other vampire, one I did not trust, I would not have allowed the request to have been made in the first place."

"I wouldn't be as calm as you if someone was asking to sink fangs in you."

"You are young," Lenorre stroked up my side, "and though I can be just as possessive, there are those I trust."

"You trust her not to mind-fuck me?"

"Kassandra, if I was going to..." Eris stopped when Lenorre raised a hand.

"If I were you and wanted a taste of Kassandra's blood I wouldn't finish that sentence. Yes, I trust her not to use her wiles on you or to breach the boundary of politeness." She touched my cheek. "I trust you."

"Then trust me when I say no."

"As you wish," Eris said. "I would not have asked had I known you were so loyal to Lenorre."

"When did you get the impression I wasn't?" A bit of anger clouded my tone.

She held my gaze a little too intensely for comfort. "Do you want the truth or would you prefer I leave some words unspoken between us?"

"Oh, no. Pray tell, what gave you the impression I'm not loyal?"

"The way you look at me." Her words hit like a fist, stealing the breath from my lungs for one harsh moment.

"Just because I find you attractive doesn't mean I'd do anything about it."

"Mayhap. I was hoping you would."

"No reaction?" I asked Lenorre, who was as calm and reserved as a statue.

"Kassandra, you expect me to react like a human. I am not human. I do not think or feel like one. Neither, my dear, are you."

"Wolves mate for life," Rosalin said. "We're pretty monogamous and possessive. Well, most of us. I could think of a few exceptions."

"Is that what it is?" I asked Rosalin. "If I was in Lenorre's position I'd be freaking the hell out."

"It is nothing more than a sharing of blood," Eris said.

"No, it's not. It might be for you, but for me it wouldn't be. It would feel too much like cheating."

"How can it be cheating if your lover is giving you permission? We're not going to bed together."

I tried for honesty. "I've seen the way you look at me. You've seen the way I look at you. Why should we risk crossing the line?"

Eris offered a pleased smile. "You fear you would want to cross the line with me? Would it be so simple as one bite and you would want to crawl into my bed?"

I was growing increasingly uncomfortable. It was a weird situation to begin with. Lenorre's palm played idly against my side. She squeezed my hip, making me look at her.

"I don't know, but I can tell you one thing. Even if I was tempted to cross that line with you, Eris, I wouldn't let myself."

"Then," Eris said, "I misread you and offer my apologies. I will find other food this night. There may come a day when you are not so afraid of me, Kassandra."

"Don't get your hopes up, Eris. I'm not afraid of you. I just don't share my blood casually."

"Your depth only makes you more intriguing."

"If it matters at all," Rosalin said, gracefully interrupting the tension, "I'll still open a vein."

"Then," Lenorre spoke quietly, "go. Kassandra and I shall retire for the evening."

She gave me a smoky look and my stomach started flipping all over again.

Retire, my ass.

CHAPTER TWENTY-ONE

By the time I finished brushing my teeth and emerged from the bathroom, the bed looked like a really good place to sleep.

Lenorre sat propped against the pillows, still wearing her silky pajamas.

"You look comfy," I casually noted.

She sank lower, arms reaching above her head as her fingers laced around the wooden beam that connected the bedposts. The gesture reminded me of her bound wrists and I stifled a shudder of pleasure.

Lenorre stretched, lifting her body slightly off the mattress. The last few buttons on the midnight blue shirt were left undone, falling open as she teased me with a glimpse of her pale, flat stomach. "Oh, I am," she purred, twisting her hips slightly in the stretch, showing off her hourglass figure, "very, very comfortable." Her voice was breathy. The look she gave me managed to convey more desire than her words.

I was wearing The Two Points shirt she'd given me, which was long enough to cover my black bikini-cut underwear. "Guess what I forgot?" I put a sway in my walk.

Lenorre held a hand out and I took it. "I am glad you forgot them."

"You would be." I laughed as she pulled me into the circle of her arms. Burying my face in the bend of her neck, I inhaled the scent of her.

"You are tired?" she mumbled against my hair.

"Mmm-hmm," I breathed. "I got up early to go to work. Not all of us spontaneously combust in sunlight."

She laughed and swatted my thigh, gently. When I jumped, expecting more than a playful swat, she laughed again. "Do you plan to work tomorrow?"

"I told Rit to call me if she needed me. There's no point. I don't intend to juggle any more cases until I've figured out what happened to Timothy and where Alyssa is." Lenorre nodded, then twined her silk-clad leg around mine.

"If you wish to go to sleep," Lenorre drew the tips of her fingernails lightly across my exposed thigh, "I shall understand."

"I don't mind touching right now, but I don't think I'd survive a repeat of last night. I might not spontaneously combust but I might spontaneously pass out again."

Lenorre stopped moving. "Ah, yes. You did spontaneously pass out." She grinned. "I do not think the bed would survive a repeat."

I laughed. "No, I don't think so." I snaked my arm around her back and played my fingers over the dip the position had created at the base of her spine.

Lenorre kissed me and I returned the kiss, exploring her mouth until my head reeled and I was dizzy with desire.

"How did I ever say no to you?"

Her accent sent a shiver of pleasure through me. "You were scared and being quite stubborn."

"True enough." I brushed my lips across her cheek. "So were you."

"I was reasonably determined."

"Oh, really? Is that what they call it?"

"Yes."

I had to fight not to shudder when her breath tickled my neck.

"Why did you tell Eris if I gave my permission, you'd let her sink her fangs into me?"

Lenorre nipped my neck. I jumped, letting out a sound that was uncomfortably close to a girlish yip.

"Oh, Kassandra, you have been too long in your hiding amongst the humans."

I frowned. "Rosalin told me biting isn't always erotic for a vampire."

"She is correct. At times feeding is just that." She propped herself up on one elbow, gazing at me with those silvery eyes. I traced her jaw with the tips of my fingers.

"If my attraction was so obvious to Eris, I imagine it was obvious to you?"

Her head lowered and her lips brushed my palm. "It was."

"And that doesn't make you jealous?"

"You are not the type of woman that likes to feel guilty," she said. "You struggle with your desires, between those of wolf and human. Now there is a new addition to your personality."

"The raven."

"Yes, the raven. As well as the mark The Morrigan placed on your soul."

I agreed, again. I'd pretty much known the second bit of information from the moment I found my spiritual path and The Morrigan. I also knew she wasn't an easy Goddess to walk with. So far, I'd been right. The words "difficult to fathom" came to mind.

"I don't think the raven has actually shown any personality changes," I said. "Not like when I was infected with lycanthropy."

"The raven is very different from the lycanthropy virus."

"What does all of this have to do with Eris?"

"You are going through a transition. You are adapting to our relationship, overcoming your fears, as well as dealing with outside influences," she said. "I know you well enough by now to be certain you will not do anything to betray me, but you in turn need to know I give you that same amount of devotion. You have the freedom to make your decisions as you see fit, and I will not judge you harshly for them."

"You were jealous when Rosalin and I slept together," I mentioned mildly.

"There is friendship between you and Rosalin. I did not want that friendship growing into something more intimate and for you to lose your heart to her. That is why I was initially upset. Do you remember when I told you if you lost your heart to another, it would divert all of my plans?"

"Oh, yes. I'm still trying to figure out all of those plans."

She pulled me suddenly against her, and my thigh slid easily between her legs. "This," she said, "was my plan."

"Not a bad one."

"I do not think so." Her voice was as smooth and rich as velvet. "Kassandra, you may find yourself physically attracted to other women. So long as I am the keeper of your heart, I am satisfied."

I shook my head. "I don't get that."

The look she gave me told me she'd seen much more of life than I had in my twenty-six years. "How many women have you slept with?"

"That's the worst question to ask your lover."

"But you will answer honestly, won't you?"

"You really want to know?"

"I asked, did I not?"

I had to think about it, to make sure I wasn't pushing anyone out of mind. I'd forced myself to forget some of them. "Five."

"You had only been with three women before Rosalin and me?"

I nodded. "All of which were long-term relationships, or at least I thought they were at the time."

"How many women have you kissed?"

"More than five."

"Do you see now how I know your loyalty will not falter?"

I shook my head.

"You admitted you were attracted to Eris, but it is as you told her. You are not a casual person. What happened with Rosalin was because you are not used to controlling your wolf on a sexual level. I would not feel threatened by Eris if you grew a fondness for her…" She shrugged. "I still do not believe I would feel threatened. Intrigued, mayhap. I have seen the way she calls to you."

"Are you saying Eris is fair game?" I was confused.

"No." She swept back the long onyx curls of her hair. "I am saying if something happens between the two of you I will deal with it when and if it happens. I am telling you that so long as you are honest with me I will not get angry."

"I would."

"If a woman threatens to take more of your heart than I have, if she threatens to take more of you than I have, then she will pay dearly. Does that knowledge of my emotions make you feel any better, my love?"

"Yes, but I can think of something that would make me feel even better."

"What?"

"Falling asleep in your arms."

Lenorre pulled me against her and I nestled my knee more deeply between her legs, resting the side of my face against the silken cloud of her curly hair. I wiggled, moving until I was able to bury my face in the bend of her neck. The warm scent she wore lulled me to sleep, but I clung to her unique, personal scent, breathing her in like the cool night air she reminded me of.

CHAPTER TWENTY-TWO

There weren't any lights on when I woke. Lenorre didn't have a clock in her room, so it was impossible to tell what time it was. I crawled out on my side of the bed and flicked the switch just inside the bathroom door. My jeans were where I'd left them on the marble countertop, my cell phone still in the back pocket. I pressed the button on the side to illuminate the screen. It was twenty minutes till four. Lenorre was still awake, somewhere.

My stomach rumbled, letting me know why I'd woken. I was hungry. I put the jeans back on the counter and snatched a dark green robe from the hook on the wall. Lenorre had enough robes to dress a small army. If it had been my apartment I would've walked to the kitchen wearing nothing but my undies and a T-shirt. As it was, others lived here, and I didn't know quite a few of them. Walking around half-naked in front of strangers just isn't my thing.

I headed for the main room beyond the labyrinth of hallways, doing a little better at finding my way without getting lost. Every one of the many hallways in this place looked nearly identical to me. I followed a map in my head—forward, left, forward, right. Lights glowed along the stone walls, making my shadow dance as I walked by. A spill of bright light at the end of the last hallway told me I'd made it to the main room all by myself. Point for me.

I heard voices speaking softly and stopped, eavesdropping.

"Her power is intriguing," Eris said.

"It is not her power that intrigues me," Lenorre replied almost idly.

One of them rose from her seat. "Her beauty, then?" Eris's voice came from farther in the room.

Lenorre laughed lightly. "It is *her*," she said with emphasis. "Need there be any more reason than that? You are drawn to her for your own reasons. Must I explain my reasons to you? Perhaps you should be searching the depths of your own feelings instead of trying to penetrate mine, Eris. Why are you drawn to Kassandra?"

I leaned against the wall, listening, trying not to make any noise. Which was hard to do, since vampires hear as well as any lycanthrope. I didn't want to participate in the conversation, but I was curious as to what they were saying about me.

After a long moment of silence Eris responded. "I do not know." Her tone was thoughtful. "She is a complex and passionate creature, unlike the women that fall at my feet begging for a nightly embrace."

I didn't know how I felt about being called a *creature.*

"Kassandra would not throw herself at anyone's feet." Lenorre sounded mildly amused. "Unless it is what she desired."

"I have noticed. She's quite capable of taking care of herself, isn't she?"

"Yes. Dare I say," Lenorre put a little faux-awe in her tone, "that you have gained a certain amount of respect for the woman you once deemed my pet?"

Eris laughed then. "I was wrong. Has Rosalin told you her news?" She changed the subject so abruptly they almost lost me.

"That Kassandra has claimed her as one of her wolves?"

"Yes."

"Rosalin informed me some hours ago."

"I think your wolf is blossoming."

"I believe you are correct."

"She has the mark of an alpha," Eris said. "Is she aware of such?"

"Yes."

"And?"

Lenorre didn't respond and I wondered if she shrugged.

Lukas Morris had told me the white in my hair was the mark of an alpha because it was the same color as my fur. Of course, he'd told me that before I'd littered his chest with silver bullets. But Lukas hadn't been the first to say that.

"How do you think Sheila will react to this news?"

"She will view it as a threat to her control over the pack and a personal challenge."

My stomach chose that moment to rumble, and the room beyond fell silent. I mentally cursed it.

"Kassandra, you may come out now. You were more than welcome to interrupt the conversation at any moment, but it seems your stomach has decided to accomplish the task for you." Lenorre's voice carried throughout the room.

I stepped around the corner. "You knew I was listening?"

Eris's brows rose an inch. "I do now." She turned to look at Lenorre.

The smile Lenorre gave her was devastatingly impish. It suited her, making her storm-cloud eyes sparkle mischievously.

"How much of our conversation did you overhear?" Eris asked.

"You have no idea why you're attracted to me and Sheila will throw a hissy once she finds out I've claimed Rosalin. Right?"

"I'm not fond of being spied upon."

"Get used to it," I said, "because if you're talking about me and I'm within hearing distance I'm going to spy." I clutched the robe around me, finally summoning the will to walk into the room. "By the way, I have no idea why you're attracted to me either. Unless you're just into difficult women and I'm the first one that won't throw herself at your feet." I wasn't sure where the snide comment came from. I couldn't hide the resentment in my voice. I wasn't entirely sure where it came from either.

Eris's beautiful features were empty of any reaction, like she'd thrown on an impenetrable mask. I'd worn that expression before and seen it on other cops. It was a way of hiding. She didn't want me to know what she was feeling or what she was thinking. I was fine with that.

My stomach ruined the moment again, grumbling loudly. If I didn't eat soon, I'd get a stomachache.

"Come." Lenorre stood and offered her hand to me. "We will find something for you to eat."

"Thank you. That would be nice."

❖

I had thought the hallway led to more rooms, but I was wrong. Lenorre showed me to an underground kitchen, and though it was small, the dining room connected to it was vast. A long wooden table with intricately carved chairs sat in the middle of the room, with a candelabra chandelier over it. The table could've easily seated twenty people. Lenorre struck a match and lit three long red taper candles set in a candelabrum that was placed at the middle of the table, not bothering with the ornate chandelier. The walls of the room were almost a peach color, but too light to be peach and too bold to be beige.

I ended up eating a bowl of fruity cereal, sitting across from Lenorre and trying to ignore her watching me.

She finally broke the silence. "Did our conversation bother you?"

I finished the last of the cereal. "I don't know. It made me a little uncomfortable."

"Why?"

"Why were you talking about me in the first place?"

"Eris was trying to figure herself out through me."

"How does that work?"

"She apparently believed if she could pinpoint my attraction to you, it would explain her own."

"But it won't."

She gave a half nod. "Correct, and I believe there was more truth to your retaliation than you knew."

I shrugged. "I'm getting used to women being attracted to me because I'm either something to conquer, someone to play with, or someone to use for their own benefit."

"Your past?" Lenorre asked in a gentle tone.

"Yeah. Rearing its hideous head."

She seemed to understand. Lenorre didn't ask me about my past and I was grateful. She didn't expect me to rip my heart open and spill its contents on the table between us. I'd learned some lessons, and several had been harsh. I remembered those especially, but even when I looked back over the pages of my history I had tender moments, though those often hurt the most. The sweetest memories have a way of reminding us that not everything is absolutely bad or absolutely good.

I'd tried to run from love, but one way or another, love always catches a person off guard.

"What are you thinking?" she asked, without seeming to pry. She had too much grace and elegance. She would ask a question when curious about something, but was as unobtrusive as possible.

"That everything happens for a reason," I said, "and that nothing in life is set in stone."

Lenorre smiled rather melancholically. "Love is stronger than stone."

I sighed. "I'll agree it's a very strong force, but it's still capable of dying."

"Think of love as a garden," she said thoughtfully. "Everyone knows if you do not tend to it, it will not grow. But in order to have a truly beautiful garden one must pull the weeds."

I laughed. "Are you comparing my past relationships to weeds?"

The corner of her mouth twitched. "I might be. Does the thought amuse you?"

"Yes, and strangely, it makes sense."

Lenorre bowed her head. The long curls of her hair framed her porcelain face like some mythological painting of a dark Goddess. Her startling eyes met mine in a way that made the breath catch in my throat. The candlelight reflected off her pale features, and she tilted her head slightly to one side. "Does it?"

My pulse quickened, thudding against my ribs.

"Yes," I said, mouth inexplicably dry. I blinked and her chair was suddenly empty. Arms wrapped around me from behind.

Her breath was hot against my ear. "Truly?"

I flinched, making one of those girlish sounds. I tried to get out of the chair but Lenorre pinned my wrists to the wooden arms with supernatural quickness and held me prisoner. I tried to turn to look at her, to see what expression she wore, but her face was too close.

"Lenorre?"

She knocked the chair out from under me, using her grip on my wrists to swing my body around in a graceful motion. I tried to catch my balance, nearly losing my footing before she picked me up and set me on the table. She grabbed the sash on the robe, jerking the tie loose. I made another startled sound, but this time it wasn't girlish. Somewhere inside me the wolf's eager anticipation was adding fuel to my leaping pulse.

"Yes, Kassandra?" She spread my legs with her hands.

"You didn't throw me near one of the candles, did you?"

She grinned, flashing petite fangs. "Now," she murmured, "would I do such a thing?"

Lenorre moved too quickly for me to form a response. She put a hand on my chest and pushed me backward on the table. I obeyed as her hand caressed down my body, her fingertips sliding beneath the band of my underwear. I heard the bowl of milk tip over and crash to the floor, then drip in a steady stream over the edge of the table.

She drew the underwear down my legs in a sensual glide, baring the most intimate part of my body to the warm candlelit room.

"Remove the shirt." Lenorre spoke in a silken voice from where she stood between my legs. I could feel the smooth finish of the wooden table against the back of my knees, where my legs draped over the edge. "You may keep the robe." Her hands swept across my thighs, making my body ache with desire. Her voice dropped into a breathy whisper. "I want to watch the candlelight dance across your breasts."

Her demand made a shiver run through the lower part of my body. I did what she asked. If she had told me to ditch the robe, I would've done that too, albeit against all of my modesty. I sat up, shrugging out of the hunter green material, letting it slide down my arms. Lenorre stepped back, watching me with eyes like storm and sea fog. The chill of her power caressed my skin, causing my nipples to harden. I crossed my arms over my chest and tossed the shirt to the dining-room floor.

My hair was long enough to cover my breasts. Lenorre reached out, guiding the long tresses across my shoulder. I inhaled deeply. The merest brush of her fingertips caused my body to stir. The hair tickled along my skin, falling in a silken veil down my back.

"Lie down." The chair legs scraped against the stone floor.

Lenorre pulled the chair to the table, looking like some dark queen upon her throne.

"Kassandra?" she asked, and I realized that I'd been staring at her. The breath filling my lungs was shallow.

I reclined, holding myself up on an elbow as I slipped one arm through the sleeve of the robe, then the other. It wasn't about being covered, though the thought had crossed my mind. If we were interrupted I wanted to be able to dress quickly. I don't believe in giving free shows, or any shows at all, for that matter. The material was undeniably soft against my skin, and the sensation of that softness was comforting. All of my senses heightened, and each touch echoed throughout my body in a wave of subtle pleasure.

Her hands wrapped around my calves as she pulled me across the table. Startled, I managed to catch myself, keeping my gaze on her as her hands caressed the back of my thighs, stopping at my ankles. "Put your feet on the arms of the chair."

I braced the soles of my feet against them, and her hands wrapped around my ankles like shackles. My heart gave one startled thump that beat above the other beats as her mouth brushed the arch of my foot. Her tongue flicked out and I couldn't decide if it tickled or felt good. I tried to draw away and her grip tightened as she held my legs in place. I was transfixed by her beauty as her mouth traced an invisible path up them.

She watched me, sliding her hands up the back of my thighs, dangerously close to more intimate parts. A flood of warmth pulsed between my legs.

"Lenorre," I breathed, tossing my head back when she cupped my ass in her pale hands. "What are you doing?"

A breeze swept across my body, almost like a draft of air, but it wasn't that. Her power caressed me like a lover, causing my nails to scrape loudly on the surface of the table.

"Feasting," she said.

If I had thought one little brush of power was something, I had been wrong. It was only a taste, a sample of what she was capable of. Her power soared up my spine like a gasoline-soaked rope set on fire, causing my back to arch off the table. The room swam in streamers of darkness as my hips rose and fell. Her hands were suddenly on them, holding me down. Her nails dug into my skin, creating small crescent moons as she held me against the rising moon of her power, and as if her power were the moon, she called, but not to the beast. She called to my body.

I caught a glimpse of the candlelight reflecting in her eyes in an eerily cat-like fashion before the power hit me like a wave and took me under. It tore a long moan from my mouth, brought my back off the table again. I felt her hands again, like a weight wrapped around my ankles, pinning my feet back to the chair. My entire body thrummed with energy. A flicker of fear rose in me, but her power took me under its spell again. From the tips of my fingers to the soles of my feet, heat sailed through my veins, coursing over every inch of my body, and where it touched, every muscle contracted. As if coaxed by an unseen hand, I cried out and clawed the air, searching for something to grab on to, for something to tear in the moment of passion's chaos.

The table was cool against the side of my face. My breath came too quick and too deep, and my vision was blurry with the aftermath of orgasm. I wiped the sweat away from my forehead and drew in a deep, slow breath, trying to teach my lungs how to work again, trying to remember I had a body. I turned my head enough to see Lenorre lounging in the chair, watching me with a dark, triumphant expression.

I tried to speak, and my mouth was so dry I had to swallow. "Did you…" I breathed. "Did you just mind-fuck me?"

"No." She noticed the fear I didn't try to conceal. "Kassandra, why are you afraid?" She looked utterly perplexed, as if she couldn't fathom someone being intimidated by the fact their vampire girlfriend had just rocked their world without so much as laying a fingertip on any sexual bits.

Spent, I lethargically pulled my legs on the table and she let me go. My hands shook where I drew the robe closed, covering the front of my body.

"Kassandra?" She searched my face.

"That was," I tried to find the words, "too strange for me, Lenorre. It felt great, but it freaks me out a little that you weren't even touching me. Okay?"

"Kassandra," she said slowly, carefully. "It was my power that brought you. How is it any different from what we did earlier? I did not *enchant* you. I merely focused my energy and brought you. How different is it from your witchcraft?"

I laughed, nervously, suddenly very uncomfortable. "No one has *ever* done that to me, Lenorre. Absolutely no one. It's not humanly possible." I couldn't summon the will to meet her gaze, half ashamed at my own fear, half angry it existed in the first place.

And that's why you're freaking out, I thought. *Idiot, you're not human. You think shape-shifting is humanly possible?*

Lenorre gave a frustrated cry and hit the table with the palm of her hand. The table shook with the impact and I jumped.

Her power made her eyes surreal and misty.

"No," I said.

She grabbed my thighs, jerking me forward again with little gentleness. I used my arms and shoulders to catch the impact, trying to keep the back of my head from hitting the hard surface. Her mouth was suddenly between my legs, erasing any sense of panic that had threatened to rise. She licked me, her tongue swirling in an intricate circle around my clit. I tried to pull away from her out of sheer stubbornness.

Lenorre grabbed my hips, anchoring my body to her mouth. With her mouth between my legs, I didn't know whether to run or grind myself against her face in pleasure.

I forced myself to struggle, to fight against her. Lenorre gazed up my body, tearing her mouth from my mound. "Stop!"

Like someone had slapped me across the face, I did so, my pulse pounding. With her power riding her, she sent an intoxicating thrill through me.

The thought of Lenorre forcing me to surrender all of myself to her excited me beyond thought. I wanted her to take me. I wanted her to fight me, to dominate me. I didn't care if it was the wolf's desire or my own. I wanted her to win me, to prove herself strong enough to sway me.

Her nails dug into my hips, and the pain was sweetly delicious. She positioned her mouth between my legs, sealing her lips over me and sucking my clit roughly into her mouth, so roughly I cried out in pleasure and pain as her fangs grazed me. Her tongue found a rhythm, coaxing me to obey. I writhed on the table like the wet and aching thing she made of me. I fought in vain. She held me to her mouth as our wills battled.

She drew it out for a long time, bringing me to the height of pleasure and keeping me there, suspended, filled with a need so heavy it hurt to bear it. I cried her name in a half moan. I pleaded with her. I begged her for release. I apologized in an attempt to coax her to bring me. How long she drew it out, I could not say. It seemed like it had gone on for hours, until I had finally given up hope, destined to ride the waves of pleasure, to burn like the phoenix in the flames of my own aching desire.

It built inside me, like some great wave seeking a shore of release that it could not find. Tears burned at the corner of my eyes and I cried. My body shook with silent sobs as all the pain, all the emotional baggage I had carried with me sank in the face of Lenorre's passion. My hips bucked as she drove my body to that emotional ledge once more. The orgasm built again, threatening to burst. I cursed, crying out in frustration. I expected her to pull away, but she did not. At last, she conquered me completely. Her tongue brought me with a ragged cry of pleasure while the tears stained my cheeks.

Afterward, I lay unmoving. I was still crying when her arms encircled my body. Lenorre cradled me protectively and tenderly against her, carrying me with ease.

"Thank you," I said when I could finally summon the will to speak.

Lenorre said the only thing she needed to. "You're welcome."

I rested my head against her shoulder and closed my eyes.

CHAPTER TWENTY-THREE

I rolled over yawning and got a mouthful of Lenorre's velvety curls. Gently, I plucked the tresses out of my mouth and found a few of them were my own tangled strands. She was still out. Lenorre slept (if that's what you want to call it) on her back. Her arms were crossed over her chest.

"Stereotypical vampire," I mumbled, placing a kiss on her cheek and slipping from between the cool satin sheets.

No, not all vampires sleep with their arms crossed like that. Lenorre lay on her back a lot, but some mornings she died holding me. I didn't like moving her when she was dead, and I didn't want her dying with her face near my neck, because that meant she'd wake with her face near it if I couldn't get away soon enough. A vampire plus a neck equals what? Therein lies my point.

The robe was at the foot of the bed, folded neatly over the wooden beam that mirrored the headboard. I picked it up, slipping it on. I needed some coffee and then a shower. First, I needed to find clothes to put on under the robe. I didn't feel like trying to play cover-the-peek-a-boos to keep from flashing anyone. Rosalin was probably awake. The rest of the vampires would be just as dead as Lenorre.

I didn't have any clean clothes, which gave me an excuse to rummage through Lenorre's walk-in closet. It was decent-sized, with an obscene amount of silk. I found a pair of silk red pants with a drawstring and a matching button-up shirt and slipped them on, tying the drawstring and folding the waistband under so the pant legs wouldn't drag on the floor—a trick we short people learn early on in life. I ran the silken sleeve of the shirt through my hands, trying to decide if I wanted to wear it, then brought the material to my face, inhaling sharply. It smelled like clean detergent, but beneath that scent was Lenorre's. I slid it on and grinned when it came down to my knees.

The kitchen was bright and sunny. Someone had drawn back the shades on the window in the dining room. I squinted into the brightness.

Rosalin peeked out from the kitchen. "Pancakes?"

"Coffee," I mumbled, distracted by the strange reflection on the window. Once I could approach the sunlight without squinting I peered outside.

The backyard was just as huge as the front yard. I think both were too big to be called yards. Acres, maybe, but not yards. The sunlight bounced off the crystalline body of water where rocks were stacked neatly to create a beautiful waterfall that trickled into the pool. It was strange to see it uncovered so late in the year. Maybe it was heated. A beautiful gazebo was off to one side.

I turned to find Rosalin standing patiently behind me holding a mug of coffee.

"Cream and sugar, right?"

"Yes. Thank you."

"No problem. You look very festive. It's still a little early for red and green, isn't it?"

She glanced down, looking at the pants, and gave a small laugh, shaking her head. "You raided Lenorre's closet, didn't you?"

I took a sip, my shoulders easing with the first taste. The real cream and sugar she'd put in it blended perfectly with the coffee, not masking the coffee's flavor, but enhancing it.

"I didn't bring another change of clothes."

"You could've asked me for something. I'm closer to your size than Lenorre is." She grinned, showing a row of perfect white teeth. "Though I have to admit, you look cute in oversized clothes."

I shook my head. I never understood how Rosalin was always in such a good mood. Then again, she hadn't just woken. One of these mornings, I should jump up and down on her bed like a maniac while she was sleeping. That sounded like fun. I'd like to see how coherent and cheerful she was in the morning then. Rosalin made me feel grumpy.

She went into the kitchen and returned carrying a white mug with a rainbow on it. From where I was standing, the contents smelled like spearmint tea.

"Gods," I said, sitting at the end of the table. "Even your fucking mug is cheerful."

She laughed, nearly spitting out her mouthful of tea, then swallowed audibly. "What?"

I tilted my head to the side. "How do you do it? How are you always in such a good mood?"

She shrugged. "I don't know. 'Cause when I'm awake I'm awake?"

"Apparently."

"I don't charge to the coffeemaker first thing in the morning."

"I don't charge."

"Seriously?" She laughed and I gave her an unfriendly look.

"Either way," she said, "I'm not a coffee addict like you are."

I shrugged. "That makes a little sense, but not much."

She sat in the chair next to mine. "I had a *very* good time last night."

Her words were so unexpected that instead of drinking the sip I'd taken, I ended up inhaling most of it. After I was done coughing, I blinked at her. "What?"

"I wish I had a camera. The look on your face."

"What look?" I cleared my throat.

"I totally caught you off guard." She started grinning again and I stared at her. There weren't any marks on her neck, but if there had been, they would have already healed. I didn't need the marks to know Eris had bitten her. She was damn near glowing.

A twinge of something flashed through me. Jealousy? Anger? Fear? I couldn't tell, but whatever it was I carefully squashed it down and ignored it.

"You slept with Eris?" I didn't have any reason to feel...this. Where the hell was it coming from? I didn't even know Eris. Why would it bother me if Eris and Rosalin slept together? I tried to bring my thoughts to a quick halt.

She blushed, as if remembering what had transpired. "Well, no, not technically. I can see why you're intimidated by her. She's very…intense."

"She doesn't intimidate me," I said carefully. "I rejected her offer because I didn't want to cross Lenorre."

"Lenorre told you she didn't mind if Eris embraced you," she said, and somehow managed not to make the word *embrace* sound intimate. "She gave you permission to make your own decision. You turned Eris down because you're attracted to her and you were afraid you couldn't keep being bitten by Eris from turning into something sexual. I was in the room, remember?" She seemed a little upset.

"I remember," I said calmly, "and maybe you're right, but it's not because she intimidates me."

"Kass, you are, just admit it. She intrigues you too."

I gave her a cold look. "I won't admit to that."

"She's very good at what she does, you know."

I took a very careful sip so I wouldn't choke this time. "So?" I said, but it came out more defensively than I'd planned.

Rosalin shook her head. "I have never known someone with so many hang-ups."

"You make me sound like I'm a prude because I wouldn't let her bite me."

"You're not a prude. You're just difficult and highly selective."

"I am. And, obviously, I made the right decision. I didn't want things to get out of hand between us, and since it got out of hand with the two of you—"

"Oh, no," she said with a wicked grin, "Eris is about control, remember? She's a pro-domme."

I didn't want to hear any more. I got up, walked into the brightly lit kitchen, and rinsed my mug out in the sink. Then I placed it on the top rack in the dishwasher, trying to keep myself distracted. I didn't need to be thinking about Eris and Rosalin in the same sentence. Admittedly, I considered Rosalin one of my best friends. It's strange, no matter how old we get we still manage to maintain the idea of a best friend. Rupert was a good friend, but more like a brother. I worked with Arthur and got along with him most of the time, but sometimes his jokes went overboard and just irritated me. Rit and I worked together, but we'd only been out to have coffee once in the three years I'd known her. I watched Rosalin as she walked into the kitchen in her light gray sweatpants and pink tank top.

"You're the closest thing to a best friend I have," I admitted.

"That's the first time you've actually said something really nice to me," she said, making me feel a little bad, but evidently not intending to.

"I'm sorry. I know I can be a bitch…"

"You're not a bitch. You were at first, before I got to know you, but once I did, I realized it was your way of keeping yourself safe."

"If you haven't noticed, I have a difficult time letting people get close to me."

One moment she was walking around the island and the next her arms were solid around me. I was so caught off guard for a moment that I just stood there, and when she didn't pull away I wrapped my arms around her lithe frame.

I'd break every one of Eris's Goddess-damned fingers if she hurt her. Or at least I'd try to.

With her face buried in the bend of my neck I heard the deep intake of breath as her body relaxed against mine. It wasn't sexual. It was comforting. My shoulders eased as I did the same to her, burying my face in her neck and inhaling her scent. Her perfume smelled soft and feminine, but beneath it was the earthy scent of wolf, of family.

"I would've preferred being promoted to more than just a friend," she said. "I'm glad I'm your best friend and all, but being with you was fun. A lot of fun."

I stood there, my face still buried in her soft skin, and tried to be uncomfortable but failed. Maybe it was the soothing scent of another wolf. But somewhere inside me, I trusted that she wouldn't try to turn the situation into anything more than it was. I spoke against the fall of her auburn hair. "You had amazing sex with Eris, remember?"

"I can't help it." She sighed heavily. "I like sex, even if it's just getting off on some woman's fangs."

I took a step back. "I know you do."

"So do you," she said, grinning again.

I clasped her shoulder. "Yes, but I like sex with my girlfriend. Besides, I thought you said most werewolves were monogamous. Whatever happened to that?"

Her eyes flicked to the marble counter by the sink. "I told you there were exceptions to the rule. We're both dominant females. We're allowed to pick and choose." She shrugged. "I just haven't found the right one, and until then I intend to enjoy being single." She met my gaze and gave one of her fleeting smiles, but not before I'd seen the hurt look.

I touched her arm and she dropped her gaze to my hand. "I don't like seeing you hurt." I spoke softly. "If you need to talk, you know I'm here. You'll find the right woman, eventually."

"I miss being in a relationship," she said abruptly. "I miss snuggling, and movies, and dinner, and learning about my partner's little quirks. Lately, it's just been sex."

"Maybe it's because you're giving the sex away without a relationship contract."

"A relationship contract?"

"Yes," I said seriously. "You offer your body without asking for any form of commitment in return. When you make it look like what you're offering is just sex, women will take it and leave it."

"I told *you* I was interested in a relationship."

"You beat around the bush about it and I wasn't ready for one."

"You got into a relationship with Lenorre." Her tone was bland, but I could feel the tension behind her words.

I took in a deep breath and spoke carefully. "There was something there I couldn't run from."

"With me? How was it with me?"

"You were good," I murmured, remembering. "I honor the experience, Rosalin. You're the only other wolf I've been with. I just didn't feel that soul pull and, be honest, you didn't either. It was just lust and metaphysics."

"You're right. But I am very fond of you."

"I'm fond of you too."

"You and I both know we make better friends. I just want someone, you know?"

"I know." What else was I supposed to say?

"I still think we would've made wondrous fuck buddies."

"And it's back to sex. I swear, you think about it more than I do."

Rosalin laughed. "I think we're about even in that area. I'm just more open. You keep yours all bottled up and unleash it at random moments."

I couldn't help but give her an amused look. "Are you saying I'm explosive?"

"When it comes to emotions you can be."

"I'm not that bad."

"No," she said with a grin, "you're not *that* volcanic."

"Thanks, Ros," I said lightly, hopping up to sit on the island counter.

Rosalin rested her shoulder against the cabinet by the stove. "Are you going to the party tonight?"

"What party?" I asked, then remembered. "Are you referring to Lenorre's Samhain Masquerade?"

"Yeah?"

"She hasn't invited me." I gave a small shrug. "I'm not much of a party girl. I can't believe she's trying to swing this thing with such short notice."

"It'll work," she said confidently.

"How? Especially if she's wanting all of her vamps to dress up in these exquisite costumes. How can they get them so quickly?"

"Lenorre's got connections. She's not dressing all the vampires, just the ones working the floor. She's already hired a handful of skilled tailors and seamstresses."

I shook my head. "I don't get it."

"She has her ways," Rosalin said again, but this time in a cryptically pretentious tone.

I slipped off of the counter.

"Where are you going?" she asked.

"Home. I need a shower."

"Lenorre has a shower."

"I need my shower, and my clothes."

She made a little "o" with her mouth. "I'll tell her when she wakes."

"Thanks. I'll go get my stuff and leave."

Rosalin nodded. Remembering her words, I stopped in the doorway and turned. "Fangs?"

She blinked at me. "What do you mean?"

"You said something earlier about getting off on some woman's fangs." I gave her a sly look. "What was that about, exactly?"

Her lightly tanned cheeks flushed a shade of rosy pink.

"Oh," I took a step toward her, "if it's making you blush so hard you have to tell me."

She took in a deep breath and said as casually as she could, "I got off when Eris bit me."

"That's possible?" I asked, then remembered my night with Lenorre. Rosalin opened her mouth to respond and I held up a hand. "Never mind, don't answer that."

I went back downstairs and grabbed my backpack, swinging it over my shoulder. Remembering I was still wearing Lenorre's clothes I dropped the bag and pulled out a wadded pair of jeans, the Two Points T-shirt, and some socks. Lenorre must've put the shirt in my bag. I didn't recall it being in her hands on the way back to the bedroom last night. Then again, I had been utterly exhausted, both emotionally and physically. So, who knew?

I slipped the shirt on over my head, folding the crimson pajamas and laying them across the back of the armchair. I pulled on my shoes and scanned the room, making sure I wasn't leaving anything behind that I needed. Leaning over the bed I placed a soft kiss against Lenorre's forehead. It was still some hours 'til sundown. I dug the car keys out of the front pocket of my bag and left.

CHAPTER TWENTY-FOUR

My cell phone was ringing. I finished buttoning the black–and-red striped overshirt and followed the irritatingly loud sound to my overnight bag. Pushing my towel behind my right ear, I answered the unrecognized number.

"Hello?"

"Is this Kassandra Lyall?" a woman asked. "This is Gwen. Gwen Cunningham."

"It is. What can I do for you, Mrs. Cunningham?"

"Alyssa," she said. "My daughter. One of her friends from the neighborhood just came over. Would you like to speak with him?"

"Sure. Put him on."

I sat on the couch, dressed, with the exception of the towel on my head. I shifted, trying to get into a comfortable position with the small-of-the-back holster. I could usually ignore the discomfort of the gun when I sat. The trick was putting most of my weight on my shoulders. I often did it unconsciously now, but wondering what news this friend of Alyssa's might have, I'd totally forgotten about the gun. They have a way of reminding you you're wearing them.

"Hello?" He sounded young, with a thin, nervous voice.

"Start with your name. Then tell me everything you know."

"Alec. My name is Alec Wright. I live a few houses down the street. I grew up with Lyssie," he said, then corrected himself. "Alyssa. She said she'd call me last night, that she was going to check on Timothy." His tone gave away the rise of panic he was experiencing. "She didn't call."

"Are you friends with Timothy?"

"Yeah. We go to the same school."

I nodded, though he couldn't see my response. "Alec," I said softly. "Where did she go? Do you know where she went?" If I could get a lead on Alyssa I was pretty sure I had a clue to Timothy's location. Well, you've got to know where someone is to go check on them, don't you?

"Kind of. There's a vampire." The boy swallowed audibly. "Lyssie called him the Count of Counts. Said he promised he'd give her and Timothy a lifetime together. That he'd give her the power to save her mother. I told her it wasn't a good idea, but she wouldn't listen to me. She told me the cops found Timothy and how that piss—ticked the Count off."

"Alec," I said in a firm tone. I didn't need him distracting himself with thoughts of "I should have" or "I could have" and was afraid that's where he would go. "I need to know where Alyssa went. If you tell me, I can save her. If you tell me, I can save them both."

"I don't know. Lyssie said they met the Count of Counts in an abandoned church downtown. I...I don't know what street it's off of." His voice cracked. "All I know is it's near the vamp club. I'm sorry," he said, and I wasn't exactly sure to whom he was apologizing. "I'm really sorry. I should've stopped them. I should have told someone sooner, but I promised. She made me swear I wouldn't tell."

I could hear Gwen on the other end saying, "It's okay, Alec. It's not your fault."

"Alec, I want you to stay with Gwen for a little while. Do you think you can manage that?"

"Yeah, I'll call my parents and let them know."

"Good. I'll see if I can get someone to come sit with you guys for a while, all right?"

"Why?"

"I don't think it's safe for you to be outside without an escort. The sun will set soon. You've just given me information that may or may not put your life at risk." I paused, deciding I sounded a little too harsh. "I seriously doubt it, but if you're connected to Alyssa and she breathes word of it to the bad guys…"

I heard his quick intake of breath. A little bit of healthy fear can keep you alive—going bat-ass crazy does not.

"I won't."

"You'll stay inside after dark?"

"Yes. I swear."

"Good. Tell Gwen I'll call her or someone else will later tonight."

"I will."

I flipped the phone closed, took the towel off my head, and headed for the bathroom to finish getting ready. It looked like I might miss Lenorre's party after all.

CHAPTER TWENTY-FIVE

Blue folds of night crept across the land like indigo fingers. I stood in front of my living-room window watching the last strands of light be extinguished like flames sinking into an ocean. Then I stood there for Goddess knows how long. The sky took on a velvety darkness, until I could see the points of the crescent moon pricking the darkness like ivory antlers in the night. I relaxed, feeling the moon's glow like a breeze against my skin.

The doorbell chimed unexpectedly, shattering my thoughts. I drew the Pro .40 in a one-handed grip, quietly tiptoeing toward the door.

"I heard you draw your gun, Kassandra." Lenorre's voice flowed like molten chocolate. I unlocked the door.

Lenorre looked like she was dressed to go to a business meeting at the club. A pair of ash-colored slacks clung to her hips. A white button-up blouse was partially hidden behind a matching ash jacket. Her hair had been pulled back and was clasped at the neck, though a few stray curls of shimmering onyx cascaded rebelliously like black tears against the sides of her face.

In black jeans and a burgundy T-shirt, I looked a little underdressed standing next to her. The only thing I was wearing that was even remotely dressy was the black-and-red top buttoned over the tee.

She stepped into the room without invitation.

"I thought a vampire had to be invited into a person's home?" I asked.

Her heels were quiet against the soft-carpeted floor, and she glanced around the room, slowly taking everything in. Her silvery gaze finally met mine. "That's a foolish notion. You haven't been reading the books I loaned you, have you?"

"I haven't had time." I shut the door and locked the dead bolt.

Lenorre lounged on the couch, watching me as I went into the kitchen and grabbed a can of Diet Coke from the fridge. I wiped the top of the can off with a napkin.

"I like your apartment," she said.

"Thanks." It was the first time Lenorre had ever been here. Why was that weird to me? I shook my head.

"What?" Lenorre asked.

I shook my head again. "Nothing."

"What were you thinking?"

I should've been more aware of my actions around her if I didn't want her to ask questions. "It's…"

"Kassandra."

"You make my apartment look bland."

The corners of her mouth twitched. "And how exactly does one accomplish such a task?"

"Don't try to play coy vampire with me. If you want me to say it, just ask."

She stood from the couch in one smooth motion. When there were only a few inches of space between us, she said, "I would like to hear you say it."

"You're prettier than my decorating job. Happy?"

She laughed and stooped to kiss me, brushing her lips across mine. "You do realize you are as well?"

Something low in my body did a trick for her then, a little flip.

"I don't know whether to take that as an insult to my decorating abilities or a personal compliment. It's really not hard to outshine my decorating job."

Lenorre gave me a playful look. "That was rather implied, yes."

"Ouch." I laughed, then moved to the matching leather armchair, not sitting in it, but propping my butt against its arm. "I've got a lead on Alyssa and Timothy."

"Yes?"

"Apparently, one of Alyssa's childhood friends knew about the entire ordeal. Have you ever heard of the Count of Counts?"

Her gaze darkened like a storm. Her lashes closed, hiding whatever emotion was hidden in their silvery depths.

She said one word, filled with an angry heat like I could reach out and burn my fingers on it. "Yes."

"Tell me."

"He calls himself the Count of Counts." Lenorre spoke slowly. "He sneaks into a territory and overthrows the established Count or Countess."

"Are you saying he's snuck into town after your throne?"

"That is what it would seem." Her tone held a hint of tiredness. She wasn't truly tired, because vampires don't crave sleep. Maybe she was weary. After a few centuries of dealing with vampire drama, the shit probably got old.

"From what Alec told me, he lured Alyssa into his lair with the promise of strength and immortality," I said. "She wanted to be with Timothy, and I'm guessing he played on Timothy's curiosity. It sounds like he also promised Alyssa the power to help her mom."

Lenorre nodded. "The Count of Counts is not an honorable man. Be that as it may, there are some rules in our society he might adhere to, such as taking only a willing victim."

"Yes, but I imagine he lured them in without allowing them to read the fine print."

"Precisely. He seduced the children with his offer." She shook her head. "It is not a promise he will follow through on. Of that, I am sure. His reputation precedes him."

"Will he kill them?" I asked what I had to ask, what I'd been wondering since I'd hung up the phone with Alec.

Lenorre stared at me for several moments and finally said, "No, I do not think so. He will keep them as his pets and, more likely than not, use them as fodder."

I fell back into the chair, my knees draped over the arm. "Wonderful. Just fucking wonderful." I sighed. "I have to get those kids out of there. I don't care what it takes. I'll tear the son of a bitch apart fangs first if I have to."

"I know." She stood to pace around my coffee table, looking beautiful and thoughtful. She often paced when she was deep in thought. It made her seem almost human, but not quite. She still had an air around her that marked her as "other." But she was damn good at playing human when she wanted to. She'd had centuries to perfect the art.

"We must devise a plan of attack." She stopped, scanning my ceiling.

"No." I shook my head. "You can plan all you want, but plans rarely go as you want or expect. Besides, I think that's what the son of a bitch is expecting. If he's after your throne, he's waiting for you to make your move. We have to catch him off guard. He'll be anticipating an organized attack."

"And what do you suggest, my love?"

"Seek and destroy," I said as some unfathomable wave of strength swelled within me, spiraling out of my mouth, calling to my wolf, calling to the raven, calling upon my ties to the Morrigan. "We hunt. We take our prey down. We use the element of surprise."

"No. I admire your courage, your anger, your desire for justice, but we must go in with clear minds or all will end in chaos." She gave me a determined look. "We mustn't plan every move, but we must set options in place, options to fall back on and use if things do not go according to the original scheme. We are going in blind if we do not devise something."

"Either way," I crossed my arms over my chest, "we're going in blind. The only difference is that I want to go in with guns blazing."

"No," she said, and this time her answer was harsh and definitive. "No. This is vampire business, Kassandra. We do not just walk in and destroy. There are ethics in place."

"That's a pretty idea, Lenorre, but you don't negotiate with the bad guys. The bad guys don't give a shit about ethics or morals, vampires or no. You'll waste your time negotiating with him and he'll screw you over." I steeled my gaze on hers.

She stood absolutely still, like some gorgeous lifelike statue in the middle of my living room. "How skilled is your friend Rupert?"

"He's skilled."

"I want you to call him and see if he will join us." She strode toward the front door, pausing to cast a glance over her shoulder. "We will meet at the manor in an hour's time."

"So, that's it?" I asked, a little excitement fluttering in my stomach. "Tonight?"

"One hour." She slipped out the door, leaving behind the warm, sensual scent of her perfume and a flicker of hope. It didn't surprise me that Lenorre had shown up unannounced, nor did it surprise me that she'd figured out where I lived. Lenorre might not have been an investigator, but she was a Countess vampire and had eyes and ears all over the city. Lenorre would've made a damn good PI. More than likely, Rosalin had told her where I lived. Yet, why she'd decided to come over instead of waiting for me to meet her in her own home, I didn't know. I did know that if I asked she would've given me a mysterious smile. Such was Lenorre.

Either way, I hoped we would take out the Count of Counts and find Timothy and Alyssa, preferably alive. If my suspicions were right and Timothy was undead, that's better than dead, isn't it?

CHAPTER TWENTY-SIX

I wasn't against coming up with a good strategy. A lot of the time I devised spur-of-the-moment plans, and so far…I'm still alive. Obviously, I'd made mistakes in the past. I'd been trained to follow procedures and protocol, but I'd too often seen them crumble like grains of sand in the wind, especially when dealing with the preternatural. Anger and momentary stupidity made me want to charge into the abandoned church full force and try to take out the Count of Counts. I understood that. The wolf wanted that… wanted to hunt, to kill. It would've been so easy for her, for us.

Which is why I was sitting on the couch between Eris and Rosalin. Zaphara sat across from Rupert. He'd let me know when he arrived that he too hadn't found anything on Sheila Morris. Either she was careful or I was paranoid. I had a feeling it was the former.

Lenorre stood deathly still by the fireplace.

She had gotten her way. In the end, we were trying to make a plan, or at least lay the foundations of one. If it failed there had to be a plan B, which in my book always involved trying to stay alive and not get anyone else killed.

Currently, the most important thing was to get Timothy and Alyssa out of the Count of Count's deceptive care.

Lenorre interrupted the silence, her voice as cold as dry ice. "The Count of Counts is mine," she said at last. "If he believes he can overthrow me, then it is only fair I give him the opportunity to try. I am within my rights to challenge him."

"I agree with you," Eris said. "Yet he does not play by our rules. What then, Countess?"

Lenorre shook her head slowly. "I will be the hands of his undoing. I want you and Zaphara on guard. If the Count accepts my challenge you are to take out any of his henchmen that try to interfere with the duel. I have no doubts he will try and bend the rules, if not break them outright."

"Lenorre," I said. "I care about you, but I don't care much for your plan."

"Kassandra." She knelt before me and touched the white streak in my hair, allowing it to slide through her fingers. "This is what it means for me to be Countess. I must protect my people." Her expression was one of compassion and understanding. She knew I loved her. I hadn't understood until then just how much she realized, or really how much I felt, but the idea of her challenging another vampire didn't sit well. The idea of losing her sent a chill through my heart like a splinter of ice.

"This is as much my business as it is yours. I have people to protect, too."

"And I know you will do your best," she said, "as I will do mine."

"The Count of Counts has defeated many formidable opponents," Eris noted in a casual tone, as if we were all just friends gathered around to sip tea and enjoy the fire.

"Do you doubt her?" I asked, not because I was angry, but because I truly wanted to know.

"No. You are the one that doubts, not I."

What Eris said was somewhat true. My worry made me uneasy, thinking Lenorre was putting her very existence at risk. She was one of the most powerful vampires in Oklahoma, but I couldn't squash the little voice inside myself that told me there's always someone out there bigger, stronger, and ready to kick your ass.

Was she more powerful than the Count? Could she defeat him all on her own? I wanted to believe she could, but reality wouldn't let me. The risk was too great.

Overestimation of your abilities can get you killed. I don't care if you're human, vampire, or the freaking Easter Bunny.

"I take it Rupert and I are supposed to get the kids?" I asked, suddenly depressed. Where was my anger? I needed it. I knew how to work with anger, to wield it like a sword. It helped me to deal, damn it.

I looked at Rupert. He'd been quiet for most of the conversation, listening intently. It wasn't obvious by a glance, but I knew he was armed. He always was.

"I'll help," Rosalin added.

Suddenly, I had an idea. Lenorre knelt by my legs, still watching me.

"What is it?" she asked.

"I can scout ahead. We don't know how many vampires we're dealing with. You said earlier we were going in blind without a plan. I'm fairly confident I've got enough control to shift to the raven." I didn't really doubt I'd be able to. Lady knew the actual shift itself was very different from the wolf. It wasn't painful. If I fought my beast, especially on a night when the Moon Mother calls, it hurts like a bitch and a half. Yes, in fact, I did learn that the hard way.

The corner of her mouth twitched. "There is one fault in your idea."

I blinked. "That would be?"

"What happens when you shift back?"

"The naked thing. Right. There is that."

"Naked thing?" Rupert asked. "Do I want to know?"

"Not really," I said.

Rosalin said, "Kassandra is naked after she shifts into a birdie."

"Birdie?" Rupert asked. "What?" He looked so genuinely confused I knew I'd failed to mention the whole raven thing. How do you tell your best guy friend you're a freak?

You let others do it for you.

"Kassandra has been Goddess blessed." Lenorre glanced at him. "The Morrigan has granted her a gift."

"Kass, I have no fucking idea what your girlfriend is saying."

I sighed. "I don't know how to explain it, Rupert. I'm not just a werewolf anymore."

"You are truly so ignorant of the blood in your veins." Zaphara's voice held an edge of surprise and disbelief.

"What are you talking about?"

Zaphara looked at Lenorre. "You have not told her all of the truth, have you?"

"I do not know if she is ready to hear it."

"Oh no," I said, "someone better fucking tell me something."

Zaphara seemed to wait for a signal from Lenorre. When Lenorre nodded, Zaphara looked at me.

"Kassandra, you were never purely human."

CHAPTER TWENTY-SEVEN

The room seemed to be spinning, even though it wasn't. I was never human? She had to be toying with me again. My entire family was "normal," that I knew of. How could I be any different? Besides, witches and clairsentients weren't inhuman. In fact, most of the psychics and witches I know are purely human.

"Why do you think I allowed Zaphara to kiss you?" Lenorre asked.

"I have no idea." My words had an irritated edge. My wolf was unsettled, pacing, testing the walls of my shield. I was ready to hunt, and now I was pissed off because of yet another fucking surprise. A surprise my own lover had known but not bothered to tell me.

"Kassandra, I tasted your power when I kissed you. There is fey blood in your veins."

I bit my bottom lip, then laughed, full-throated. "You're insane. I'm not a faerie."

"She didn't say you were a faerie," Eris commented. "She said you have fey blood in your veins."

"What is your ancestry?" Zaphara asked, watching me as if gauging my every reaction.

"Irish, English. Hell, I don't know for sure. I'm a mutt."

"How much do you know of your Irish descent?"

"Very damn little."

"Zaphara," Lenorre addressed her, "tell Kassandra what you know. If you openly place your cards on the table she will be more receptive to hearing your words. If she is to call on the raven tonight, she needs to know sooner rather than later."

I gave Lenorre a look that said she should tread lightly, but, of course, it didn't faze her. She was made of stronger stuff. Then again, as a Countess, she has to be.

Zaphara nodded, pushing the aubergine-tinted tresses out of her face. "Your Goddess calls to you through your blood. Your blood is genetically receptive to her magic. This does not make you a pure-bred." The words sounded a little condemning and I did my best to ignore her arrogance. "An ancestor," she said, "and a pure-bred faerie would produce a human and fey being such as you are."

"So you're saying one of my long-lost ancestors fucked a full-blooded faerie? If that were true, wouldn't the blood run throughout my entire family? I've heard stories of faeries running off with humans before." I tried to remember everything I'd read, but it'd been a long time. "I was under the impression that when a fey chooses a human consort the human never steps foot out of Tir na nÓg, the otherworld, or whatever."

"Human and fey blood mingle unpredictably," she said, answering my first question. "The gene may be passed unnoticed, diluted in one body and undiluted in another. It is unpredictable," she repeated. "No, it would not be obvious in others in your family. Also, practicing witchcraft and being more sensitive than the rest of your family may have awakened the ability, triggered the gene, so to speak." She gave me a serious look. "There is some truth to every myth. Some fey, however, choose to spend only one night with a human outside of the fey realm. Thus, your ancestor may not have been captured. In fact," I gave her my full attention, "you may well descend directly from a fey, and not the human side. Have you ever heard of a changeling?"

"A changeling is a faerie child swapped with a human child."

"Or a mixed-blood child left outside of a human household to be adopted and to live among the humans."

"What about being a werewolf?" Rupert asked. "I thought only one virus could exist in a host?"

That was a very good question.

"You speak of a virus," Eris said, "not of genetics."

"Lycanthropy is not generally genetic. Only a few branches are," Zaphara said. "Neither is vampirism genetic. The fey are an entirely different species, with a DNA structure similar to humans'. This is why we have been able to breed with them much like the elves."

"You're fey," I accused her. "That's how you know so much about this, isn't it?"

Zaphara smiled widely. "It took you that long to figure it out, little witch? If you had known yourself, you would've recognized what I am."

"Well, excuse me for having never met a faerie before."

"And now you can say you have had such a pleasure."

"You're awfully tall." My words sounded casual, but the look I gave her was not. I knew the truth, but I was partially trying to be irritating. Zaphara probably wouldn't like being reminded that most people thought faeries were small and cute. No, if one actually studied, the first fey to set foot on Irish soil were a tall and very advanced race known as the Tuatha Dé Danann.

"Many different species of faerie exist," she said. "I thought you studied mythology?"

"I did, but forgive me for being a little rusty, oh great faerie poo-bah."

Faeries and elves, like werewolves and vampires, had been accepted into our culture, but we didn't see much of them. They kept to themselves, preferring isolation from their human cousins. Some fey were far stranger than human, but the sidhe and the elves resembled humans enough to be able to procreate with them.

"Kassandra, do not seek to play games with me or I too will play games with you," she warned.

"Fine. You're Tuatha Dé Danann. You're sidhe?"

"That is what the mortals began calling us."

"Hell," I said, "it's written in every mythology text I've found—Daoine Sidhe, Tuatha Dé Danann… What's the other one?"

"Aes Sidhe," she pronounced smoothly. "There's also the Leanann Sidhe. They began calling us *sidhe* based upon the mounds we sought sanctuary in once the humans began to overpopulate the land of Eire. If you must know, we prefer being called the Daoine Maithe."

"The Good Folk?"

I was rewarded with a slight nod for my translation.

"You're making my head spin," I told her. "This is way too much to take in right now."

"You chose a path that awakened your blood, not I."

"True enough, but I am so not in the mood for a history lesson right now. There are so many damn accounts it's difficult to discern the truth from fiction."

"I am glad you are able to perceive that much, witch."

I narrowed my eyes at her and said bluntly, "You're a cold bitch, Zaphara."

"The coldness that runs through my veins runs through yours."

"I am not cold."

"I'd argue that," Rupert said. "You can be cold."

"I'm pragmatic, not a cold-hearted bitch."

"And you think the fey are not pragmatic?" Zaphara shook her head.

"She's right," Rosalin said, meeting my gaze. "Some would misinterpret your pragmatism."

"As what?"

"As being cold."

"Whatever." I directed my gaze back to Zaphara. "Where were you going with the little history lesson?"

"You have powers available to you that you have yet to uncover and learn to harness. I can teach you how to use the magic that your blood, and your Goddess, grants you."

"And what do you gain in return?" I let my suspicion cloud my tone.

"Something to occupy my time."

I didn't really believe her. I was sure she could find other things to do, but whatever. She was willing to teach me a few things. Where was the harm in that?

She interrupted my thoughts. "There is much for you to learn. I can teach you how to come out of a shift fully dressed." It was like a carrot dangling in front of my nose. How spiffy would it be to avoid future embarrassments and setbacks based upon nudity? Public indecency is so overrated.

"Fine," I said, looking to Lenorre. Somewhere in our conversation, she had moved back near the fireplace.

Zaphara looked at her too. "Kassandra learns quickly, so I don't think it'll take long to teach her how to manifest a few articles of clothing. An hour or two, perhaps. If we can accomplish that, it would indeed be a good idea to send her as the raven to scout."

Lenorre asked me, "Is this what you want?"

"It's not a matter of what I want or don't want." I tucked a stray hair behind my ear. "I really don't like being nude after a shift. I already get that with the lycanthropy. If I can avoid it… Then yes, this is what I want, but it's also what I need to do in order to save Timothy and Alyssa. If it doesn't work I could always fly back to the club and change there."

"That's not really convenient," Rosalin said. "We should wait a few blocks away. We'll let Kassandra find the church, do a little spying, and then we'll follow her in."

If I really, truly wanted to avoid a little lesson session with Zaphara I could've told someone to ditch some clothes for me in the alley, but again, that was out of the way, and I could still get caught. Being charged with public indecency isn't really my cup of coffee.

"Let's just do it and get it over with."

"Shall we go somewhere more private?"

"Yeah, that would be ideal."

"You may use my room," Lenorre said. "I will be there in a moment."

I got up and went to her, standing on my tiptoes to press a gentle kiss against her pale cheek. "Wish me luck."

"All of the luck in the world," she said, her fingertips stroking over my shirt and to my lower back before I regretfully turned and followed Zaphara to Lenorre's bedroom.

On the way down, I kept reminding myself it was worth it.

CHAPTER TWENTY-EIGHT

I was sitting on the edge of Lenorre's bed, waiting for Zaphara's instructions, when Zaphara strode across the room, silent and deadly in her boots. She sat on the couch. "Come here," she said, "sit in the chair."

I moved, falling back into the matching velvet armchair, and kept my mouth closed.

"Anything you do not wish to lose in your change, I suggest you remove now."

I didn't want to ditch the clothes, but I had to ditch the gun. I wasn't willing to lose the Pro .40 or the small-of-the-back holster. I took the gun and holster off the belt, laying it on the empty piece of couch closest to me, then unbuckled the belt and tossed it on the couch as well. I unbuttoned the overshirt and draped it on the back of the chair.

"You might want to remove more than that, little witch."

"Fine," I grumbled, unlacing the knee-high combat boots and kicking them off to the side. "Satisfied?"

Zaphara shook her head, the long tresses of her purple-black hair dancing across her shoulders. "We must start with less. Once you gain a feel for how this particular magic works you will probably catch on more quickly." She gave a nudge of her head in my direction. "Remove your pants and shirt. Your undergarments will be sufficient to practice with."

"This better not be one of your damn schemes," I said, pushing the black jeans down my legs. I kicked them off into the middle of the room, then raised the shirt over my head and let it fall to the floor.

"Are you capable of shifting at will?"

"I've done it a few times, yes."

"Do it."

I drew in a long breath through my nostrils. Calling upon the wolf and raven were two different things, like embracing two different elements. Where the wolf was earthy and solid, becoming the raven was like trying to capture fire and air. I went to my knees in front of the armchair, forcing my mind to quiet, forcing myself to look within. I searched for that place inside my soul that contained the spiraling essence of raven.

Feathers as soft as silk...

Eyes that were cunning and wise...

I felt heat then, mingling with an unseen breeze, like the soft fanning of ebony wings.

Whether I opened myself up or the raven soared through me, I was not sure. The world fell away, until I could no longer smell the air-conditioned room. I opened my eyes, having seen the shadows dance around me before... I watched them swell and stretch around me now, until everything in the room was in blackness, until even my body was shrouded in the depths of misty shadows like some magical veil.

A shadow doesn't feel like anything, not to the skin. The darkness that rose around me was not cool or warm. I had no logical explanation for the magic in my veins. Zaphara's explanation made more sense than anything. I was not human. I was magical, and I had two options. I could accept and embrace the blood in my veins, or I could ignore and despise it. Why should I ignore the truth? I've always firmly believed in that. The first goal of a witch is "Know Thyself." I knew myself, and so could travel the path of acceptance. At least, that's what I believed. In practice, I could be a bit more stubborn than that. But I was coming to terms with my wolf and my raven. If I could do a bit more to make those terms work for me instead of against me, I would.

I felt no shifting of bones, lengthening of the spine, or any bursting sensation like when the wolf surfaced. I gave myself over to the raven and allowed my mind to slip, recalling what it felt like to be the raven, and somewhere in the middle, she and I met. I became her, and she in turn became me. We were animal and woman, bound together by blood and magic.

I shook my feathers, as if I'd just come in out of the rain. There was no rain in the bedroom, but when the shadows left, a dampness clung to my soul, a trickling sensation that I could only presume was the after-effects of the magic.

"That you have gained the control to summon the raven at will is a very good sign," Zaphara said. I cocked my head and her face loomed in my vision. I did a little hop and skip, catching enough air beneath my wings to perch on the arm of the chair. I watched her, waiting intently for her instructions.

"The ability to harness magic comes at an early age for the fey," she continued. "With fey blood comes fey magic."

"You're about to lose me," I clicked at her.

"You understand, but wonder what that has to do with you?"

I bobbed my head.

"Your blood may be diluted, but I am surprised you had no signs during your childhood. By the way, Kassandra, do you think I can understand you?"

"I don't know," I smarted off in a series of clacks. "Can you?" My remark definitely lost its effect coming from a beak.

"If you are not able to force words from your raven mouth," she leaned forward, her gaze intensifying, "you need to learn to project your thoughts onto the one you are speaking with. If you do not become adept at one or the other, you will not be able to communicate beyond the raven's natural ability."

I cocked my head to the other side and blinked at her.

Like this. Her voice echoed not in my ears, but through my mind, like some great gong being struck. Her mouth was closed. Her eyes were suddenly more like the gemstones they mimicked, like gazing through the stone itself, never-ending, multifaceted. It was at once a beautiful and disturbing sight.

Do you think you can accomplish this much before we pursue more complicated endeavors?

I felt like I was getting a headache. If I could've glared at her, I would've. I didn't like having her voice in my head. No matter what form I was in, it was unnerving. How many humans were diagnosed with schizophrenia when they were actually being toyed with by faeries?

Kassandra, her sultry voice flowed through my mind, *you must visualize. All magic comes with the ability to use visualization as a focal point. You are a witch, surely you know how.*

I pushed my words at her, pictured them resounding off the walls of her brain like she was doing to me.

Volume down, I said.

She looked at me with an empty expression.

So sorry. Her words were a sarcastic hiss.

Whatever. How do you not hear all of my thoughts?

A thought directed to oneself stays within. It is when you direct your thoughts outward that you project them, that I grasp them.

Greeeat.

When you shift back, do you do so by visualization?

I had to think about it. The first time I'd accidentally shifted, I returned by visualizing and remembering what it felt like to be human. Anytime I had tried after that, I did so intentionally using visualization as a guide.

Yes.

Then the problem of your nudity lies in that you are not pulling your clothes back with you.

What do you mean?

Are you visualizing them, or merely your human skin?

I guess I focus on what it feels like to be human.

Then focus on what it feels like to be human and clothed.

It's that easy?

Zaphara's head dipped forward.

I tried to shrug and nearly succeeded in losing my balance. I'd have to avoid that particular move.

Here goes…

I hopped into the seat, spreading my wings, and brought images to my mind. But most important, I remembered what it felt like to be human, to feel my blood pounding through my veins, to feel the cushion of the chair beneath my ass. I brought the small sensations to mind, such as the coolness of the air-conditioned room against my skin. I let the physical feelings of the raven fall away, separating myself from her, like peeling off a cloak. I released the feeling of the seat beneath my clawed feet and imagined sitting, but this time, it was different. I had been wearing clothes, granted not much, but enough that I focused on what I had been wearing. The way the straps of the bra felt on my shoulders. The way the fabric felt between my legs, covering, shielding. I sensed the shadows rising.

Do you think you can do that with more than undergarments?
She was still in my head.

I opened my human mouth and said, "Zaphara, get the fuck out of my mind."

"As you wish," she said, and a sly look filled her eyes. "Your answer?"

I ran my hands over my body, and sure enough…I'd emerged in the same undergarments I'd shifted in. I gave a sigh of relief. "Yes, I think so. That was easier than I expected it to be."

"Aye, 'tis not a difficult task. There are far more onerous ones."

"Peachy," I said, then had to ask, "Will everyone understand me if I project my thoughts?"

She shook her head. "A human will not comprehend. A gifted psychic might, but a human will not grasp your thoughts unless they have some magical training."

"What about Rosalin and Lenorre? Would they understand?"

The door to the bedroom opened as Lenorre entered the room. "I will understand," she said. "I take it she succeeded?" She wasn't asking me the question, but she turned to look me up and down, confirming I was wearing clothes, kind of.

"Yes," Zaphara said and stood, her eyes searching my face. They no longer had their crystalline quality. "If you are capable of holding the image in your mind, you will return from one shape to the other in the attire. Yet," she said, "if you shift nude you will not have any clothes to bring over."

"What if the clothes are destroyed?"

"You may bring them back whole."

"I can't believe I'm asking this, but back from where?"

"The Other World." She laughed at my expression. "That was not a question you were ready to have answered. You will grasp the meaning in time."

"That's the thing. I'm not sure I want to grasp the meaning."

"You will," Lenorre said. "It is in your blood."

I looked at her and sighed.

"We will not bother going by the club first," Lenorre explained. "We will go and hunt the strays that have trespassed in our territory. Kassandra," she looked at me with a commanding air about her, "get dressed. We leave in a half hour."

I said the only thing I could. "Aye, aye, Captain."

Lenorre and Zaphara both looked at me with interest and perplexity.

"What?" I asked, then grinned. "Oh, sorry. Aye, aye, Countess?"

"You never cease to be a smart-ass, do you?" Zaphara asked.

"Rarely."

Lenorre shot me a disbelieving look. "Very rarely."

I gave her a soft smile. "You know me so well."

Lenorre laughed. "Better than you think I do."

"I believe you." She crouched to pick up my clothes and offered them to me with one hand. "Thanks." I took them and slipped the shirt on over my head.

I could shift into my human form without showing up naked in a room full of vampires.

Goddess be praised.

CHAPTER TWENTY-NINE

I was driving, with Lenorre in the passenger seat next to me, and Zaphara, Rosalin, and Eris in the backseat. Rupert followed us in his sporty Cobra Mustang. An awkward feeling fluttered in my stomach. Something about our plan wasn't right.

I sighed. It was surprisingly quiet for a car full of five people. Okay, two werewolves, two vampires, and a faerie. Not really people at all. Maybe silence did make sense.

"Something is wrong," I said, watching Lenorre shift in her seat.

"What do you mean?"

"I can sense it. Something's wrong with our plan. It's going to fall through." It's difficult to explain unease when you can't pinpoint the reason for it. There's no logic behind sensing something unexpected is about to happen. You merely sense it and know.

My forearms felt naked. Usually, when I went out on a hunt I wore the wrist sheaths Rupert had given me a few years ago. Most wrist sheaths come with throwing knives, but the ones I had left at home were more like miniature daggers that covered my forearms completely. I had a moment to regret not wearing them, but I'd made a quick decision. The gun at the small of my back was a comfort, but it, like most weapons, was a human comfort, a human need. I may be a werewolf, but I'm not invincible. The pentacle scar on my chest served as a daily reminder of my weakness. I felt vulnerable, and I couldn't figure out why.

"You are uneasy." Eris's haunting voice carried from the backseat. "Why? What do you sense?"

I shrugged, stopping at the stop sign before driving under the overpass. I made a left turn, giving the car some speed to merge onto the highway. It was Samhain and a Friday night, which meant we weren't the only ones out and about, but I had a strong feeling we were the only ones about to go up against some fang-faced bad guy.

"I don't know," I said finally. "Won't it look strange?" I glanced over my shoulder at her gorgeous features. "The four of you standing only a few blocks away."

"It is Halloween," she said. "How strange will it look?"

"Like you're out kidnapping kiddies. Why don't you just wait at the club?"

"No." Lenorre shook her head. Her hair was still pulled back at the nape of her neck. "If we wait there it will take too long to reach you if you need us."

"How many vampires will spot a raven and start yelling witch?" My tone was sarcastic, but I was serious.

"She has a point," Zaphara said.

"This is what we'll do. I'll park two blocks away from the church. You stay in the car, and when I'm done scoping out what we're up against, we'll either go in or make a better plan. Deal?"

Eris laughed. "I think I know now why she is uncomfortable."

"Indeed."

"What?" They were all looking at me.

"I get it." I felt Rosalin's eyes on the back of my head. "You're freaked because you're not in control."

"No, that's not why I'm freaked. I'm not freaked, actually. I'm just…uncomfortable."

"Because you're not in control."

"Look. You may be right, to an extent. I'm used to hunting alone. I've hunted with Rupert. I think I'm uncomfortable hunting with all of you. Does that make sense?"

"Why would you be uncomfortable with us?" Zaphara asked.

"Kassandra feels that it is her responsibility to keep everyone alive," Lenorre stated a little too perceptively.

Was that it? Was I just uneasy because I felt if something happened to any of them, it would be my fault? Once I decided it was true, I grudgingly agreed.

Eris and Zaphara laughed.

I narrowed my eyes. "I'm not worried about you two," I said heatedly. "I'm sure you can hold your own."

The laughter didn't exactly stop, but it lessened a bit.

"Either way," Eris cooed, "I'm touched."

"Don't be."

Zaphara said, "You care about us," in an amused tone.

They were teasing me.

"I think I'll just ignore them," I said, more to myself than anyone else in the car.

Lenorre's voice helped distract me. "That would probably be for the best."

CHAPTER THIRTY

I didn't risk driving by the not-so-abandoned church. I parked two blocks away like I said I would, at a corner gas station we had passed on the way into the neighborhood. Rupert killed his headlights, slipping the dark purple Mustang in behind my Tiburon. Surprisingly, there weren't a lot of people out. A woman with light hair cascading around her shoulders and dressed as a sexy devil walked by holding on to the shoulders of a three-foot ghost and a pirate boy only a few inches taller than the ghost. Strappy pink slippers flashed from beneath the white sheet. I turned the key, killing the engine.

"Well?" Rosalin asked. "I just thought of something. It'll look funny having a bird fly out of our car."

"No one will see me."

"A human might not see you," Zaphara said. "I certainly would."

I unbuckled my seat belt, letting it snap back with a hiss. Reaching behind my back I took the Pro .40 and its holster off my belt and handed the gun butt first to Lenorre. The safety was on, as always, unless I was about to put a bullet in someone.

"Hold on to this for me," I said. "I don't think I could manifest the gun quite yet, and I don't want to risk losing it." I unbuckled the belt from around my waist, sliding it through the belt loops and handing it to Lenorre after she took the gun. With nimble fingers she lifted the edge of her shirt, tucking the gun down the front of her pants. The gesture managed to flash a nice line of flesh.

I bent over and carefully drew the gun out. "You've watched too many movies, and I'm not comfortable with the idea of you accidentally shooting your precious bits, vampire or no. You only shove a gun down the front of your pants in emergencies." I started threading the belt through the first loops of her slacks. "If you have the loops," I said, "use the holster." Then I thought to ask, "Have you ever used a gun?"

She took it from me, clicked off the safety, and pulled the slide back, sending a round into the chamber. "Does that answer your question, Kassandra?"

I swallowed, forcing myself not to turn into a puddle of werewolf in her lap. There's something undeniably sexy about a woman that knows how to handle a weapon.

"Well enough," I said, taking the holster and thrusting the belt through it. "Think you can draw this way?" I took the end of the belt through the last of the loops, sliding it through the buckle, then gave it a good tug to make sure it was sturdy and secure. Voilá.

She turned the safety lock on and reached behind her back, putting the gun into the holster. The holster was canted, which took some getting used to for a quick draw. A lot of the cops I worked with didn't wear small-of-the-back holsters. If you get knocked down by a bad guy and happen to land on your back, it's quite painful. Most cops wear a hip holster or a shoulder holster. A lot of female cops opt for hip holsters, because breasts can get in the way of a cross draw or a draw from a shoulder holster. Fortunately, my breasts are small enough I could pull off wearing a shoulder holster without that problem.

"You've made your point. Be careful your shirt doesn't ride up over the holster, or you'll give everyone a peek-a-boo and scare all the humans."

"You're stalling," Rosalin said, with an edge of shock to her tone.

I flicked my gaze to her as she leaned forward in her seat. "What?"

"You're stalling."

I smiled and knew it wasn't a happy smile. "A little bit."

"Why? This is what you do for a living, isn't it?"

"Ros, every time a person goes into something like this they never come out the same. You always remember."

"I'm going with you, then," she said with an edge of stubbornness to her tone I didn't hear very often.

"No, you're not," I replied just as determinedly. "You're going to stay here in the car with the others."

"But you don't want to do this, and I can't bear to watch you have to do it alone. Lenorre?" she said pleadingly, as if asking her for help.

"No," I said again, more firmly, "I am doing this alone. You're more than welcome to come in once I've checked out what we're walking into. Until then, you get to keep your furry ass in that seat and wait."

Her honey eyes widened in a puppy-dog look. I shook my head. "Rosalin, no. I'll be fine." I tried to reassure her, even if my words turned out to be a lie. "I have more experience doing this than you do." I began removing the overshirt. I could do this. Zaphara had shown me how to do this. I could shift fully clothed. All it took was visualization and being confident in my abilities. I drew in a deep breath, willing my mind to concentrate.

"I am going in with you."

It was Zaphara's voice this time, which caught me off guard. I hadn't expected that.

"Absolutely no—"

"Do not think to tell me no, little one. Your voice may override Rosalin's, but never mine."

I closed my eyes. I would not get pissed. I would not get pissed. I would not...

"Lenorre," I said through clenched teeth, "we're wasting moonlight."

"I do not dictate Zaphara's every move," she said. "If she wishes to go with you then I cannot oversay her wishes. Though I must admit I do not think it is a bad idea."

"Fine, but whatever you do, don't get us killed."

"It is not us I shall be killing." The threat in her words made goose bumps break out over my arms.

I opened the car door and stepped out, shutting it on Zaphara. She could open the damn door herself. I was pissed. I couldn't help it. I wasn't afraid Zaphara would get me killed. In truth, if something happened to her I would feel somewhat responsible. I may not have liked her, but I didn't dislike her enough to ask her to take a bullet. Or whatever else might be waiting for us.

The church was two blocks away. I headed for it at a quick stroll, slinking into the shadows along the edge of the sidewalk, disguising myself. I'd had a knack for going unnoticed whenever I wanted to as a child. I used that talent now, moving silently and sticking to the shadows.

The sidewalk circled around the blocks. Hedges decorated the edge of the backyards. Other than the lampposts on every corner, the neighborhood was dimly lit.

A rustling noise in the bushes made me pause for a moment. Where was Zaphara? I hadn't heard her approaching. Had she decided to remain in the car after all? The bushes rustled again, and my heart pounded. Being on guard often meant being paranoid, but it was better than getting killed. I turned slowly, jumping when a streak of black bolted out of the bush. It moved so swiftly, as if its paws weren't even touching the pavement. The cat stopped under the orange wash of the next street lamp, drawing back its ears.

"Zaphara?"

Keep your mouth closed, wolf. We do not have all night, remember?

Guess so.

Shift here, she said, her fluffy tail flicking as she darted behind a small circle of trees on the side of someone's lawn. It was dark enough to provide cover. I crossed the street and did what she said without arguing.

As I'd done earlier, I let go of my human body and brought the raven into mind, touching the brim of heated air and pulling it around my body like a cloak. I was getting better control and shifted quicker than any of the other times. The magic swam around me, like an invisible cloud. I was drowning in mist without feeling, then suddenly it was gone.

The black cat loomed in my vision. The fear hit me. My heart gave one huge pound and I flew into the tree overhead, breathing a little too fast.

Kassandra! Zaphara's voice vibrated against my skull. *Control your magic! Do not let it control you!*

Magic. That was right. I breathed, allowing my chest to puff up before releasing the breath. The cat was just Zaphara, I reminded myself, nothing to be afraid of, nothing to pick a fight with.

You did that on purpose, I said.

Zaphara gave an evil little chuckle that sounded utterly wrong coming from a feline.

I opened my wings, arching my body, following an invisible current as I dived-bombed her. The cat yowled, flattening itself to the ground as my beak barely missed the top of its furry black head.

Karma. I projected the thought to her.

I cupped the air beneath my wings, pushed it down, and soared. Zaphara's irritated voice followed me.

Kassandra!

Next time you think to try and get one up on me, I said, *you should remember I'm damn good at revenge.*

Zaphara gave an irritated hiss below me, darting across the street as she followed my flight.

I caught the steeple between my feet and held on. Truthfully, I was afraid of heights. If I thought about it I almost went into a panic, but I was learning to ignore it. Then again, I still wasn't flying that high, which helped. Zaphara's slinky form darted across the steps leading onto the porch.

How will we get inside?

I pushed off the steeple, bouncing across the scratchy rooftop, and peeked over the edge.

I haven't thought that far.

You should, said the cat, sitting back on its hind legs, *as I find it highly unlikely that they have a pet door.*

Check around back. I dove off the roof, trying not to panic as my stomach dropped. Zaphara gave another flick of her tail before slinking into the bushes that surrounded the building. The only windows were made of stained glass. Being more for art than functionality, they were fixed. The only way to get through them would be by breaking them. Though fragile, the noise factor wouldn't work. *I have an idea.*

Zaphara sprinted across the front of the yard. *I cannot see a way to get inside using the back of the church.*

I said I have an idea, I told her again.

Share it, Kassandra.

You think we're faster than any vampires?

That depends entirely on the vampire. Why?

I started walking back and forth across the branch, gazing at the double doors that led to the main part of the church. There were two boarded-up windows in front of the church.

If I could get one of the vampires to open the door, one of us could slip inside and crack a window.

Brilliant, she said sarcastically, *and if any vampires happen to spot us? What do think they will do?*

To a bird and a cat? We're insignificant.

They might kill us just for sport, Zaphara said, *and one of us would have to shift back to open a window.*

Then don't get caught.

You are telling me not to get caught?

You're the one going in when the big bad vamp opens the door, I told her as I flew onto the porch. *I trust your ability to remain unseen and to stay alive and my ability to play the crazy, confused bird part for all it's worth.*

This I cannot wait to see.

I'm a smaller target. There's less chance of them catching me, kitty cat.

If you want to keep your feathers, do not call me that.

I began tapping on the boarded window in a rhythmic manner. It sounded faintly like Morse code. Tap-tap-tap. Tap-tap. I waited a second, listening. Tap-tap-tap. I still couldn't hear anything on the other side.

TAP-TAP-TAP!

Then it came, the sound of heavy footfalls, of hurried and careless footsteps. I'd never heard a vampire make so much noise. One of the doors creaked open.

TAP-TAP-TA...

I stopped tapping when the vampire walked out.

"What the fuck do you think you're—" He caught sight of me.

"Kra?" I cocked my head to the side. The male was young, with long wheat-colored hair that fell in a braid. He was wearing a blue shirt with a pair of torn jean shorts. I never understood wearing a long-sleeved shirt with shorts.

TAP-TAP-TAP.

"Shoo!" He waved his arms at me.

I opened my beak and let fly a series of clacking and screeching insults, then jumped onto the porch, fanning my wings out and shaking them at the vampire like demented maracas.

"Get the hell out of here!" he said in an angry whisper.

"Kree," I said softly. No.

He lifted his foot and I darted between his legs, catching his bare skin in my beak.

"Kra!" I crooned my victory, ambling out of his reach.

"Stupid bird!" The vampire hissed, fangs dribbling with spittle. Why did some vampires do that when they went all vampiric on someone? The whole slobbery fang thing was so unattractive.

I began making a series of clicking noises, strolling toward the steps.

The vampire got to his feet, grumbling something about tearing out every one of my feathers.

Uh-huh.

I jumped to the second step, taking my sweet-ass time.

Zaphara?

Hmm?

Get ready to bolt.

Such a shame, this is quite amusing.

Ready? I'm about to really piss him off.

He was moving slowly, like a kid trying to catch a wild animal.

I jumped down to the next step, then the next. He hurried. I stopped and he stopped, trying to be inconspicuous like some horrible cartoon character.

Come on, dip-fangs, make a grab.

The vampire finally lunged at me. I took three quick hops, pushed off the walkway, and launched myself into the air, then dove into the thicket of branches just in time to see him fall on his face.

Nice. Zaphara was a sleek black streak as she bolted into the building.

I'm in, she said.

Good, I thought, *now let's start taking these fuckers out.*

Feeling a little battle lust?

Maybe I am.

We are supposed to wait for the others.

You need to get me inside. Go find a secluded window and let me in, damn it. I scratched my head against a branch.

The sound of her scoff filled my mind for a brief moment. I'd wait in the tree until she found an unguarded window.

The vampire on the porch was wiping blood off his mouth.

"Pierce your lip?" I crooned softly, cocking my head.

CHAPTER THIRTY-ONE

The vampire had given up and gone back inside. It seemed like I'd been waiting in the tree for a good twenty minutes when I finally lost my patience.

Zaphara?

No response. I wobbled across the branch, having to stretch my legs. It was a bitch trying to do nothing. I wasn't used to waiting, probably because I sucked at it.

Zaphara, don't play games with me. What's taking so long?

Still nothing, only the soft sounds of the breeze, the hum of a car here and there, and distant noises of kiddies exclaiming, "Trick or Treat!"

This hadn't been a good idea. They shouldn't have come with me. It was too risky. Oh, I understood some of the reasoning behind Lenorre's determination to be present and to take care of the Count herself. If she didn't, she'd only appear weak in front of the vampires in her keep.

A barely audible trilling meow came from the ground below. Zaphara stared at me with those wide amethyst eyes. Even in her animal form they were strange and inhuman, not quite animal.

Finally!

I found a way in, but I do not think going back is a good idea.

Why?

We are badly outnumbered and they would notice us slipping through the back.

By how much?

A dozen. Her feline head tilted to the side, ears swiveling as if she was listening to something I couldn't hear.

And? I was irritated. Why did she have to draw everything out? Couldn't she just tell me?

The two children you were looking for…I may have found them. What do they look like?

I turned my head, getting a better view of the black, shadowy figure on the ground while Zaphara scratched the back of her front leg with her hind leg. The gesture was amusing. She played the cat very well.

Short brown hair, tan skin, dark eyes. That's what Timothy looks like. I saw a few pictures of Alyssa at her parents' home. She has long blond hair and blue eyes.

There's more than one of those.

What?

Kassandra, we need to leave.

Her ears flattened against the back of her head as she turned to look toward the church.

Zaphara, tell me what's going on. What do you mean there's more than one of those?

Please, Goddess, don't say it. I had one of those moments when you don't want to know, you don't want to hear the evil truth, because you already have a pretty damn good idea what it is, but you have to know, you have to face the reality of that truth.

You know what I mean. We must go. Now!

I didn't have time to form a response. Zaphara was like a blink in the darkness. One moment she was there, the next she had disappeared. I had no idea where the fuck she'd gone.

The two double doors to the church were suddenly flung open, as if they'd heard her command. The same vampire I'd pissed off emerged, followed by three other vamps.

"It wasn't normal," he said. "That bird was seriously fucking with my head. It wasn't just a bird. I know it wasn't."

"You're so full of shite," an accented female voice said. "What the 'ell was a bloody budgie gonna do to you? It was just a bird! And as you can see, it's gone." She motioned toward the yard.

I tilted my head again, trying to get a better view. She was shorter than the male vamps that surrounded her. One of the others stepped forward, running a hand through his long black hair. "She's right. I don't see a bird."

"I swear a bird was out here, a big black annoying bird. I'm not lying. Why would I lie?"

"I don't doubt you saw a bird," the woman said. "I doubt the bird was more than a bird."

The vamp with the long dirty blond hair that had tried to kill me began to fidget. "I'm telling the truth. It tapped on the window. I came out. It started baiting me. It didn't act like a normal bird. Normal birds don't walk right between your legs!" He motioned at the part of his leg I had sliced up, but the wound had already healed. He was a vampire, after all.

"Maddox." The vampire with black hair said his name like a command. The vampire that had been standing apart from the group came forward, bowing from the neck up. "M'lord, what have you?" His tone was rather unfriendly and sarcastic, as if he didn't like the other vamp. His name somehow suited him. He was built, more built than any vampire I'd ever seen. His salt-and-pepper hair was cut short, almost to the scalp. The black shirt he wore looked like it struggled not to rip against the bulk of his muscles. The way he held himself made me think he was an older vampire. I couldn't exactly pinpoint it, but I got a strong sense his resentment had to do with being bossed around by the newbies. I'd be pissy too.

The vampire with long black hair wrapped an arm around the woman's waist. She was wearing a bright red dress that clashed with the red fall of her hair. The dress was strappy and slinky, swaying any time she moved even the slightest, giving an illusion of Hollywood glamour. Goth boy was wearing a red-and-black zoot suit. Most vampires had a taste for fashion, but some of those tastes were a bit eccentric. The outfits alone might've worked, but together they looked cheesy.

"Sorry, Brody, there's no budgie," she said to the younger man.

Goth boy turned to Maddox, who stood waiting for his orders with more patience and reserve than I would've been able to muster in his situation. "See to it Brody does not speak of this. If Master hears his insanity about birds he's liable to kill him just for a laugh."

"It is done," Maddox said. "Come, Brody. Will you be quiet or must I give you another lesson on the power of silence?"

Brody looked scared shitless. I didn't have to smell it. It was written across his features. He bowed his head, his hair falling like a silken curtain to hide his features.

"I'll shut up. But I know what I saw."

"Just cram something in your mouth," the woman said.

"Come, children," Goth boy said cryptically. "The night is young." At his command, they went back inside the church. Maddox turned, looking out over the yard. He wasn't a fool. The others might be, but not ol' Maddox. With a bang, he shut the two doors.

Well, that was certainly interesting.

Are you quite done? I jumped at the sound of Zaphara's voice. She slipped out from beneath the cover of bushes near the porch.

Yeah, I didn't know you were still here.

I couldn't leave you alone.

I didn't intend to do anything stupid. Just eavesdropping.

If they had noticed you they might've killed you. She headed for the corner of the street.

I swooped from my perch, following her to the parked car. She was right. I would've been in deep shit had I been spotted, at least where Brody was concerned. Was he beginning to feel a little mentally unstable?

I did learn one thing, I told her, trying to fly at the same pace she was walking.

What did you learn? How to hide in a tree?

Besides that. Brody is the weakest of the vampires on the porch. Goth boy is arrogant, full of himself and his abilities. The woman is so in love with Goth boy that if he said jump, she'd ask how high, and Maddox is not one to fuck with. He means business.

Terrific, that gets us where?

You really aren't very good at this, are you, Zaphara? I flew ahead of her, glancing back. *It tells us where to drive the sword. If we seek information, Brody is our best bet. He's afraid of Maddox, and I'm pretty sure Maddox is the vamp that does the devil's work.*

I thought you did not believe in the devil?

I don't. It's a figure of speech.

The black Tiburon came into view. Rupert was standing outside, propped against the Mustang. I landed on the hood of his car. If I could've communicated with him, I would've told him his ass should've been sitting in the car. As it was, I did my best to give him a scolding look.

"What?"

I shook my head. Why bother? It's not like he'd understand me anyway.

Zaphara was suddenly walking toward us, boots silent on the concrete. "You should have stayed in the car." She said exactly what I'd been thinking.

"I'm not the type of guy that just stands around and does nothing," he said, and I couldn't argue with him, not only because I wasn't able to communicate with a human, but because I knew how he felt.

We were hunters. Hunters don't sit around twiddling their thumbs when they have game to catch. I was finding that bad little vampires made for very interesting game.

CHAPTER THIRTY-TWO

Lenorre drove my car to her mansion since I'd opted on flying home. I beat them to the house, shifting on the porch and sighing with relief when I managed to include my clothes.

The Tiburon halted in front of the house and Rupert pulled in behind Lenorre, parking and getting out of his car.

Zaphara stepped out of the passenger side and held the door open for Eris. Rosalin crawled out on Lenorre's side.

Lenorre came around the front of the car. "Zaphara has told me of what happened at the church."

I nodded. "Can this wait until we get inside? We need to talk to Rupert and tell him what happened. He's a part of this now."

Lenorre's hand caught mine and there was sympathy in her gaze.

The look confused me. "Zaphara didn't tell me everything, did she?"

"I am afraid not. Come, my love. I shall abide by your wishes and speak with you of this matter inside."

"You're always so proper." It wasn't really a complaint, but I suddenly felt grumpy. I didn't want to know everything else, damn it. It was bad enough Zaphara had been implying the Count of Counts had a bunch of kiddies locked somewhere in his church. Then again, maybe I was wrong, but it was one of the few terrible possibilities that came to mind.

Lenorre smiled, showing the tips of her fangs. "I'm English, Kassandra. Would you expect anything less of me?"

She pulled me against her and I didn't argue, melting into her. "Can't teach an old dog new tricks?" I mumbled.

She laughed, holding me close as we walked toward the house. "In my case, an old vampire."

❖

"The church is not very large," Zaphara explained. I crossed my arms over the dining-room table, listening. "I found another way in," she looked at me, "through an underground storage room in the back. There's a window just above ground level. I believe," she said slowly, "that Rosalin and you could fit through it."

I really didn't want to squeeze through a window on bad-guy turf. It wouldn't be the first time I've had to, since I was the smallest cop on the force. Sometimes, my size was more curse than blessing.

I suddenly remembered I'd promised to call Arthur. I'd found a lead, and I hadn't even thought of contacting him until now. Wonderful, he would be upset with me, but if it kept his ass alive it was worth it. If I called Arthur he'd want to bring a team in to help us take down the Count of Counts. For a human, that was a suicide mission. In fact, I wasn't too sure it wasn't a suicide mission for us.

"Kassandra?" Rosalin asked.

"I'm listening. I need to call Arthur."

"If you contact him and try to bring him into this it'll be a mistake," Rupert said. I gave him a look. He was the only human in our group, but he had nearly the same training I had when it came to dealing with bad guys and monsters. He'd definitely had more experience being a hunter than I had. I'd even admit that his knowledge and abilities were most likely greater than mine.

"I know," I said softly, "but he'll be pissed when he hears I've left him out of the investigation again. He's been getting irked with me lately because I keep doing that to him."

"It's your job," Rupert said. "You're the one that can handle it. Not many cops left on the local police force know how to deal with the supernatural, Kassandra. Too many of them opt out of the training because they think it's evil."

"That's true."

"So just forget about Arthur. We've got to figure out how to save those two kids."

My heart suddenly felt heavy. "I'm afraid the Count has more than just Timothy and Alyssa."

Rupert never flinched. "How many?"

I looked at Zaphara. "Tell us what you saw."

"We were outnumbered by nearly a dozen. When I went in, there weren't any vampires near the storage room. However, most of them are gathered in the main room. Including the Count himself. He has set up a throne where the pulpit once was. I do not think it would be safe sneaking in through the back, but it is an option." She took a deep breath. "You won't like what I'm about to tell you, Kassandra."

"I know, but if I remain ignorant we won't get anywhere."

"Some of the children have been changed," she said. "If your Timothy was there, I did not see him." Her amethyst gaze went to Lenorre, who was sitting next to me. Lenorre's hand stroked my thigh, probably in an attempt to comfort me, but it did more. It distracted me. I shuddered and forced myself to focus.

"The Count of Counts has begun somewhat of a cult following. He is taking children and turning them. Lady only knows what he's doing to them." She shuddered in disgust and gave a disapproving look. It was the first time I'd seen Zaphara do that. It was good to know she had some morals.

"What can we do?" I said to myself more than anyone else in the room. "Lenorre's still got her Samhain Ball to attend. There's got to be a way to take this bastard down—"

"If it means anything, I think the sooner we kick his ass, the better." Rosalin leaned forward eagerly, her wolf in her eyes. The energy of her beast called to mine, tickling the hairs on my arm and making me suddenly warm. I closed my eyes, shielding. Control is strength.

"It's not a matter of just rushing in and kicking his ass," I said. "You've got to remember that lives are at risk in a war, both theirs and ours. You have to weigh your options. Rupert, any ideas?"

He drummed his fingers on the tabletop. "Yeah."

"Care to share?"

"You won't like it."

"Why?"

"It involves putting you at the front line of this war. How do you feel about delivering pizza?"

"Son of a bitch. You can't come up with anything better than that?"

"We're limited on what we're able to do, Kass. Unless we resort to brute force, we're screwed."

"Do I get to put my gun in the pizza bag?"

"If that's where you want to put it."

"Fine, tell me the plan. I'll tell you if I can do it."

"We both know you can, Kass."

"Silver bullets will not accomplish much against a vampire," Eris said. She'd been quiet the entire time, taking in our conversation.

She was right. The only thing a silver bullet would do was slow a young vampire. Unless you were shooting point-blank and blew a decent-sized hole in the heart, a bullet to a body part just irritated most vampires. The way to kill one involved a sharp wooden stake made out of oak. It was a good idea to bless the stake, but religion wouldn't protect anyone against an angry vampire.

"I'm fresh out of stakes," I said.

"I'm not," Rupert said.

"You just happen to carry a spare?"

"Kass, you know me. I'm always prepared."

"Are they blessed?"

"No. I figured you could do that."

"Get me the oil I need and I can bless them. Unfortunately, holy water doesn't do shit."

"Neither do crosses," Rosalin added, "right?"

"Religious emblems won't do anything," I told her. "It's the combination of the wood and pine oil their bodies reject."

"The blessing helps ensure the stake's potency," Lenorre said. "You could still impale a vampire with oak and pine, but it is more effective if you infuse the wood and oil with your energy."

"I didn't know that," Rosalin said. "Could I help?"

"You can get me the oil I need." I slouched in my seat, briefly touching Lenorre's hand.

Rosalin went into the kitchen, and I heard a cabinet door open and close before she walked back out carrying a bottle of pine cleaner. I bit my lip, trying not to laugh.

"The main ingredient is pine oil," she said, swaying the bottle from side to side.

Rupert chuckled. "Let's get a bucket and marinate some stakes."

"It's not a barbecue," I said. "Where are they?"

"I've got a gym bag full in the car. I'll go get them."

"Will the pine cleaner work?" I asked Lenorre for reassurance.

"Yes. I think it will." She scrunched up her nose. "Looking at it puts me off."

"Then why do you have it in your house?" I asked, amused.

"I do not use it."

Rosalin beamed, clearly proud of herself. "Nope, that's me. I'll go get a bucket."

"I'll help you bless them," Zaphara said, glancing at Lenorre and Eris. "As I'm sure the vampires in the room will probably want to leave."

Lenorre stood and I squeezed her hand. "Is it that bad?"

"At a distance, it does not bother me overmuch," she said smoothly. "However, I would prefer not to smell the scent of highly concentrated pine cleaner."

"I agree with Lenorre," Eris said. "I would rather not participate."

Lenorre bent at the waist, placing a soft kiss against my cheek.

"We'll come get you when we're done."

Rupert still hadn't gone out to get the stakes like he said he would. "Think you ladies could find what we need for Kassandra's disguise?"

Eris and Lenorre exchanged a look. "Most likely," Lenorre said. "If all else fails we will order pizza."

"Lenorre!"

"Do not worry, my love." She smiled widely enough to flash her dainty fangs. "I would not kill someone just for their uniform."

Eris said, "I'm not opposed to tying them up in the basement." She actually winked at me.

I turned back to Lenorre. "I don't want you charming them out of their uniform, either."

"Why would I do that? You would be surprised what a person would do just for money."

I shook my head. "Go. Rupert, get the stakes."

He nodded, following them out of the room.

Eris turned around, looking over her shoulder. "You would look cute in a uniform."

Since I couldn't tell if she was joking, I didn't say anything. Rosalin walked in, placing an empty bucket on the table, then poured the entire bottle of cleaner into it. Without thinking I inhaled a deep whiff, then coughed uncontrollably.

"Holy fuck," she said, plugging her nose. "No wonder they bolted."

I tried to breathe the air in through my mouth and choked. The smell of pine and chemicals was so strong I could taste it on the back of my tongue like I'd just taken a swig of it.

"We'll need gloves," I said.

"And nose plugs," Rosalin added.

Zaphara chuckled from her seat at the table. "Apparently, wolves don't much like the smell either."

Neither one of us disagreed. It wasn't necessarily the pine, as much as the concentrated amount of pine. Werewolves and vampires have a stronger sense of smell than humans. I didn't know about Zaphara. If so, the Daoine Maithe tolerated it better than the two of us.

Rupert emerged from the foyer. "Smells like my grandmother is in here." He dropped a navy blue gym bag on the table and unzipped it to pull out a handful of long wooden stakes. "Just drop them in?"

"Sure," I said, struggling to breathe past that suffocating smell. "Why not?"

He dropped them into the bucket one at a time.

"Would you prefer I bless the stakes?" Zaphara asked.

I nodded, holding onto the edge of the table. "I'm having a hard time concentrating and trying not to gag."

Once the bucket was full, Zaphara took it. Her hair draped around her face, framing the paleness of her skin, the dark line of brow. Her features were slack, utterly serene. In truth, we were closer to cursing the stakes than we were to blessing them. We had to infuse them with the energy of our intentions. Obviously, our intentions were for them to kill a vampire. In my book, that seemed more like a hex than a blessing.

She drew a symbol in the air with her right index finger. The symbol blazed like a violet shadow hanging in the air, and a breeze of warm energy tickled my arms.

Zaphara looked at me. "The Raven has granted you more than just a mask to wear," she said, her voice dripping with power as thick as molasses. "It seems she has granted you the gift of sight as well."

I watched as the seven points of the star dimmed, gradually bursting with white light and disappearing altogether, like it had never been there.

"Do you know what you have just seen, Kassandra?"

"You drew a septagram. The Faerie Star."

"Good. Very good, little witch."

"I didn't see anything," Rupert said.

"You wouldn't," Rosalin said. "I didn't see it either, but I felt it." She shuddered.

"What did it feel like, wolf?" Zaphara asked her.

Rosalin took a step back, her shoulders hunched forward protectively. "Power," she said, "it felt like power."

Rupert spoke up again. "I didn't feel anything either."

"Rupert," I said softly.

"I know. I'm human. I wouldn't."

"You would if you were a psychic," Zaphara said.

"Somehow," he said, "I feel like I should be grateful I'm not."

❖

It would've been best if we had soaked the stakes in the pine overnight, to ensure the wood absorbed the oil. Unfortunately, we didn't have that much time. Rosalin emptied the bucket in the sink and set about drying the excess liquid off the wood. It would do.

Lenorre had found a dark blue polo shirt with a popular pizza logo on it. Apparently, Trevor had delivered pizzas for a bit of extra cash before he met Isabella. He wasn't a big guy, but the shirt was still long. I'd had to borrow a pair of drawstring khakis from Rosalin to fully pull off the disguise. We'd also found that Rosalin and I wore the same size shoe, even though she was a few inches taller. She'd loaned me a pair of blue-and-white running shoes, which felt weird and slightly uncomfortable because I wasn't used to their shape and weight. I was used to boots, skate shoes, and the occasional heel. Given a choice, I'd have preferred the boots or the skate shoes, whether they're ideal to run in or not.

Trevor had also provided us with a hot bag. The bag Rupert had thought about using wouldn't have fooled anyone. In fact, if I wasn't quick enough the smell of pine would give us away. We gathered around the kitchen table, and I busied myself with putting the small-of-the-back holster on. I pulled the baggy shirt over it, which hid the gun, unless someone was looking for one. Rupert confirmed for me that it wasn't noticeable.

"Done," Rosalin announced as she finished putting the nine stakes I would carry in the bag. We had fifteen stakes in all, which meant Rosalin, Zaphara, and Rupert each got two. I got stuck with the rest. Lenorre and Eris assured us they didn't need them, probably because they didn't want to touch them. It made sense; I didn't want to play with silver. I couldn't imagine the vampires wanting to play with their bane, either.

I would take out the vampire who answered the door, if the delivery disguise confused him long enough. The others would follow my lead. We would go in and kill them one by one, until we faced the bastard himself, the Count of Counts.

"Something is missing." Rosalin eyed me curiously. "You need to pull your hair back. You need a hat too. Hold on."

She went upstairs, returning with a khaki baseball cap and ponytail holder. "It doesn't have the logo on it, but it'll work."

"I look horrible in baseball caps."

"It's a good idea, Kass. You're not going to a fashion show. Shut up and put the cap on."

"Thanks, Rupert." I took the headgear from Rosalin. "Next time we go hunting you get to wear a dress. Okay?"

He chuckled while I pulled my hair up, tucking the ponytail into the hole at the back of the cap and securing it on the top of my head.

"Now," he said, "we're ready."

CHAPTER THIRTY-THREE

I tossed the pizza bag over my left arm, leaving my right hand free to go for the stake or, if need be, for my gun. I'd parked the Tiburon on the street corner, and the others had ridden with Rupert. They wouldn't make their move until I was done taking down the vamp at the door.

As casually as I could I followed the sidewalk to the steps in front of the porch. Climbing them, I unzipped the bag. It'd make it easier to go for the stake if the vampire got suspicious and tried to kill me before I could say anything. Considering the strong smell of pine that leaked from the bag, I was pretty sure shit would hit the fan if the vampire got a whiff of it. I had to be quick, very quick. It was quick or dead.

I paused at the door, taking a deep breath to steel myself, then knocked lightly. Vampires have excellent hearing. I wanted only one vamp to answer the door. It wouldn't accomplish anything if they all came running.

One of the double doors opened to reveal the same vampire I'd tormented earlier. His features contorted in confusion.

"Pizza?" I said, trying to sound cute and utterly harmless. Lady knows, there isn't enough Xanax in the world to truly accomplish that, but I tried.

"We didn't order any—"

With speed known to most lycanthropes, I slipped my hand inside the hot bag, wrapped my fingers around the damp stake, and thrust it into his heart, putting my entire body into the motion. He stumbled backward.

His breath wheezed out as he slipped to the ground. Quietly, I used a hand on his shoulder to keep him from falling with a loud thud.

"Pizza..." His mouth opened and closed like a fish out of water, gasping silently. It wasn't like in the movies. He didn't dissolve into a batch of dust or instantly decay. He just died.

"Not bad," Rupert whispered. "You're pretty fucking fast. I barely saw you."

I took it for the compliment it was. "Thank you," I said, wiping the blood on my borrowed T-shirt.

Zaphara ducked into the doorway, touched the vampire's forehead, and murmured something I couldn't understand. A warm breeze of power trickled over my skin.

"They will not see him."

"I can see him," I said.

Her smile was grim and dark. "You were watching when I cast the spell. The only thing a vampire may notice is the smell of blood."

"One down," I murmured. "Eleven to go."

"We should split up," Rupert said.

"Eris and I will go find the Count," Lenorre said, "as that is where our battle lies."

"Kass," Rupert said, "who do you want to go with?"

"I think you should go with Zaphara," I told Rupert. "I have faith she'll keep your ass alive."

"I can take care of myself," Rosalin said. "I don't need you to babysit me."

"Rosalin. This is not the time, nor the place. I want you to come with me."

She looked like she was ready to argue when I shook my head. We split up into three groups. Zaphara and Rupert would go through the main part of the church with Lenorre and Eris to fight the vampires there. That was where most of the vampires were, according to Zaphara. Rosalin and I would search for the kids. Some of them might've been changed, but we would see how many were redeemable. *Redeemable.* It wasn't a pretty thought.

First, we had to find where they were keeping them. Zaphara had seen the ones that were changed in the main part of the church, but she hadn't seen anyone that looked like Timothy Nelson. That was either really bad news, meaning he was dead, or he was being held prisoner somewhere. If it were a choice between two evils, I'd prefer he was unharmed and locked up somewhere.

We spotted doors to our left once we emerged from the entryway. I opened one and listened. Nothing. The church was two stories high, so one of the doors led upstairs. Zaphara had explained the layout as best as she could before we left. A small kitchen, a basement, and a storage room were toward the back, and an upstairs was probably where Sunday-school classes were held when the church was in service.

Sounds of fighting broke out in the other room.

"That's our cue," I said, opening the first door to find a moldy-smelling bathroom.

I walked lightly, as quietly as I could. Rosalin followed suit. I opened the second door to find a set of stairs.

We slipped up them, emerging into one of the hallways Zaphara had described. A door at the end of the hallway opened and the vampires I'd seen earlier from the porch, the redhead and Goth boy, strode into the hall. They stopped.

"Well," he said. At first, he looked confused, then the confusion turned into a hard, arrogant look. "Greetings. I'm afraid we didn't order anything."

"I'm pretty sure you did," I said, handing the pizza bag to Rosalin. She took it, steadying a stake in her other hand.

"I think they're here to play, Dommie," the woman said in what sounded like an Australian accent.

I drew the Pro .40, clicking the safety off and instinctively aiming at his heart. I was pretty sure Rosalin could handle Red. Goth boy seemed the more threatening of the two.

He looked at the gun with an arrogant smirk.

"Go ahead," he said, spreading his arms wide and taking a step forward. "Try me."

"My pleasure," I said, and squeezed the trigger.

The bullet hit him, his body jerked, but he stood his ground. He placed two fingers over the hole in his heart, smearing the tips of his fingers in the blood, and lifted them to his mouth. "Not a bad shot," he said, licking the blood from his fingers like a cat bathing. "I'll give you credit for that."

Before I could say anything else, Rosalin rushed the female vampire in a blur of speed. It distracted me for a moment, giving Goth boy the time he needed to attack me. My back hit the wall and his hand wrapped around my throat, threatening to crush my windpipe as he picked me up off the ground. I drew a ragged breath over the grip of his fingers and growled.

"Not good enough," he said.

"Bite me." I raised the gun between our bodies. He saw the movement, tossing me to the side like a rag doll. I braced myself, allowing my elbows to take the impact when I hit the ground, keeping my forehead from slamming into the carpet. A woman screamed. It didn't sound like Rosalin.

"Trisha!"

Rosalin's clawed hand came into view. In her hand she held a mass of pulsing meat. My mind didn't want to register what it was, but once I looked and saw the hole in her chest, I knew. The smell of blood hit me like some sweet metal.

The vampire's heart fell to the ground with a meaty thud.

The wolf growled through me, her anger falling from my human lips. I discarded the gun, snatching one of the stakes.

Goth boy heard me, heard the growl rolling from my chest. He started to turn, but it was too late. I hit him, plunging the stake into his body like a blade. I jerked it out and pulled my arm back, ready to land another blow.

His raised hand fell away as he sank to the floor, no longer undead, but truly dead.

"That wasn't the smartest idea."

"It worked," Rosalin said in a growling voice, "didn't it?"

"I thought you couldn't shift partially." I retrieved the hot bag of stakes and my gun.

"I can't," she said, voice strained.

Rosalin went to her knees in the hallway as she tried to fight the change. I watched the struggle etch her features, until finally she gave herself to it. The beast rose to the surface, spilling out over her skin in a tide of red fur that was a subtle blend of gray, cream, and dirt red. A red mask circled her eyes, traveling the length of her snout.

She came to me where I knelt, bumping against me in greeting, and I buried my hand in the soft fur at the base of her neck.

I scratched behind her ears. "Come on."

Rosalin trotted down the hall. She passed each door and sniffed like a K-9 dog looking for drugs. When we reached the end of the hallway, she stopped at the last door.

"Here," she said, speaking carefully with her wolfish mouth. "I smell vampire."

I held the gun in a one-handed grip. Rosalin stood next to me, bigger than a Great Dane in her wolf form. Before I could say "Go," she threw her furred body into the door. A muffled scream came from the room beyond as it collapsed.

Vampires didn't scream, did they?

Chapter Thirty-four

The room had been transformed into a makeshift bedroom. Whoever had been in here last had left the overhead light on. A bed covered with a pink-and-white floral comforter stood in the middle of the room. Someone had apparently lived in the church before the vampires had taken over. Even though I'd never seen the Count of Counts, I had a hard time believing the floral decorations were a part of his touch.

Then again, most bad guys have a huge weird streak.

An old wooden desk was pushed into one corner of the room. A nightstand next to the bed held one of those lamps with the body of a vase.

Rosalin followed me, her ears flattened against her skull as she scanned the room. The muffled scream sounded again. I stayed against the wall. The worst thing you can do in a fight is walk out into the open without checking to make sure no one's there.

"Do you hear that?"

Rosalin nodded, keeping as low to the ground as her height would allow and slinking along the opposite wall.

I heard a noise, almost a knock, but not quite. The lamp wobbled on the nightstand.

"Shit." I holstered the Pro .40 and walked around the bed.

"Keep an eye on the door," I told her as I picked up the lamp, jerking the plug out of the wall. Someone was in the wall behind the nightstand. Call me careless, but I was betting it wasn't a bad guy.

I put my hand flat against the horrendous wallpaper. "Timothy?" I asked, lowering my shields slightly. I sensed a presence of cool energy but couldn't tell if it was him.

The next blow vibrated against the palm of my hand. It had to be him. "Get away from the wall," I said. "If you can hear me, get away from the wall." I waited for the space of a few heartbeats, then picked up the nightstand. I didn't care how much noise I made. The only thing I suddenly cared about was getting whoever was behind there out. I really hoped the others were kicking some ass in the other room.

I slammed the rickety wooden nightstand into the wall. The corner of the table caved part of it, but not enough. The nightstand broke and splintered on impact. I grabbed the edge of the hole in the wall, bracing myself with my foot against the baseboard, and started tearing pieces of plaster away with my bare hands. I could've shifted, could've called the beast to the surface, but it was unnecessary when I could just as easily dig a hole with my human hands.

Tearing the plaster away allowed some of the light to shine into a small room beyond.

Timothy was slumped over on his side, his arms shackled behind his back. A strip of dirty cloth speckled with blood and saliva was bound between his lips.

"Timothy. Oh, Timothy, what have they done to you?"

A bass growl shuddered across my spine. Every hair on my body suddenly stood at attention.

"He wasn't cooperating," a masculine voice said. I whirled around to find Maddox's huge frame standing in the doorway. Rosalin sank low, her ears drawn back, ready to attack. Her own bass growl rumbled against her chest, building as it flowed out of her muzzle. She snapped at the huge bulk of vampire in the doorway, snarling and showing her sharp teeth. Maddox either didn't care or didn't feel particularly threatened.

His eyes met mine across the room. At first, I thought his pupils were dilated, but then I realized they weren't. His irises were as black as his pupils.

He took a step forward, and Rosalin snapped again. He stopped, finally looking down at the massive werewolf.

"I don't mean any harm," he said.

"I'm supposed to believe that?" I slowly reached behind me to draw the Pro .40.

"I want to help."

Rosalin gave another threatening snarl, discouraging him from stepping into the room. Not many vampires wanted to wrestle with a werewolf. Maddox was built like a bodyguard, like he was used to throwing people around, so I imagined he was stronger than most vampires. In truth, the two of us against Maddox were probably an equal match when it came to strength, but alone...alone either one of us would probably have gotten our butt kicked.

Maddox didn't make a move to step into the room. He turned, looking down the hallway. "Get the boy," he said as I heard a door slam shut somewhere. "I'll take care of the others. Once you get the boy, ask him about me. Find out for yourself if I'm trustworthy." He turned and, in a blur of speed that belied his heavy bulk, disappeared.

I'd torn apart enough of the wall to reach in and touch Timothy's shackled arms. His legs were restrained at the ankles. He wiggled, trying to get closer to me, to help me get him out of the dark prison. I got a good grip and pulled, dragging him over the jagged edge of plaster. I jerked him against me, turning him around, and tore the knot behind his head.

The corners of his mouth were bloody where the gag had begun to tear into his skin. His head lolled forward and I put a hand on each of his shoulders, bracing him, holding him upright. He blinked, as if he was having a hard time fixing his gaze on any one thing in particular.

"He's..." Timothy's voice was hoarse like he'd been screaming for hours. He coughed, trying to clear his throat, which made my heart hurt. He was just a boy.

"He's okay," he said at last. "Maddox. He was bringing me food. He got in trouble for me." He cleared his throat again. "That's when they put me in the wall."

The youth that had been in his eyes the last time I saw him alive was no longer there. That cool energy, the smell of night air...

I put two fingers under his jaw. "Let me see."

He did what I asked. Slowly, as if it pained him, he opened his mouth to reveal a set of fangs.

"I told you not to. Why?"

"I had to know." He shivered. "He's got Alyssa. He'll turn her."

"He hasn't done it yet?"

"He saved it for tonight."

I touched the shackles at his wrists. "Let's get these off you."

Gently, I helped him turn around so I could get a closer look at his bindings. The metal clasps were secured around his wrists by a lock in the middle. Blood gleamed on both his wrists. He'd struggled against them. If a vampire was weak enough to be unable to snap a lock, he had to be starved. I curled my index finger around the top loop of the lock and pulled, popping it out of place. I did the same to the lock between his ankles.

"That's the best I can do right now. Are you okay?"

I could tell it hurt him to move his arms. Vampire or human, being held in the same position for too long would eventually hurt. He looked at the metal bracelets. "I'm fine."

The wall in the hallway shuddered before I heard footsteps approaching. I drew the gun, aiming at the doorway, and didn't lower it when Maddox appeared. His hands and one side of his face were covered in blood.

"We have to go," he said.

We stared at one another for several moments while I debated whether to trust him. Timothy had said the vamp was on our side. I hoped he was right.

"Fine," I growled, "but pull any stupid shit, and I will make sure you are well and truly dead."

"Understood," he said, motioning us out of the room.

"Do you know what's going on downstairs?" I asked him.

"Your friends have discarded the Count's pawns. We need to be with them when they face the Count himself."

I didn't argue but followed him. Rosalin took up the rear and we placed Timothy in a protective circle between us.

If anyone wanted him, they'd have to get through us first.

CHAPTER THIRTY-FIVE

The main part of the church looked like Christianity's idea of the apocalypse. Vampire bodies were strewn across the pews, children and older vampires alike. Their blood created pools in the white carpet. I walked down the aisle and toward the scene at the altar.

The Count of Counts stood by his throne in an old-fashioned suit of blue crushed velvet. Black lace blossomed at his neck and wrists. Eris knelt in front of the small stage. A blood-soaked sword lay idly on the floor, like she'd dropped it. The muscles in her arms twitched as if she braced herself against some unseen force.

"You think you can defeat me?" The Count's laugh unnerved me because it was not the laugh of someone in his right mind.

I started to ask Maddox why Eris was kneeling, but then I looked past my shields. I didn't see anything, but I sensed it. The energy and power in the air was unmistakable.

The Count of Counts wasn't just any old vampire. He was a psychic vampire and he was feeding off Eris.

Without thinking I strolled forward. "You're fucking pathetic," I said loudly, forcing my voice to carry across the entire church. His power wavered, interrupted. Good, I wanted to spoil his party. The Count of Counts gazed at me with clear blue eyes. Most of his face was hidden behind thick black brows and a lush black goatee.

"Look at that," he said joyously. "Another toy to play with. I must thank you, Lenorre, for bringing your most powerful assets to my party."

Maddox stepped up beside me, drawing the Count's attention to himself. The Count's eyes widened a fraction. "You traitorous—"

The Count staggered, bringing a hand up to his cheek. His fingers came away with blood.

He turned like a raging lion on Lenorre. "You will pay for that!"

Lenorre did not give the Count the satisfaction of a reply.

"Traitor?" Maddox's voice was thick with scorn. "You call me traitor? You murdered my Countess. You unsettled our people and placed your puppet to rule in her stead. You came here thinking to do the same and there would be no consequences. You are the traitor."

I drew the Pro .40, sighting down the barrel at the bridge between the Count's eyes. His attention shifted back to me.

"You would not da—"

Yeah, actually, I would. I pulled the trigger and chaos erupted.

Maddox rushed the Count, hitting him like a battering ram, sending both of their bodies to the stage floor.

The Count sprang to his feet, blood flowing from the bullet wound. "I'd kill her again just to hear her sweet pleading."

Maddox threw a right hook that sent the Count's head whipping back at an awkward angle.

The two began fighting in earnest. The Count blocked Maddox's next punch, using his forearm to sweep it aside. He dealt a blow to Maddox's midsection, hard enough I heard something crack.

I cursed, trying to get a good shot, but the fight was speeding up. The sound of blows fell faster, heavier. Maddox and the Count moved across the stage like angry blurs. Fucking vampires, they moved too Goddess-damned fast.

Lenorre helped Eris to her feet and they turned, focusing on the fight in front of them with expressions of utter calm. The Count stumbled dramatically as Maddox landed another blow on the side of his face.

The Count's entourage had probably been the only thing that had kept Maddox from kicking his ass sooner. Watching Maddox fight like some pissed-off vampiric elephant, I was happy I wasn't the Count.

The warning howl of Rosalin's wolf made every one of my senses rock to high alert. I spun around.

"Kassandra!" Timothy cried.

Crippling pain shot up my right leg, searing like fire. Hands like steel clawed at me. My right leg gave out from under me, taking me to my knees. The child vampire reared like a snake about to strike again. Blood swelled under my newly torn khakis. I hit her with the back of my hand, sending her small frame colliding into one of the pews.

She sprang back like a jack-in-the-box, a river of my blood spilling down her chin, and hissed ferally.

The wolf didn't like that. She pushed against the surface and snarled. The vampire lunged and I dodged, grabbing a handful of her coppery curls.

There was drying blood on the front of her apricot gown. Whatever wound had been dealt, her body had healed.

The vampire child swung at me, trying to tear at my body with her nails as if she thought they were claws. The wolf's growl built deep in my chest.

Her body went completely slack. "You would hurt me?" she asked in a small voice.

The world slipped out from under me. She was just a child. How could I hurt her?

The gun in my hand felt heavy, so heavy. The wolf's anger sailed through me, igniting the blood in my veins, pushing the vampire's mind-fog back. One predator knows another's tricks.

"Oh, please," I growled, and shoved the barrel into the soft skin of her neck.

Beyond the sound of something crashing, I heard the bullet hit stone.

The child vampire fell to the floor in an apricot heap.

I scanned the church, right and left, sighting down the barrel and each pew as I made my way back toward the head.

Maddox hit one of the pews, toppling it over as he tried to get back to his feet.

Lenorre and Eris, holding bloody swords, stood at opposite sides of the stage with the Count between them. Surrounded by death and violence, Lenorre was still calm, as if she had all the patience in the world. Power turned her gray eyes the color of liquid mercury.

I steadied the gun on the Count of Counts.

"You think your little gun can hurt me?" he asked, voice strained.

Blood pumped from the wounds they had dealt him. Somewhere in his fight with Maddox, Lenorre and Eris had managed to catch the Count off guard.

"No," I said, my voice sounding unnaturally calm, "but they can."

Lenorre and Eris rushed him in a blur of supernatural speed and strength. I kept the gun sighted on him. Eris drove her sword high through his chest, piercing his heart, tearing a ragged, pain-soaked scream from his mouth. Their movements perfectly in tune, Eris dropped to her knees to stay out of Lenorre's way, allowing her Countess to deal the final blow. Lenorre's slimly muscled arms drew back and, like a beautiful, deadly Goddess, she effortlessly sliced through the Count's neck with the bloodied blade.

He collapsed and, as his body swayed forward, his head fell to the floor like a rejected ball.

❖

Lenorre strode toward me, the bloody sword swinging at her side, drops falling behind her like vampiric breadcrumbs leading to death. One side of her face was smeared with blood, clumping in the curls that fell against her cheek. I waited for her to say something, but she didn't. She placed her empty hand on my back and pulled me against her, her lips meeting mine in a kiss so hard I nearly lost my balance.

I slid my hands up the sides of her torso, careful of the Pro .40 still in my right hand. My hands followed the base of her ribcage, curling around her back. As soon as my hands brushed over her spine, I felt the sheath there. The nylon protection created a slight interruption in her clothing, but if I hadn't been touching her, I would've never known it was there. No wonder she and Eris had turned down our offer of weapons.

She drew away from the kiss. "I understand it is not quite the time and the place…"

I put a finger over her mouth. "I know. I'm just glad you're alive." I hadn't realized until then how much of the worry I'd managed to push aside in order to fight. I cupped her face in my hands, carefully pointing the gun away from her as I guided her mouth back toward mine.

"Alive," she murmured, amused, and bowed her head to kiss me again.

Something heavy bumped my healing leg. "Hug?" Rosalin's wolfish voice made Lenorre and me both pause.

"You just had to ruin the moment, didn't you?" I asked, but used my gun hand to pull Rosalin against me. Her furry head bobbed in answer to my question. Whether I had meant to do it or not, I had claimed her as my wolf, and I needed her as much as she needed me. The amount of blood in the room was making my wolf pace, but my shields were strong enough to keep her at bay for the moment. I wanted to change, to let her run and hunt the way she needed to. But she'd have to wait a bit longer. If I decided to howl before the full moon…maybe, just maybe, I'd ask Rosalin to go with me. It actually sounded kind of fun. Strange that.

I scanned the room, looking for Rupert and Zaphara, and a tide of fear caused my stomach to turn. I was about to ask where they were when Lenorre answered my thoughts. "After we broke through most of the Count's people, I sent Zaphara and your friend to rescue the children."

"They're okay?"

"Yes."

"Good."

Eris came to us, rubbing her temples.

I gave her a quizzical look. "Are you okay?"

"Let us just say I am glad the Count is dead," she said sourly, obviously unhappy. "I never thought I would experience another headache."

I couldn't help it. The corner of my mouth twitched into a grin. "I've got some Excedrin in the car if you need it."

Her sea-green eyes peered out at me through a mask of the Count's blood. "I truly hope you are being sarcastic."

"Gee, aren't you grumpy?"

She wiped the sword she carried off on her shirt. "You would be too, had you been prey to his power."

"Alyssa!" Timothy exclaimed, suddenly bursting through our little group and running toward the two double doors at the corner of the room. Rupert and Zaphara held the doors open, as a group of children and teenagers walked through.

Timothy pulled the small blond girl to him, hugging her gently.

"These are unharmed," Rupert said. "The Count was keeping them locked in a basement. None of them had been changed yet."

"For that," Lenorre said, "we are lucky."

"Indeed," Eris added.

Zaphara stood off to the side, grave and quiet.

"You did well," I told her. "Thank you."

She didn't say anything, only gave a cryptic smile and a slow bow of her head.

Such was Zaphara.

"Call your little police friend," Lenorre said, "so we may go and clean up. We still have a party to attend."

"Do I have to go?" I resisted the urge to pout. The last thing I wanted was to play dress-up with a room full of vampires. I'd had just about my fill of them tonight.

"Oh yes," Eris said, "Lenorre had an outfit made especially for you."

"How do you do it?" I asked her. "You wait until the last minute, yet everything still goes as planned."

"I have my ways."

I shook my head and reached into my pocket. It was empty. I'd left my cell phone in my other pants. I usually carried it everywhere. Yes, even when I had to go hunting down the bad guys. The world doesn't stop just because there are bad guys. I had, however, learned the hard way to remember to turn the ringer off. A ringing phone often draws a lot of unwanted attention when you're trying to be sneaky.

Rupert held his cell out to me. "Use mine."

I dialed Arthur's number, walking away from the group, ready to get an earful about how I never told him what was going on, how I was just another human, and how I had to stop taking the police cases into my own hands. Even if I managed to save the day, they still weren't happy. One of these days, I feared Arthur would uncover my secret. You can only wear a disguise for so long. Eventually, the mask comes off and the truth is revealed. Until then, I'd just pretend I'd forgotten all about calling him.

Hey, it was partly true.

Chapter Thirty-six

The cops had arrived and handled the rest of it. I was right, Arthur was pissed that I hadn't clued him in, but like always, he was ultimately grateful I'd done my job.

Arthur had been staring at Timothy with a look I couldn't read. "What am I supposed to tell your parents?" he finally asked.

"I'd prefer it if you didn't tell them anything."

"You want me to lie to them?"

"Technically, Officer, telling them I died isn't a lie."

"Detective Kingfisher."

"Detective Kingfisher, I will tell them when I'm ready to confront my mother."

At that, Arthur chuckled, shook his head, and said, "I wish you luck, boy."

They checked every one of the dead vampires, confirming they were indeed super-beasties and that we hadn't killed any innocents. Zaphara had removed the spell from the vampire in the entryway when one of the cops tripped over it.

The few children that had been turned were young enough that either the process of being turned or being the Count's pets had broken their minds. They had to be executed. Lenorre and Eris had taken care of that part. Which I was grateful for, since I really didn't feel like it was my place. Child vampires are just a little creepy. They give me the heebies. There, I admit it.

The cops would help the rest of the children return to their parents, since some of them were from different states, and a few weren't even from this country.

Alyssa had been safely returned home. Timothy, on the other hand, was granted permission to stay with Lenorre as one of her vampires. We learned Maddox had cornered one of Eris's patrons outside the club and tried to send a warning, but no one took it seriously. He didn't know who else to go to and stay alive in the process. The Primes would cast a vote deciding his fate, but I had a feeling he would be staying with us. I think, for Timothy's sake, it wasn't a bad idea.

When Lenorre asked Maddox why he betrayed the Count, his reasoning seemed pretty solid. The Count had murdered his previous Countess. So Maddox had gained the Count's respect and traveled with his band, watching as the Count sought another conquest. When I'd asked him what had happened to his previous clan, he'd told me the Count's puppet still ruled, as was the case in all the areas where the sick bastard had managed to overthrow whoever held the vampire community together.

The need for vengeance in Maddox's gaze was hard not to notice. Perhaps, he would only stay for a while. I sensed his desire for revenge would far outweigh his desire to be content living in Lenorre's domain.

Alyssa's mother filed for a divorce and placed a restraining order against Dennis Cunningham. Timothy spent most of his nights with Alyssa and her mother, making sure they were safe. He wouldn't talk to his own mother or father. The only family member he would associate with was his brother. And although his brother was still coming to terms with his baby brother being a vampire, there was no question he'd stick around.

Rupert was still helping me keep an eye on Sheila. Considering the situation with Rosalin, whether we found anything on Sheila or not, I had a feeling it was a good idea. I didn't intend to let anything happen to Rosalin, and since I had claimed her, but she remained the Beta in Sheila's pack, I needed to keep an eye out for trouble. As usual.

The masquerade ball at Lenorre's club wasn't as unpleasant as I had anticipated. Then again, she assured me we only had to stay through one dance and long enough for her to put in an appearance. That made me a little happier.

Lenorre wore a black tux tailored to fit the contours of her body, showing her figure off to perfection. She'd clasped the curls of her hair at the back of her neck and worn a white fedora. As always, she looked gorgeous. She and Eris were the only two vampires who had opted out of dressing up in masquerade garb and had worn a tux. The rest of the vampires had swirled beautifully out onto the dance floor, appearing like the dark and mysterious strangers they were. The crowd had gone wild, scurrying for a chance to dance with one of them.

The dress Lenorre had picked out for me was revealing, but not overly so. The straps were tiny enough I couldn't wear a bra. The back was low-cut and made me feel like I was half naked. The sheer strips in the material over my stomach showed off the skin underneath. Oh, I'd argued about the dress, but in the end I'd lost. The expression on Lenorre's face when I was fully dressed was enough to keep me in it, though I had a niggling feeling she'd like the dress a lot more when she was tearing it off. Between my thoughts and Lenorre's heated looks, I was thrumming sensually.

She'd somehow managed to talk me into wearing the mask that went with the outfit. The black feathers of the raven mask matched the black satin dress. The patches of my bare skin that peeked through the solid black material were suddenly very white. The skirt kept trying to tangle about my legs like a waterfall of satin, and I had to force myself to focus on following Lenorre's lead, as she knew how to dance. Another benefit of lycanthropy was being able to move gracefully, without letting on that I had no idea what the hell I was doing.

The night proved to be romantic, even with the hunting that had come before it. Lenorre managed to talk me into one more dance. The tune was slow, with an edge of seduction that made the dance seem more intimate, more meaningful. With her body against mine, I let all thoughts of the confrontation with the Count and Sheila Morris disappear.

Eventually those thoughts would catch up with me. But for tonight, Lenorre held me and I followed her, inhaling the sweet and spicy scent of her perfume.

Beneath the perfume was the smell of my lover.

My Lenorre.

About the Author

Winter Pennington is an author, poet, artist, and closeted musician. She is an avid practitioner of nature-based spirituality and enjoys spending her spare time studying mythology from around the world. The Celtic path is very close to her heart. She has an uncanny fascination with swords and daggers and a fondness for feeding loud and obnoxious corvids. In the shadow of her writing, she has experience working with a plethora of animals as a pet-care specialist and veterinary assistant.

Winter currently resides in Oklahoma with her partner and their ever-growing family of furry kids, also known as "The Felines Extraordinaire."

Winter can be contacted at winterpennington@gmail.com
Blog: http://www.winterpennington.blogspot.com/
MySpace: www.myspace.com/akissofwinter

Books Available From Bold Strokes Books

The Long Way Home by Rachel Spangler. They say you can't go home again, but Raine St. James doesn't know why anyone would want to. When she is forced to accept a job in the town she's been publicly bashing for the last decade, she has to face down old hurts and the woman she left behind. (978-1-60282-178-1)

Water Mark by J.M. Redmann. PI Micky Knight's professional and personal lives are torn asunder by Katrina and its aftermath. She needs to solve a murder and recapture the woman she lost while struggling to simply survive in a world gone mad. (978-1-60282-179-8)

Picture Imperfect by Lea Santos. Young love doesn't always stand the test of time, but Deanne is determined to get her marriage to childhood sweetheart Paloma back on the road to happily ever after, by way of Memory Lane-and Lover's Lane. (978-1-60282-180-4)

The Perfect Family by Kathryn Shay. A mother and her gay son stand hand in hand as the storms of change engulf their perfect family and the life they knew. (978-1-60282-181-1)

Raven Mask by Winter Pennington. Preternatural Private Investigator (and closeted werewolf) Kassandra Lyall needs to solve a murder and protect her Vampire lover Lenorre, Countess Vampire of Oklahoma all while fending off the advances of the local werewolf alpha female. (978-1-60282-182-8)

The Devil be Damned by Ali Vali. The fourth book in the best-selling Cain Casey Devil series. (978-1-60282-159-0)

Descent by Julie Cannon. Shannon Roberts and Caroline Davis compete in the world of world-class bike racing and pretend that the fire between them is just professional rivalry, not desire. (978-1-60282-160-6)

Kiss of Noir by Clara Nipper. Nora Delany is a hard-living, sweet-talking woman who can't say no to a beautiful babe or a friend in danger a darkly humorous homage to a bygone era of tough broads and murder in steamy New Orleans. (978-1-60282-161-3)

Under Her Skin by Lea Santos. Supermodel Lilly Lujan hasn't a care in the world, except life is lonely in the spotlight until Mexican gardener Torien Pacias sees through Lilly's façade and offers gentle understanding and friendship when Lilly most needs it. (978-1-60282-162-0)

Fierce Overture by Gun Brooke. Helena Forsythe is a hard-hitting CEO who gets what she wants by taking no prisoners when negotiating until she meets a woman who convinces her that charm may be the way to win a battle, and a heart. (978-1-60282-156-9)

Trauma Alert by Radclyffe. Dr. Ali Torveau has no trouble saying no to romance until the day firefighter Beau Cross shows up in her ER and sets her carefully ordered world aflame. (978-1-60282-157-6)

Wolfsbane Winter by Jane Fletcher. Iron Wolf mercenary Deryn faces down demon magic and otherworldly foes with a smile, but she's defenseless when healer Alana wages war on her heart. (978-1-60282-158-3)

Little White Lie by Lea Santos. Emie Jaramillo knows relationships are for other people, and beautiful women like Gia Mendez don't belong anywhere near her boring world of academia until Gia sets out to convince Emie she has not only brains, but beauty and that she's the only woman Gia wants in her life. (978-1-60282-163-7)

Witch Wolf by Winter Pennington. In a world where vampires have charmed their way into modern society, where werewolves walk the streets with their beasts disguised by human skin, Investigator Kassandra Lyall has a secret of her own to protect. She's one of them. (978-1-60282-177-4)

Do Not Disturb by Carsen Taite. Ainsley Faraday, a high-powered executive, and rock music celebrity Greer Davis couldn't be less well suited for one another, and yet they soon discover passion has a way of designing its own future. (978-1-60282-153-8)

From This Moment On by PJ Trebelhorn. Devon Conway and Katherine Hunter both lost love and neither believes they will ever find it again until the moment they meet and everything changes. (978-1-60282-154-5)

Vapor by Larkin Rose. When erotic romance writer Ashley Vaughn decides to take her research into the bedroom for a night of passion with Victoria Hadley, she discovers that fact is hotter than fiction. (978-1-60282-155-2)

Wind and Bones by Kristin Marra. Jill O'Hara, award-winning journalist, just wants to settle her deceased father's affairs and leave Prairie View, Montana, far, far behind but an old girlfriend, a sexy sheriff, and a dangerous secret keep her down on the ranch. (978-1-60282-150-7)

Nightshade by Shea Godfrey. The story of a princess, betrothed as a political pawn, who falls for her intended husband's soldier sister, is a modern-day fairy tale to capture the heart. (978-1-60282-151-4)

Vieux Carré Voodoo by Greg Herren. Popular New Orleans detective Scotty Bradley just can't stay out of trouble especially when an old flame turns up asking for help. (978-1-60282-152-1)

The Pleasure Set by Lisa Girolami. Laney DeGraff, a successful president of a family-owned bank on Rodeo Drive, finds her comfortable life taking a turn toward danger when Theresa Aguilar, a sleek, sexy lawyer, invites her to join an exclusive, secret group of powerful, alluring women. (978-1-60282-144-6)

A Perfect Match by Erin Dutton. The exciting world of pro golf forms the backdrop for a fast-paced, sexy romance. (978-1-60282-145-3)

Father Knows Best by Lynda Sandoval. High school juniors and best friends Lila Moreno, Meryl Morganstern, and Caressa Thibodoux plan to make the most of the summer before senior year. What they discover that amazing summer about girl power, growing up, and trusting friends and family more than prepares them to tackle that all-important senior year! (978-1-60282-147-7)

The Midnight Hunt by L.L. Raand. Medic Drake McKennan takes a chance and loses, and her life will never be the same because when she wakes up after surviving a life-threatening illness, she is no longer human. (978-1-60282-140-8)

Long Shot by D. Jackson Leigh. Love isn't safe, which is exactly why equine veterinarian Tory Greyson wants no part of it until Leah Montgomery and a horse that won't give up convince her otherwise. (978-1-60282-141-5)

In Medias Res by Yolanda Wallace. Sydney has forgotten her entire life, and the one woman who holds the key to her memory, and her heart, doesn't want to be found. (978-1-60282-142-2)

Awakening to Sunlight by Lindsey Stone. Neither Judith or Lizzy is looking for companionship, and certainly not love but when their lives become entangled, they discover both. (978-1-60282-143-9)

Fever by VK Powell. Hired gun Zakaria Chambers is hired to provide a simple escort service to philanthropist Sara Ambrosini, but nothing is as simple as it seems, especially love. (978-1-60282-135-4)

Truths by Rebecca S. Buck. Two women separated by two hundred years are connected by fate and love. (978-1-60282-146-0)

High Risk by JLee Meyer. Can actress Kate Hoffman really risk all she's worked for to take a chance on love? Or is it already too late? (978-1-60282-136-1)

Spanking New by Clifford Henderson. A poignant, hilarious, unforgettable look at life, love, gender, and the essence of what makes us who we are. (978-1-60282-138-5)

Missing Lynx by Kim Baldwin and Xenia Alexiou. On the trail of a notorious serial killer, Elite Operative Lynx's growing attraction to a mysterious mercenary could be her path to love or to death. (978-1-60282-137-8)

Magic of the Heart by C.J. Harte. CEO Susan Hettinger and wild, impulsive rock star M.J. Carson couldn't be more different if they tried but opposites attract in ways neither woman can resist. (978-1-60282-131-6)

Ambereye by Gill McKnight. Jolie Garoul is falling in love with her assistant. The big problem is, Jolie is a werewolf. (978-1-60282-132-3)

Collision Course by C.P. Rowlands. Tragedy leaves Brie O'Malley and Jordan Carter fearful and alone. Can they find the courage to take a second chance on love? (978-1-60282-133-0)

Mephisto Aria by Justine Saracen. Opera singer Katherina Marov's destiny may be to repeat the mistakes of her father when she becomes involved in a dangerous love affair. (978-1-60282-134-7)